Praise for Rachel Hauck

and

GEORGIA ON HER MIND

"Rachel Hauck is a hilarious and powerful new voice in
Christian chick lit. Readers will love Macy and her
high-spirited antics, while coming away with
something more than just a frothy read."
—Kristin Billerbeck, author of *What a Girl Wants*
and *She's All That*

"In *Georgia on Her Mind*, a fresh voice breezes onto the
chick lit scene and blows away the competition. Funny,
thought-provoking and heartwarming, this book took me through
a gamut of emotions. I laughed, I cried, I laughed
again and then sat very still at the conclusion, mulling over the
ending. Rachel Hauck's first venture into the chick lit genre
is certainly not going to be her last. Grab a latte, pull up a chair
and don't make any plans that can't be changed, because,
I warn you, it will be very difficult to put the book down."
—Tracey V. Bateman, author of *Leave It to Claire*

"Really fabulous chick lit is hard to find, but Rachel Hauck
delivers just that with *Georgia on Her Mind*. This book has it all:
voice and a hilarious, yet touching,
y to a happy-ever-after ending. This
d all future books by Ms. Hauck are
 as my daily iced Americano."
uthor of *Alaska Twilight*

nny! A beautiful story of how
ad to our greatest dreams. Rachel
e and capture hearts. Well done!
, award-winning author of
Coming Up Josey

Rachel Hauck

Georgia on Her Mind

Steeple
Hill
Café

Published by Steeple Hill Books™

STEEPLE HILL BOOKS

ISBN-13: 978-0-373-78574-2
ISBN-10:   0-373-78574-7

GEORGIA ON HER MIND

www.SteepleHill.com

Printed in U.S.A.

For my dad, John Charles Hayes,
who watches and waits with the
Great Cloud of Witnesses.
I miss you, Pop, but I'll see you soon.

Chapter One

To: ALLCasper&Co.
Re: Reorganization

I skim the e-mail from Casper & Company's director of operations and my boss, Veronica Karpinski.

In order to streamline our work flow… blah, blah, yadda, yadda. I scroll down farther.

Reordering of departments…

Hmm, she never mentioned that to me. As manager of customer service, I'm usually privy to such upheavals.

Starting Monday, Mike Perkins will assume manager of customer service responsibilities…

What! Mike Perkins? I reread. *Starting Monday…* Each word zaps me like an electric shock. In a panic, I snatch up the phone and autodial Lucy O'Brien. My hands shake. My stomach curdles.

My friend's phone rings a hundred times, or so it seems to me. "Come on, Lucy, pick up!"

I can't hold my tears back any longer. But I must. Crying women, crying managers of customer service, are not highly regarded.

"Unprofessional displays of emotion," is the actual phrase our CEO, Kyle Casper, used in a staff meeting after Marcia Carter lost it when she didn't get promoted to senior administrator, *again.*

These are the worst kind of tears—tears of frustration, tears of anger. Tears that take forever to stop once they start.

"I can't believe this place," I mutter, gazing again at the e-mail, enduring another ring on Lucy's end without an answer.

What is it—ten-thirty? The day has barely begun and already it's one of the crummiest of my life.

My call to Lucy bounces to voice mail. "You've reached the desk of Lucy O'Brien. I am unable—"

I bypass the message by pressing the number one.

"Lucy…" My voice quivers, so I halt for a steadying breath. "It's Macy. Call me, please."

I slap the receiver onto the cradle and pace the length of my corner window office. *What is going on? What is Roni up to now?*

Outside my office window, dark blue storm clouds swell and move across the Florida sky and I catch my reflection in the glass. Leaning in for a closer look, I give myself the once-over. Ann Taylor suit, Gucci boots, face dusted to perfection with Bare Escentuals, my shiny brunette hair grazing my shoulders. I am the picture of a twenty-first-century businesswoman.

I'm exactly where I thought I'd be at this stage in my thirty-three-year-old life—until that obnoxious morning e-mail.

I stride back to my desk, kick the chair out and sit down, hard, trying to balance the juxtaposition of emotions. Confusion mingled with anger, tears of weakness mingled with stubborn resolve. I thought I'd outgrown these moments.

It's going to be a long day.

"Macy?" My department's admin, Jillian, lurks outside my door.

Snapping out of my sulk, I pretend to be busy by reaching for my computer mouse. "What can I do for you, Jill?" I jiggle the mouse to wake up the sleeping laptop screen.

"You okay?"

I force—I mean force—a smile. "Of course. Why wouldn't I be?"

Am I yelling? 'Cause it sounds to me as if I'm yelling. I clear my throat and lower my voice. "Anything else?" I jiggle the mouse again. The screen wakes up.

The horrifying e-mail screams at me. *Loser!*

Jillian lowers herself into the cushioned chair across from my desk. "I saw you come in this morning. New boots?"

"Yes."

"They're gorgeous."

"Gucci. Bought them on my trip to Manhattan."

"How much?" Jillian doesn't mess around.

"Your week's wages." I don't mess around either. "Did you really come in here to talk about my boots?"

"Y-yeah, sure." Her cheeks turn a deep shade of pink.

"You know you blush when you lie?"

"Attila sent out the new organization chart," she blurts out, tossing a copy of the new org chart on my desk.

Attila is our code name for Veronica Karpinski. Short for Attila the Hun. I inadvertently labeled her with the moniker several years ago when she was an up-and-comer, bustling around the office commanding and conquering. To my chagrin, the name stuck. To my good fortune, no one remembers where or when it originated.

"So I see." I duck behind my laptop.

Jillian stretches toward me, whispering. "You're reporting to Mike Perkins now."

Truly, I want to scream. I can read e-mail. The tears surface again and I'm sure if I blink, even once, they'll spill over.

I click on an old e-mail from Lucy to get the horrid, I've-been-demoted e-mail off the screen.

"Anything else I can do for you, Jillian?" I ask, ready for this exchange to be over. The pressure beneath is about to cause an explosion and I can't be responsible for Jillian's safety.

"What is Attila thinking? I mean, everyone loves you. Mike is so—"

"She knows what she's doing." As angry as I am at Roni right now, I cannot be drawn into idle talk with Jillian Holmes, resident Gossip At Large. Anything I say can and will be circulated around the office.

"Well, if there's anything—"

I stand, cutting her off. "I'm good. Thanks."

My phone rings as Jillian exits. Caller ID tells me it's Lucy—thank goodness.

I stretch around my desk with one booted leg and tip the door shut. The dam holding back the tears breaks.

"Macy, what's wrong?" Lucy asks about ten times before I can suck it up enough to answer her.

"I am so angry, so, so angry," I manage between sobs. I drop my head and braid back my hair with my fingers. Tears drip onto the faux oak desktop. I wipe them away with the edge of the org chart Jillian left behind.

"What happened?"

"Attila the Hun reorganized the entire operations department."

"When?"

"Over the weekend, I guess."

"And?"

"I am no longer manager of customer service."

"What? Can she do that?"

"She just did. Flip-flop a few names on a chart and—" My head pounds from the sudden surge of emotions. Casper is a medium-size but wildly successful software company. Kyle Casper's latest brainchild, W-Book, is destined to take the World Wide Web by storm. Everyone from little Johnny to Great-Granny can create and maintain a Web site. It's as easy as W-Book.

But I digress. "You know how these things go, Luce. They do what they want. Changing departments and department heads at the drop of a hat is nothing new. I just never imagined it would happen to me."

Lucy consoles me. "Macy, you're so good at what you do. You earned that job."

"You don't think I know that? But as of this morning's

e-mail, I report to Mike Perkins, the new manager of customer service. *He* reports to Roni."

"She could have at least changed his title," Lucy notes in a soft tone.

"One would think." I'm back to fuming. There is no reason, absolutely no reason, for her to replace me. My performance evaluations do not indicate unsatisfactory work or poor leadership.

I give 110 percent to Casper & Company. I arrive early, stay late. Last Thanksgiving I volunteered to work over the holiday weekend to help secure a half-million-dollar deal. And in December I donated the last two days of my Colorado vacation to accompany the VP of sales on a client visit.

"Macy, there has to be a reason," Lucy concludes.

"Attila the Hun's lunatic incompetence?"

"Talk to Kyle," she suggests.

"He's a coward. He'll tell me to talk to Roni and then back whatever she says."

"Then talk to Roni." Lucy's full of advice I don't like.

"No. She did this—let her come to me."

"Fine." Lucy sighs. "Then live with it, no complaints."

I laugh. "Do you know me at all?"

"Since the tenth grade. I love you like a sister, but I won't spend the next year hearing you whine about what Veronica Karpinski did to you."

Lucy knows me, all right. But nothing about her honesty changes the fact that I will complain. If this were mine to own, I'd darken Roni's office door and deal. But this is her game.

I am, er, was, a department manager. *Man-a-ger.* Trainers,

tech support, sales support and documentation reported to me. I watched out over them, *my people*.

Mike Perkins… Who's she kidding? The staff can't stand him. He's egotistical, all the while being incredibly goofy. Every week he comes into the staff meeting, clears his throat about a hundred times and asks, "Do any of you need the latest episode of *Xena, Warrior Princess? I've* got it on TiVo."

Every week. He frightens me.

I hear a light knock and look up to see Roni peering in, pushing my office door open.

"Luce, call ya back."

So, the coward came calling. With my back to her, I give one last swipe of my eyes with the soggy org chart, then whip around with a faint smile and invite my former boss to have a seat.

"What do you think?" She picks up the hard copy of the org chart with her manicured hand as she pulls up a chair. She makes a face. "It's wet."

"Water."

"Oh." She drops the paper back to the desk. "Well?" She crosses her legs and swings her foot up and down.

"I don't understand it." My headache intensifies. I lean against the side of my desk for support. I suppose I could sit, but somehow standing gives me sense of control, real or imagined.

"Change, Macy. We're taking the customer service department to the next level."

The dark clouds outside my window produce a rumble of thunder. I look out just as a bolt of lightning flickers to the ground like a snake's tongue. Suddenly rain rat-a-tats against the window.

"What next level?" I ask, facing Roni. "What are you talking about?"

"Mike Perkins developed a plan to weave training, tech support with product development. He's added a few new tiers to our structure. Kyle likes it. I like it."

A few new tiers? Corporate mumbo jumbo.

"I don't know what to say."

"Say you're on board." Roni smiles. Her foot is still swinging back and forth.

With bravado I ask, "Why didn't you tell me you wanted to make a change? I was a manager, Roni."

"Just business, Macy. Don't get offended." She shrugs as if it's no big deal.

Just business? That's all the respect I get from her? "I earned the job, Roni. I know this industry, our products and customers. I deserved better." I sell myself to her all over again, hoping I sound more confident than desperate.

"If you don't want to come aboard—" Her words trail off, but she looks me square in the eye.

I absorb her subtle threat. The blood drains from my brain straight to my feet and I fear I might grovel involuntarily. I have to be humble here. My newly purchased BMW Z4 convertible emptied my savings account, and my credit card is loaded with Christmas cheer.

I walk around to my desk chair. I'm not in control here at all. Might as well sit. "If Mike is manager, what do I do?"

"What you love," Roni says, expectant and puffed up, looking as if she just announced a resolution to world hunger. "Hands-on work with the customers, training and traveling. Our team needs your experience."

I rocket to my feet, crashing my desk chair into the credenza. "Go on the road?"

"Exactly!"

"No, Roni, no. I've been there, done that. I own all the T-shirts. I won't have my life controlled by the schedule. I have a life, a boyfriend."

Yes, Chris, my boyfriend. A thought flutters through my mind. Was I supposed to call him about lunch?

"Think of the frequent flyer miles." She stands, smoothing her light wool skirt. "That's the job we are offering you, Macy."

Frequent flyer miles. There aren't enough miles in the entire airline industry to entice me back into being a road warrior. No way.

I need air. I jerk my Hermès Birkin bag from the bottom desk drawer and snatch my London Fog trench coat (both part of the Christmas cheer on my credit card) from the brass hook on the wall.

"Where are you going?" Roni follows me down the hall.

Through a tightly clenched jaw I let her know. "Anywhere but here."

Chapter Two

❧

I dial Chris's cell and office phone, but he doesn't answer. Chances are he'll show at our place, Pop's Diner, eventually.

I park close to the door and dash inside, dodging raindrops. Snippets of my conversation with Attila the Hun replay in my head.

Mike Perkins. Go on the road as a trainer. Been there, done that! If you don't want to come aboard...

I slide into a booth by the door. Elizabeth, the waitress, sees me and comes over, snapping her gum.

"What'll it be?"

"Double order of fries. Make sure they're hot." I'm blowing a day's worth of Weight Watchers points and I want it to be hot and salty.

"Starting out a little early, aren't you?" she asks, jotting down my order.

"And a large Diet Coke." I wrap the edge of my napkin around my finger. *I've lost my job….*

Whoa, wait. If I'm no longer a manager, what happens to my salary? What about raises and bonuses? I'd planned on this quarter's bonus to replenish my savings account and pay for Christmas.

I drop my forehead to the tabletop and try not to cry.

If Mike is me and I'm, well, still me, but a plain-Jane techie, do I have a plain-Jane salary? Does he have my salary? I've heard of that happening before. A person is reorganized to a different job where the pay is conveniently less.

I feel a swoon coming on. Do women still swoon?

I've just been shoved off the career path of the upwardly mobile into the proverbial ditch of the down-and-out.

I lift my head when Elizabeth sets down my Coke. "Having a nice day?" she asks.

"No." I tear the paper off my straw.

My cell phone chirps and I answer hoping it's Chris. But it's Lucy, which is just as good.

"I'm at Pop's," I say when I answer.

"Macy, oh no. It's not worth it."

"Too late. I've ordered double fries."

She sighs. "I'm on my way."

Lucy O'Brien hasn't eaten junk food since a 1994 *60 Minutes* exposé. If I'd said I was standing on the ledge of the Melbourne Causeway about to plunge ninety feet into the Indian River, she couldn't have responded with any more urgency.

So seeing Lucy, a slender, redheaded *Florida Daily News*

investigative reporter, dash into Pop's like a superheroine almost makes me laugh. Almost.

"I got here as quickly as I could." Lucy slides into the seat across from me, stowing her umbrella and pulling a wet wipe from her purse. She towels off the table.

But it's too late—my cheeks are fat with fries. I wash them down with a slurp of soda.

"That stuff is going to kill you, Macy." Lucy wrinkles her nose and sticks out her tongue. "How you and Chris eat this stuff is beyond me."

"This won't kill me. Veronica Karpinski will kill me." I shake a long salty fry under her nose.

She shoves my hand away with a "yuck" expression on her face.

I bite the fry. "You do not know what you are missing, my friend."

"Veronica Karpinski can only 'kill' you if you let her." Lucy makes air quotes around the word *kill*. As if either of us thinks this conversation is literal.

"She's doing a pretty good job of killing my Casper career."

Lucy taps my hand. "You're going to be okay, Macy. This whole thing will straighten itself out, and you know what? I bet you'll be Roni's boss this time next year."

"Are you crazy? She would never, *ever* let that happen. She eats, breathes and sleeps that place. She broke off her third engagement because the guy asked her to take one weekend a month off work."

I hold up my drink glass for a refill.

"What does Chris say about all of this?" Lucy asks, ordering a cup of herbal tea when Elizabeth brings me a new drink.

Good question. "I tried to call him, but he's not answering his phones. Maybe I'll run by his office...."

Lucy's hazel eyes pop wide and her gaze is fixed on something behind me. "Oh, no, don't look."

Of course, I look. There's Chris, finally, dashing into the restaurant. Now the sun is shining. I lift my hand to *woo-hoo* him over to our table, but he's with a petite, smiley, bleached blonde wearing low riders and platform shoes. The two of them are wet and laughing.

"Who is she?" I wonder out loud.

"Not his sister," Lucy mutters out of the corner of her pinched lips, and points out how snugly his hand is resting on her hip.

"Maybe a friend?" I pretend the slicing pain in my chest is indigestion. His hand is *not* that snug on her hip. Not really.

"Oh, for crying out loud, Macy, get a clue. I told you not to eat this junk. It's decaying your brain." Lucy shoves me out of my seat. "Go see what he's up to."

"Chris?" I bellow without considering where I might take this scene.

"Macy." He jumps away from the blonde as if he's been bitten by a dog—that would be me, I guess.

"What are you doing here?" he asks.

"Early lunch." I cross my arms, glaring at him, studying her.

With a confused look on his face, he asks, "Did we have plans for today?"

Obviously neither of us is paying much attention to this relationship. "I tried to call you," I say, arms still crossed, eyes still fixed on this cozy couple.

"I've been out all morning."

"I guess so." I smile at the blonde.

Chris fumbles forward. "This is Kate Winters. Kate, um, this is, um…"

"Macy Moore." The buffoon forgot my name. If we weren't in public I'd kick him in the knee, then the other knee.

"It's nice to meet you." Kate offers her hand.

She seems innocent enough. Intuition tells me if I want the truth about this situation, she's my best bet.

With a faux chuckle I commence my investigation. "You two work together?"

Kate laughs. "Oh, no. I just moved into my new apartment and Chris is helping me furniture shop." She smiles all too sweetly. "He loves double cheeseburgers, so we came here for lunch."

Of course he loves double cheeseburgers. Odd that she would know that. "So, you two know each other from where?"

Giddy Kate jumps right in with an explanation. "I'm a graduate student at Florida Tech. Chris was my economics adjunct professor last term."

"How about that?" I give Chris a look.

Kate continues, beaming. "I didn't have classes today, so Chris took the day off to be with me."

Ah, it's becoming clear. Yes, crystal clear. Chris is cheating on me. Or cheating on Kate, I don't know which. I decide to out him.

"Kate, for the last six months I've been Chris's girlfriend. At least I was until about five minutes ago."

"Chris?" Kate stares up at him. Oh brother, I think she's going to cry.

Chris goes into weasel mode. "Kate, Macy, I…"

All at once Lucy is beside me, jerking me toward the door. "Come on, Macy. He's not worth the effort." She hands me my soda, refilled. Drops my coat onto my shoulders and slips my purse onto my arm.

"Six months, Chris. Wasted." What a rotten, weaseling, two-timing scoundrel. I stop at the door and offer Kate a word of advice. "Runnnn!"

Lucy pushes me into a nippy February drizzle.

"What is going on?" I gaze heavenward, arms raised. The dissipating rain sprinkles me. "Lord, hello. It's me, Macy Moore, Your friend. What are You doing to me?"

Lucy shushes me. "People are staring."

"Let them stare." I flail my arms about, the contents of my cup sloshing over.

"Macy, really." Lucy grabs at me, indignant.

"What was I thinking, Lucy? Chris Wright. Ha! More like Chris Wrong," I shout toward the restaurant, hoping he'll hear me. "Did you see her? Him with her?"

"Yes, I saw."

How did I not see this coming? Grad student, indeed.

"That's what I get for dating a man who likes to play with other people's money. Nothing is sacred to him." Like the mature woman I am, I kick a newspaper stand and nick my fancy boots.

"Macy, please, gather yourself."

"Gather myself? Lucy, my career has tanked, my boyfriend is…I don't know…dating another woman and this…drink…is watery." I head for my car, flinging the drink into the nearest trash can, and wipe my chilled hand on the sleeve of my coat.

"Where are you going?" Lucy trails me.

"Home. I need to think, sort this out." I regard my dear friend for a second, then stride over to where she's standing and give her a hug. "Thanks for being there for me."

"I'm coming over tonight."

"Bring Chinese."

Chapter Three

Arriving home, I decide to do what any woman of my education and stature would do—pout. Pity party for one, please. I change into my party outfit, a ratty pair of red sweats.

Earlier, I couldn't get Roni's attitude out of my head. Now I can't stop picturing Chris with that incredibly cute woman.

In the mirror over my couch I check my appearance. My hair is matted together from the rain, my eyes are puffy and red, and black mascara residue has pooled under my eyes and left streaks on my face. I look like a member of Cirque du Soleil.

Comparing myself to a perky Florida Tech grad student right now is stupid. But stupid hasn't stopped me before.

It occurs to me as I fall onto the couch that in this dark hour I should pray. But dialoguing with God feels, at the very least, hypocritical. We haven't been on intimate speaking terms for a few months, and going to Him now because my life is in ruins doesn't seem right.

Okay, maybe that's when one *should* run to God. But quite frankly, when I met Chris I sort of took over the rudder of my life. "Thanks, Lord. I have my career and a good man. I'll take it from here."

I flop over onto my stomach, bury my face in a thick, fringed pillow and punch the sofa cushion until my arm tires three whacks later. (Mental note: renew gym membership.) I backtrack over my life with Chris to determine where it went wrong.

I met him at a community work party, cleaning up parts of downtown Melbourne, right before my thirty-third birthday and right after my biological clock sent its first alarm: Hello, you're a thirtysomething, Macy.

That shook me. I desperately wanted a career and life outside my small hometown of Beauty, Georgia, but I never, ever wanted to be one of those workaholic women who wakes up at forty-five and says, "Oops, I forgot to have a family."

So, with baby bells still chiming, I ran into Chris a few days later at Pop's and he asked me to dinner.

He took me to the Chart House—very nice!—and we simply clicked, as if we'd known each other forever. Suddenly getting married became a priority. I hadn't met a man like Chris in a long time—handsome, goal oriented, sweet, well-spoken and moneyed. My personal I-don't-want-to-be-an-old-maid fear factor precluded asking God for His opinion.

So this is where that plan has brought me. Brokenheartville. Drat.

The phone rings, calling me out of the pity pool. I fumble to find the portable, lost somewhere under the coffee table. I bump my head reaching for it.

"Hello?" I sit up, rubbing my forehead. Winter's afternoon light falls across my living-room floor. I check the time on the mantel clock. Two o'clock.

"Macy?"

It's my neighbor across the street. "Mrs. Woodward, how are you?" The words come out slowly and high-pitched and it sounds as if one of us is an imbecile and it's not her.

"I see you came home in the middle of the day. Are you ill?"

"In a manner of speaking."

"Oh, dear. Well, I have soup on."

I wince. That's the umpteenth time she's called me for a meal this year and it's only February. I have yet to accept because I've been busy. Really I have.

"Thank you, Mrs. Woodward, but I just had lunch, and to be honest, I'm not very good company right now."

"I understand. How about for dinner?"

I wince again. "I have a friend coming over."

"Boy or girl?"

Oh, brother. "Girl. Lucy. You remember Lucy."

"Of course. I can set a place for her, too." Her voice goes up on *too* as if she's tempting me with a million dollars.

"She's bringing Chinese."

"Well, then, another night. Ta-ta."

"Yeah, ta-ta."

Lucy bungles through the door around seven-thirty with bags of Chinese comfort. I'm starved.

"Here." She hands me a few pieces of mail. "Dan Montgomery said they were in his box."

Ah, handsome Dan, the condo community's resident hunky lawyer. Think George Clooney meets Arnold Schwarzenegger.

"You look horrible," Lucy says, walking toward the kitchen.

"Thanks. I was going for hideous, but horrible is good." I glance in the couch mirror again. No, I think I achieved hideous.

"Go wash up. I'll get the plates. You do realize Dan was about to knock on your door."

"Oh, really?" That would have been the icing on the cake of my day. Opening the door to handsome Dan while looking like a dead skunk. I bet his girlfriend, Perfect Woman, was with him.

In the downstairs bathroom I scrub my face with soap. I'm too tired, too I-don't-care to run upstairs for my overpriced facial cleanser. Soap will do.

Lucy is yelling something at me. "What?" I holler back, turning off the water.

"Remember your dinner with him?"

"Him who? Chris?" Of course I remember.

"No, Dan. When you first moved into the complex." Lucy passes by with a plate of food.

I pat my face dry. "Oh, Dan, yeah."

She laughs. "You asked him where he went to church—"

"And he said, 'Check, please!'" I laugh with her. Some things aren't meant to be. A few months after our little dinner disaster, Dan started dating Perfect Woman and they've been thick as thieves ever since. I call her Perfect Woman because she has no known flaws, at least that I can see.

I light the gas logs in the fireplace, fill my plate and plant myself in the lounger. It's good to have Lucy here.

But she gets personal before my first bite of moo goo gai pan. "So, how do you feel about the Chris thing?"

"Happy and breezy, like a day in the park," I snarl. The idea of him with Kate may just ruin my appetite. May.

"Hey, I'm on your side. Be thankful you didn't get stuck with him for life."

"Eligible men don't grow on trees, Lucy. Can't just go out and pick a new one. Especially Christian guys."

She shakes her bony finger at me. "You were about to settle, weren't you?"

Egad, I hope not. "Settle is not the word I'd use."

"Are you even sure he was a Christian?"

I feel flushed. "Well, he went to church with me." When we went. "He shook Pastor Ted's hand and said, 'Good word.'"

"Oh, please."

I didn't think that would fly, but the truth is, I never really asked him much about his faith. He respected my beliefs and I liked him, perhaps loved him, and for the time being that was good enough. So maybe I was settling.

"I heard him tell Reuben Edwards the night we went to the movies he thought Jesus was simply a great man."

"Stop. This day's been bad enough." I don't want to hear it. I know. I know. I overlooked a few things with Chris. Important things. It was that biological clock, I tell you. The ringing confused me.

Lucy scoops more fried rice onto her plate. (Chinese is her only fast-food weakness.) "Just because you're thirty-three doesn't mean you have to be desperate."

"Oh yeah, I forgot. Lucy 'I-have-a-date-every-weekend' O'Brien is in the house."

She rolls her eyes at me. "I do not. Not every weekend."

Last spring she dragged me kicking and screaming to a singles event up in Cocoa Beach. "Can't go," I protested over and over. "I'm allergic to singles functions!"

My eyes watered, my throat tightened and I couldn't breathe. I needed air.

Anyway, I caved to her demands and attended this singles shindig when she reminded me I hadn't been on a date in over a year. It was a Hawaiian luau with a bonfire on the beach, roasting pig on the spit, twilight volleyball and candlelit pavilions. All serenaded by a ukulele band with its very own Don Ho impersonator. I had to admit, a very nice event.

But, as I suspected, it turned out to be the classic, textbook church singles function. Five girls for every guy, and every guy a dud—in my humble opinion. The one cool guy who showed up without a USB data stick slung around his neck, polyester pants or Velcro sneakers gravitated right past me for Lucy.

"Mace, hey, earth." Lucy snaps her fingers. "Come in, Macy."

"What?" I jump into the present.

"What about Casper? What're you going to do?"

Oh, that. Between the upheaval at Casper and the upheaval with Chris, I'm not sure how to find right side up.

"I don't know. My beautiful life…an ash heap." With that, I'm depressed. Knowing it is one thing—declaring it is another.

"Don't take this wrong…" she starts with a thoughtful expression.

"Oh no, I love conversations that start with 'Don't take this wrong.'" I brace myself for one of her friendly cuts.

"Your career was becoming your God."

"What?" Now, that's not fair.

"This last year, you changed, went berserk with work. Then you met Chris—"

"Berserk with work?" I echo, biting into my egg roll.

"You got hung up on climbing the corporate ladder and it took some zeal out of you," Lucy says.

"Zeal? You just said I was berserk with work."

She looks at me for a long second and I know she's about to utter something profound. "Your zeal for Jesus faded. Like frizzy perms and oversize belted blouses."

I'm cut to the quick. Comparing my spiritual life with distasteful '80s fashion. I fire off my rebuttal. "I'm zealous for Him by doing my job with excellence."

"Don't twist things, Macy. Your identity was becoming that whole corporate, yuppie world. The cars, the clothes, power lunches, working fifty-, sixty-hour weeks." Lucy picks up the fried rice carton and shovels another round onto her plate.

"So what are you saying? Give up on my dreams?"

"Of course not. I'm saying make an adjustment. Remember what you do in life is merely a reflection of who you are as a Christian, one who loves and serves the Lord."

Her words shake me. She's right. I didn't see it. I didn't want to see it. I hate these kinds of "duh" moments, like realizing the light has changed to red just when I've shifted into fifth gear.

"Casper obviously doesn't seem to appreciate all you've sacrificed for them, and Chris showed you how much your love means to him today. He forgot your name, Macy."

"He did, didn't he?"

"Yes, he did." Lucy reclines against the back of the couch, plate in hand, and reaches for the TV remote. She stops on the latest installment of *The Apprentice*.

"Luce, hey, do you mind?" I point at the TV with my chopsticks. "I don't need a reminder."

I wonder if Donald would fire me. Better yet, fire Roni Karpinski. "Veronica, you're fired." Hmm. I feel a little better.

Sigh. But my life is not a reality TV show. It's worse. Seeing my name on that Casper org chart dropped from the manager box into the slush pile of staff names was painful and humiliating, then running into Chris with Kate...

I wonder if I should call him and sort this out. What if he's with her? I can't bear it. I won't call. Makes me look desperate. If he's got something to say, he can come say it.

In the midst of my mental and spiritual debate the phone rings. Lucy answers and hands it to me with her eyes popping, her finger over the mouthpiece.

"It's your boss," she whispers.

"You don't have to whisper, Lucy." I yank the phone out of her hand.

"Hi, Roni." Maybe she's watching *The Apprentice*, too, and is calling to apologize.

"Macy, it's Mike Perkins."

Chapter Four

Oh. Yeah. My boss. "What can I do for you?"

"Sorry to call you at home, but you never came back to the office—"

"I had to take care of some things."

"Mmm-hmm, right. Listen, Pete Miller called from Atlanta. He needs technical help with his Web software upgrade. He's crunched for time on an e-business launch."

"I tried to send him Tim Sorenson last month, but he refused. Didn't want to pay for on-site support."

"Well, he's not refusing now. He's demanding."

Figures. "The schedule is full for the next few weeks, Mike."

"Wel-l-l-l, Jillian booked you on the 7:15 a.m. out of Melbourne."

I spring to my feet. "Me? Seven-fifteen!" My plate of moo

goo gai pan tumbles to the floor. Lucy fumbles with her plate trying to catch mine and tips the carton of wonton soup.

"Roni and I decided you're the best one to calm Pete down. Do a little company campaigning. You can install W-Book. Get him excited about our new product."

Company campaigning? The company that just demoted me? This is s-o-o-o Roni. Mike rattles off the trip details while Lucy mops up soup and fried rice and peas. Stunned, I listen to his instructions, confirming them with a series of "Mmm-hmms."

By the time we hang up, my stomach is in tiny knots. I haven't been on-site in aeons. But hey, it's like riding a bike, right? You never forget. Wanted: a three-wheeler.

I pen a mental checklist of to-dos: pack, pay next week's bills, print out my e-ticket. Oh man, my laptop is at work.

I give Lucy the lowdown. "Macy, why don't you tell him you can't go?"

"Of course, why didn't I think of that? And when he fires me, can I move in with you after I sell the condo?"

"Right. Happy trails."

Yeah, just as I thought. We continue discussing the weirdness of my day as I finishing cleaning up, taking our plates to the kitchen.

"Mace, I'm so sorry about today. I've been praying for you," Lucy says, retrieving a can of carpet cleaner from under the kitchen sink. She grabs a clean dish towel and heads to the living room.

"Thank you, Lucy." I peer at her through the pass-through. Where would I be without her friendship? She's in there cleaning up my carpet as if it were her own, praying for me, comforting me, encouraging me while I refuse to give up griping and complaining.

I can't say that I deserved this day or that God is punishing me, but I can say that if I'd been walking a little closer to Him it might not sting as much.

"Are you going to quit?" Lucy asks, returning to the kitchen, replacing the carpet cleaner.

"No, I can't afford to be a prima donna."

She smiles, leaning against the doorway. "Good. I don't want you to leave town."

I pick up the pile of mail Lucy had brought in. "I'm willing to hang out a little while and see what happens." I sigh. "But Lucy, life on the road is the pits."

"I know, but give it a chance…. Oh, you got it." Lucy points to a bright red flyer sticking out of the pile of mail.

"Got what?" I tug on the red corner and pull the piece away from the others.

"The announcement for our fifteenth class reunion."

"Already?" There, in black and red, in the bubbly verbiage of our class secretary, Alisa Bell, is a reminder to put the July Fourth weekend on our calendars and "if your address has changed, let me know!"

Alisa has never given up the job of senior class secretary. In her mind, she was elected for life. In fifteen years I don't think one of our Beauty High classmates has managed to come up MIA.

"I can't wait," Lucy says. "Reunions are so fun."

Normally I'd agree with her, but in light of recent events, a reunion sounds dreadful. "I don't know. I might skip this one. Wait for the twenty-year, where hopefully

I'll show up married to a bazillionaire and running a Fortune 500 company."

"Macy." Lucy picks up her purse and digs out her keys. "You're one of the most amazing women I know." She hugs me. "I know today was hard, but you have to believe God has a plan for you."

"I know. I know." I spend the rest of my night getting ready to leave town. The laundry I meant to do over the weekend—but didn't—has to be done. I load and start the washing machine, throw on my sneakers and drive to the office to pick up my computer.

I'm dreading this new assignment—a week on-site with an antsy, uptight customer. I mutter to God all the way to the office and back about this new phase of my life.

"Don't understand what's going on here…if You wanted my attention, You have it now…please, give me understanding…I promise to listen…."

It's late when I finally collapse into bed. My thoughts are all over the place, yet not thinking of anything at all.

Just as I drift off to sleep, the phone rings. I toy with not answering. Who do I want to talk to at this hour? No one. But by the third ring, curiosity wins out.

"Hello?"

"Macy, sorry to bother you. It's Elaine Woodward."

Elaine Woodward. Mrs. Woodward? Her first name is Elaine?

"Hi." I reach for the light.

"Can you come over?"

"Mrs. Woodward?" I call, cinching my pink robe and shaking water from my fuzzy green slippers.

The front door's ajar, so I peek inside and step subsequently into 1954. The furniture, the lamp stands, the doilies resting atop the easy chair, the entire scene straight from a '50s *Better Homes and Gardens*. I find it comforting and warm.

"Mrs. Woodward?" She's lying on the couch, one hand over her stomach and one hand covering her eyes. "You okay?"

"Macy, thank you for coming. I didn't want to be alone."

"What's wrong?" I ease down onto the edge of the sofa.

"Pain," she says with a deep breath. "Right here." She presses her middle, between her ribs.

Heart attack? Please, do not be having a heart attack. I am not EMT material. I faint at paper cuts.

"I'm going to call 911." Just the idea makes my heart palpitate.

"No, no, I don't want to bother them. I'll be all right."

"Bother them? It's their job." What is it with the senior set and their preoccupation with bothering people?

"No, let's wait. I just didn't want to be alone." She sighs with a deep moan, her face pinched and pale.

Do not tell me this is a clever ploy to get me over for a visit. If she asks me if I'd like a spot of tea, or a bowl of soup, I'll—

She moans again and I can tell she's in real pain. I feel guilty over my lack of compassion.

"Does your chest hurt? Arm numb?" I slip my hand under hers. If she says yes, I'm *bothering* 911.

"It's not a heart attack," she mutters. "Could you get me a glass of water?"

I dart to the kitchen, praying as I go. Despite the fact that I don't know what to do for my ailing neighbor, it's a relief to focus on someone besides myself.

Mrs. Woodward's hand trembles as she reaches for the glass, so I help her take a sip.

I plead, "Let me call for an ambulance."

"No, it always passes."

"You've had these episodes before?" I take the glass and set it on a coaster. "What did your doctor say?"

"I didn't tell him."

"Mrs. Woodward, this could be serious," I lecture. I rack my brain trying to remember what organ lives between your ribs in the upper stomach region. I have no idea. Well, there's $170 gone to waste for that university anatomy class.

For a while I sit quietly and hold her hand. I start to get sleepy and can't help but think how fast 4:00 a.m. will come. Then I hear the soft sounds of sleep from Mrs. Woodward.

"Mrs. Woodward?" I gently shake her arm.

She's out. I get up without disturbing her and reach for the afghan draped over the back of the couch. I cover her and click off the lights except one in case she wakes up and wants to go to her bed.

Pushing in the lock button on the doorknob, I head for home, captured in the sudden emotion of Mrs. Woodward's episode. Dark rainy night, an elderly widow all alone, over-come with pain. I would have called me, too.

The last time I saw visitors at her place was last…last… hmm, well, weird—I've never seen visitors. I don't even know if she has children or grandchildren. I didn't see any pictures on the wall or mantel.

"Hey, Macy."

"Who's there?" I tumble into a cluster of overgrown palmetto bushes, freaked. My fuzzy slipper sloshes into a pool of floating pine chips.

"Macy, it's me, Chris."

I peek between the palm fronds to make sure it's really him. A girl cannot be too careful. Yep, it's the weasel.

"What are you doing here?" I step out of the shrubs, losing a slipper. I stoop to fish it out, hobbling on one foot.

"What are you doing?" Chris asks.

"I asked you first." I wring the water from my slipper and make a beeline for my place, one slipper off, one slipper on. My pink robe flows behind me like a cape.

"I want to talk to you." He follows me.

"At one in the morning?" This day will just not end. It's spilling over into tomorrow, which is now technically today.

"I couldn't sleep." He's right on my heels, and I catch a whiff of day-old Versace Blue Jeans. I loved that fragrance until today. Until right now.

"Ah, is your conscience bothering you? Lousy cheater." I plan to leave him standing on my front porch, stewing in his own guilt with my door slammed in his face, but when I twist the knob the door doesn't budge. I shove it again.

N-o-o-o. I'm locked out—my keys are still at Mrs. Woodward's. Hoist by my own petard. I beat the door with my soggy slipper. "I…can't…believe…this…."

I drop my head against the cold exterior wall. How is this happening to me? What cosmic forces have aligned themselves to trap Macy Ilene Moore between the rock and the hard place without so much as a crowbar to wedge her way out?

Chris puts his hand on my shoulder. "You okay?"

Laugh? Cry? Laugh? Cry? Punch Chris? Definitely, punch Chris. Oh, just one good punch. But I laugh instead.

"Macy, what's going on?" He grabs my shoulders. "Stop laughing."

"I'm locked out."

"And that's funny why?"

In the cold glow of the porch light I grit my teeth and say, "Actually it's not funny. I'm just all out of tears for today."

Oops, spoke too soon. A small reservoir floods my eyes.

Without a word he produces his keys and unlocks the door. I'd forgotten I'd given him one about a month ago, just in case. How ironic for him to rescue me now after squishing my heart like a pesky mosquito.

"What's so important that you have to come creeping around at one in the morning?" I demand once we are inside. I toss the slipper into the laundry room before collapsing into my chair.

"I'm so sorry about today. I tried to call you, but you never answered." He lurks on the edge of the living room.

"Long day." I avoid direct eye contact.

"I'm sorry, Macy, about the restaurant and Kate."

I flip off my other slipper. Hmm, lint in my toes. I concentrate on cleaning my foot as if that were way more important than what Chris is attempting to communicate.

"I didn't plan for this to happen. Kate called a few weeks ago. We went out. One thing led to another…."

"Are you in love with her?"

He pauses. Dead giveaway.

"I see." My mouth goes dry, my stomach contorts and picking the lint no longer seems important.

"I know we had a good thing going. This just caught me."

"Chris, are you a Christian?" Suddenly I want to know.

He fidgets. "Well, that all depends on what you mean by Christian. I believe certain things."

Enough said. "Key, please." I rise out of the chair and hold out my hand.

"What?"

"Key. May I have my house key?"

"O-oh, right. Of course." He slips the key off the ring. "I hope we can still be friends."

"I don't know."

"Macy, don't be like this." Chris's tired irritation shows.

"You dump me, break my heart and I have to make you feel better about it? Don't put this on me, Chris."

In the wee hours of the morning my tiny amount of tolerance seems justified. What do I have to lose? I've already lost it all.

"Listen, why don't we have lunch? We can talk this out when we're more rational."

"I am rational. Besides, I'm leaving for Atlanta in a few hours."

"Atlanta?" I can tell he wants an explanation, but I'm too tired and too crabby. Besides, it's none of his business.

"Good night, Chris."

One-thirty. I crawl into bed, spent. Finally the day is done.

Chapter Five

❦

I fade in and out of sleep until my alarm beeps good-morning at four-thirty.

Why me, why now? resonates in my head. I feel shoved back to Go without collecting two hundred dollars. Did I cross wires with someone else's life?

I rouse slowly and decide to call for a cab, since this is a Casper trip. Why should my pet convertible suffer outside in the elements on account of them?

A hot shower makes me sleepier. I feel thick and stupid as I blow-dry my hair, dress in a pair of khakis and a pale blue oxford and brush my face with foundation.

I finish packing, set my bags and computer by the door, then crash on the couch exhausted until the cabbie arrives.

At five-fifteen the cabbie's horn beeps me awake. I hurry out and toss my stuff into the backseat.

Across the way, Mrs. Woodward's kitchen window glows with golden light. I should check on her. Might as well pick up my keys, too. I locked up with Chris's old spare, but I'm pretty sure it has cooties. I'd rather not travel with it.

"I'll be right back," I tell the cabbie, and scurry across the street to rap lightly on Mrs. Woodward's door.

She swings it open with a vibrant "Good morning, dear. Would you like some tea?"

I smile. "No, thanks. I'm on my way to the airport. I just wanted to see how you were feeling." Good smells waft from her kitchen.

"I feel wonderful, thank you."

"I'm glad." I spot my keys on the end table. "Are you baking?" I slip past her to snatch them up.

"I made cinnamon crumb cake. Let me get some for you to take on your trip."

My stomach rumbles, reminding me I haven't eaten. I follow Mrs. W. into her kitchen. "I'm going to ask, um—"*who do I ask?* "—uh, Drag, yes, Drag to check on you while I'm away, okay?"

She turns to me with a large square of tinfoil. "Oh, don't go to any bother. But Drag's a nice boy." Mrs. Woodward reaches out to hug me, surrounding me with the fragrance of vanilla and cinnamon. "Have a safe trip."

I take the crumb cake. The bottom of the foil is warm on my hand. "I'll see you in a few days."

"All righty."

Now, to let our neighbor Drag know he has a mission. I dart past the waiting cabbie.

"Hey, lady, ain't got all day," he hollers when I cross over to Drag's.

"One second," I say. Teach him to be fifteen minutes late.

Drag lives next door to me, directly across from Mrs. Woodward. He's a sweet guy with blond dreadlocks, and is the condo's resident surfer dude. To our knowledge, he has no known employment and no last name. He's simply Drag.

I ring his doorbell until he opens in a sleepy stupor. He looks the way I feel. Wild hair. Electric-socket wild. I didn't know dreadlocks could stand on end. He's wearing Winnie the Pooh pajamas and with eyes barely open, he mutters, "Wha'z up?" as if someone calls on him at 5:20 every morning.

I pinch my lips to keep from laughing. "I'm going out of town this week. Can you check on Mrs. Woodward a few times? She's not feeling well." I whip out a business card. "Call my cell if you need."

He nods, takes my card and shuts the door.

Okay, then. "Don't forget," I holler through the steel.

Atlanta is cold, rainy and dreary. Perfect. Matches my present state of mind. Ten years to make manager, one e-mail and one Roni Karpinski to change it all. Lucy's pointed comments about losing zeal for God while pursuing my career and Chris is a distant echo in my head moving closer, growing louder.

As much as it hurts, I'm glad it's over with Chris. I can throw away those useless rose-colored glasses and admit he wasn't the man I pretended he was.

Last off the plane, I drag my tired and depressed self to baggage claim. I'm about to yank my luggage off the conveyer belt when I hear my name.

"Macy Moore."

I twist around to see Peyton Danner wheeling her suit-case my way, and there's nowhere to hide. Rats. "Peyton, hello."

"Good to see you." She shakes my hand, looking alert and in command.

"Nice to see you, too," I parrot, grabbing the handle on my bag, trying to slough away before she realizes I'm a zombie.

But she yanks the handle on her suitcase and steps in time with me, striding as if she can make the earth move under her feet. "How's Casper these days?"

I'm too tired to fib. "Could be better." Could I *be* any duller? I feel like a partially swatted fly.

"I see."

"How's Danner Limited, and the world of corporate head-hunting?" I ask, trying to speak as though I have half a wit. Peyton Danner's company is *the* headhunter for software companies. Casper uses their services from time to time to scout new talent.

"Very, very good." She emphasizes each word.

"Maybe I'll call you." Ethically she can't ask me to call, but I can volunteer.

She flips me one of her cards. "Anytime."

Rain deluges my rental car the entire drive down I-285 to Miller Glassware. When I pull into the parking lot, the rain tapers off. Goody for me. I was hoping to sit in the car for half the morning, procrastinating, waiting for the monsoon to stop. But no—can't call the game on account of rain today.

I walk through the front door of Miller Glassware con-

centrating on the click, click of my heels against the mar-
ble tile: I think I can. I think I can.

Mike and Attila don't care that they sent me out in the
rain with a paper umbrella. They wanted to appease Peter
Miller, and I'm the only bone they had to throw.

I can do this. I have to do this. I have ten years' experience. I have core knowledge. I have the company phone list.
I plan to dial my way through the support of this customer.

Peter Miller greets me in the hall just outside his office.
He's short and balding with beady gray eyes, but exudes the
aura of a giant. "How did we get the honor of your presence
at our small site?"

"You don't want to know."

Peter regards me for a minute, probably deciding if he really does want to know. A few weeks ago, when I was manager, we'd gone around and around about support.

Fortunately for me, he's all business, and without another
word he drops me off with the IT guys. He doesn't even ask
if I want coffee—which I don't, but I'd appreciate the gesture.

I greet Al and Leroy, remembering Mrs. Woodward's
crumb cake tucked inside my tote bag. This will get me
through the day. I dig a dollar out of my wallet and ask,
"Where's the soda machine?"

"Right down that hall, first door on the left," Al tells me.

I hustle away, returning in a few minutes armed and
ready. Food and drink. What more could a drowning girl
ask for, hmm?

By the end of the day I've upgraded Web Works One and
I loaded the new product, W-Book on a test machine.

Around seven we call it a day. I'm exhausted from navigating Miller's technical jungle and for some strange reason wondering if thirty-three is truly the black hole of old maiddom from which there is no return.

The week at Miller Glassware is fraught with network difficulties, Web page hazards and technical snafus.

I spend so much time on the phone with Casper support techs that Peter Miller presents me with a four-inch gold-painted phone trophy while I pack up on Friday afternoon.

"Thanks for your hard work and support." He hands me the trinket with a grin and a glint. Wise guy.

"Nothing but the best for you, Pete." I'm sarcastic and not apologizing.

I jam the trophy into my computer bag with subtle satisfaction. It was a hard week and my guess is that Mike and Attila thought I'd fall apart, but I didn't. Makes me wonder what plans they really have for my so-called career.

(Mental note 2: converse more with God about career.)

While I survived the week, even had a little fun toward the end, this is not the life I want to lead. Life on the road stinks.

But what can I do? Dig in my heels? Wait out Mike and Roni, and leap for the first crack in the glass ceiling? Do I bone up on my technical skills and become an indispensable guru? (Shudder!) Maybe it's time to post my résumé on Monster.com? Take my toys to another sandbox. I remember Peyton Danner's card in the bottom of my computer bag.

My head hurts. Too much pondering. By the time I pull away from Miller Glassware, twilight has painted golden hues across the winter sky. I'm hit with the desire for home, for Beauty.

My hometown is only an hour north of Atlanta. Why didn't I think of this earlier? A surprise visit home. Dad and Mom would love it. And right now, so would I.

Instead of heading for the airport, I point my car toward home. (Mental note 3: change return ticket home.)

I call Dad's cell phone as I approach the edge of Beauty's city limits.

"Earl Moore."

I love the sound of his voice. "Daddy, it's Macy."

"To what do I owe the pleasure?"

"Meet me at Freda's Diner in ten minutes."

"Freda's?"

"Yes. You know, corner of Jasmine and Laurel."

"I know the place."

"Ten minutes enough time? I'm getting off at the Beauty exit right now."

"I'll call your mother."

We meet in the parking lot with hugs and kisses on the cheek.

"Good to see you, Macy." Mom's blue eyes twinkle when she smiles.

"Best thing that's happened all year, seeing you." Dad has a way of making me feel safe, that life is a grand play and I'm an Academy Award winner.

We pick a window table and Sarah Beth takes our order. Outside, the gentle routine of Beauty passes by while Mom wipes the table down with a wet wipe. Sarah Beth sets down brimming soda cups. Mom shifts them to the top right corner of the table until she's sanitized our eating area.

I snicker, remembering when Lucy swooped into the

restaurant last week to save me from my fast-food feast. She wiped down the table just like Mom. I've long suspected we were switched at birth—despite the fact that we're three months apart.

We make small talk until Sarah Beth brings the food. Burger and fries for me.

"Here we go," Dad says, holding out his hands. "Let's pray."

I close my eyes and listen to Earl Moore thank the Lord for his wife, his daughter and our food.

Then I watch as he and Mom chatter, exchanging food particles. Mom gives Dad all her salad olives. He gives her all his purple onions.

Earl and Kitty Moore, hippies—they met at Woodstock— turned Jesus freaks turned Southern bourgeois capitalists. When they met Jesus, they got married and settled in Beauty, Dad's hometown.

With Mom's blue-blood inheritance, they launched a boutique business, Moore Gourmet Sauces, peddling Mom's special barbecue and marinade sauces.

Within the first year Moore sauces had become a favorite at local restaurants and grocery stores. Then Dad went mail order, adding a recipe book. A few years ago, with me as his consultant, he launched the e-business arm of Moore Gourmet Sauces and sent Mom's specialties into cyberspace.

I don't ask much about their financial status. We lived comfortably growing up. My brother, Cole, and I had new clothes when we needed, braces and a tidy allowance. But last year the folks went to England and Greece for vacation. So the gourmet sauce business must be treating them well.

I tune in to Mom's side of the conversation. Oh, she's asking God to remove all the calories from the salad and grilled chicken sandwich.

I laugh. "Mom, you've been asking Him to do that for fifteen years." It's comforting to be in Beauty, in the shadow of my parents' routine.

"Yes, and I'll keep asking. It's worked out fine so far. I weigh the exact same as the day I married your father."

I choke on my French fry. "Mom, how can a fifty-nine-year-old woman weigh the exact same as she did when she was twenty-two?" Isn't there some scientific law against that?

"Don't know how she does it, but she's right." Dad winks at me. "Within a pound or two."

"Or five or ten," I say before diving into dinner. The food tastes wonderful. Pete Miller all but chained me to a chair and ordered me to make his e-business deadline. I popped breakfast, lunch and dinner from the vending machine. I don't want to see another bag of pretzels until the twenty-second century. Maybe not even then.

"What brings you to Beauty?" Dad sets his salad aside and asks the hard question.

I sip my soda. "Nothing really. I've been in Atlanta working. Since I was so close—"

"What's wrong, Macy? Your eyes…" Mom grabs my chin and pivots my head her way.

"Mom." I twist out of her light grip. "I'm tired, that's all. Long week." Mothers. Do they ever stop perceiving?

"Since when do you do fieldwork?" Dad's a keen one, too, and he's digging deep.

"I haven't in a while." I force a smile.

"How's Chris?" Mom asks, biting a forkful of lettuce and tomato while neatly brushing her red bangs away from her eyes.

"He's fine." If you like creepy-crawly things.

They have no idea, but their questions shine a light on my internal sense of failure. It flashes across my mind like a tacky neon sign.

Failure!

Failure!

Failure!

Sigh.

Chapter Six

❧

"Macy, you sighed." Mom's radar is blipping over Macy Land and picking up way too much activity.

Silent sigh. "Just tired."

I want to tell them what's going on. I do. But I can't. How does one tell her parents she's failed in her career and doesn't know why? That the one steady relationship she's maintained in a dozen years ended with her man in another woman's arms. And that he was a "settle" boyfriend anyway.

Do I say, "You raised an idiot"? No, not the words they want to hear. Not the words I want to say.

"Cole and Suzanne will be excited to see you." Mom weaves the conversation with gentle, casual threads.

"What have they been up to?" Cole is my younger brother. Five years, to be exact, and Suzanne is his best friend and wife.

"Suzy is about to finish school and Cole's joined her father in his business."

"Good for him," I say.

"He'll have a fine surveying career with Regis." Dad acts cool, but I can tell he's disappointed by Cole not wanting to make sauces for a living.

"Our fifteenth class reunion is this year," I offer by way of news-from-Macy. Not much else to tell yet. I tip my cup for a piece of ice, leaving out the idea that I might not attend the reunion.

"Wonderful. Chris will be able to meet your friends."

I'm confident now that she knows something is wrong, but isn't sure how to get it out of me. She's chipping at the wall hoping to find the crack.

"Maybe." I refuse to crack and continue munching on my ice.

The conversation takes a detour down a side country road. We talk easily back and forth about life in general and I avoid details about my life in Melbourne.

Dad picks up the check, leaves Sarah Beth a healthy tip and waves at Freda. Everyone, it seems, knows everyone in Beauty.

At home Dad carries my suitcase up to my old room. It looks exactly the way it did the day I left for college, the day I came home from college and the day I ran away to Florida.

Flopping onto the bed, I close my eyes, pretending I'm sixteen again and the world is still my oyster.

"How's the old room feel?"

I lift my head to see Dad leaning against the door frame. "Peaceful."

He chuckles. "You couldn't wait to get outa this room, as I recall."

"I felt pinned up in this town like I'd never been anywhere but north and south Georgia." I stare at the ceiling while reminiscing out loud.

"I was teaching you the ropes of the gourmet sauce business when Lucy called to say she'd read in the paper that Casper & Company was hiring."

"I ran home to pack."

Dad juts out his chin. "Right in the middle of my riveting account of how we bottle the sauce."

I lift my head. "Sorry about that."

He laughs, giving me the Father Knows Best eye. I hug one of the many pillows on my bed. "It worked out well, don't you think?" Until now, but I leave that part out.

"That it did."

Dad steps inside my room and straddles my desk chair. "You want to tell me what's going on?"

"Nothing's going on." I scoot against the headboard and hide behind the pillow. Is saying "nothing" a lie? I don't want to lie.

I realize I'm doomed. With Mom zeroing in on Chris issues and Dad snooping around with questions about Casper, I just might crack Humpty Dumpty-style. Calling all the king's men.

He pats the chair rungs. "I can still see you bumping down the stairs with, what, five or six suitcases, ready to move to Florida." He skips the palm of one hand over the other. "Vroom!"

The idea of running away from home at the ripe old age of

twenty-three sounds silly. But, oh, how desperate I was to bust out of Beauty and move out from under the shadow of the Moore family, and the legend of my third-grade Christmas solo.

Dad regards me for a moment. "Mrs. Riley still mentions your solo. She insists there hasn't been another one like you."

Can he hear my thoughts? "Yeah, I broke the mold." How does she remember that night? If I were Scrooge, Mrs. Riley would be my Ghost of Christmas Past.

Look, Macy Moore, look. There you are, singing your Christmas solo, "Away in a Manger." Such a sweet child.

I shake the image from my head. It gives me the willies. I sang off-key for fifteen minutes because every time the crowd applauded, I started the song all over again.

"So, how's business?" I ask.

"Rhine Flagstone of *The Food Connection* is featuring our new barbecue on his show."

"No kidding! Big time, Dad." In fact, it's huge. Good for Moore Gourmet Sauces.

"We're talking with QVC, too." He lifts a brow and waits for my reaction.

I love QVC. He knows it. Lisa Robertson is my favorite host. She could sell me a box of melted crayons and leave me with the notion I got a good deal.

But I give him a moderate reply. "QVC, eh? Interesting." My heart palpitates.

"Yep. You know, there's room for family...."

"How'd you manage to get in with Rhine Flagstone?" I ignore his thinly veiled hint.

I'm not ready to jump my corporate cruise ship for a dinghy in the middle of the Atlantic. Dad has a great business, sure, but I pined for years to get a life out of Beauty— I can't imagine returning. It'd be like double-crossing myself. And there's enough of that going on already.

Be true to you, I always say.

Dad outlines the details of *The Food Connection* deal. I smile, half listening and half analyzing my life up to now. It's been a good life, so why do I feel so bland and beige? I have great friends. I've trotted the globe for Casper, managed a staff of trainers and tech support. I've stuffed my closet with designer clothes and parked a BMW convertible in my garage.

Other than my recent career smack down and breakup with Chris, shouldn't I have some sense of achievement and satisfaction? What's missing?

"We're having a little launch party the first weekend in May. I'd love for you to come."

I tune in to Dad. "Come? To what?"

"The launch party for *The Food Connection* and Moore Gourmet Sauces. Rhine will be here, along with some of *The Food Connection* executives."

"Good for you."

"You'll come? May sixth."

"I'll check my calendar."

Mom calls up the stairs, "Earl, it's chilly tonight. How about a fire?" Her Southern lilt is intertwined with hints of her childhood in England.

Dad slaps his knee and rises. "Be right down, Kitty."

"Macy, you want some hot chocolate or tea?" Mom calls to me.

"Hot chocolate, please. With whipped cream."

"If I have any."

"See you downstairs." Dad tweaks my toes. "And think about coming May sixth."

"Okay." I flop onto my belly and rest my chin on the edge of the bed.

Peering into the present from the window of my past, I understand now that my problem wasn't this house at 21 Laurel Street, the city of Beauty, or the state of Georgia.

Nope. The problem was me, Macy Moore, and my state of mind. I thought life's answers were out *there* somewhere. Now I realize the answers are in me, in my faith in Jesus and His love for me.

Sunday afternoon Dad, Mom, Cole, Suzanne and I trail the after-church lunch herd to Sizzler. We're last in line because Mrs. Riley caught me after the service and wanted to know *all* the latest news. She's storing up so she can haunt me the rest of my life.

I gave her the view from twenty thousand feet: clear skies and smooth sailing.

She cackled, patted me on the arm and meandered down memory lane as if she hadn't heard one fluffy word I'd said. First stop, my third-grade Christmas solo. Dad, talking to Pastor Gary, heard Mrs. Riley mention "Away in a Manger" and beckoned me.

"Time for lunch, Macy."

So here I am, mooing my way down the Sizzler salad bar. Suddenly Joley McGowan, a former classmate, scurries over.

"Macy, I thought that was you in church this morning."

She wraps her svelte arms around me as if we were long-lost friends. I almost drop my plate into the coleslaw.

"Hey, Joley." I regard her casually—you know, just to see if she's sagging or bulging. Rats! She's as gorgeous as ever.

"Look at you!" she gushes, and hugs me again. "A big-time career woman. You've heard about our fifteenth class reunion, right? Of course you have. Well, I'm on the committee this year." Joley is animated and vibrant. I didn't like her much in high school, since she dated Dylan Braun, my high school heartthrob. Think fabulous smile, gentle voice, athletic, blond and hunky.

"Good for you." I continue down the line. Joley strolls beside me like a gazelle—graceful and long legged. I'm losing my appetite.

"Macy, would you please be our emcee this year?"

"What?" I stop gathering lunch. Joley's almond-shaped green eyes are locked on me.

"Well, you *were* voted most likely to succeed." She sweeps her hand in the air over my head like reading an imaginary headline. Macy Moore Makes It After All.

I grimace. "I'm a regular Mary Richards."

Her glow fades. "Huh?"

"You know, *The Mary Tyler Moore Show?* Her character was Mary Richards. Don't you watch TV Land?"

She beams again. "Oh, yes, of course."

I'm holding up the salad bar line, so I step forward. "Are you sure you want me? What about Lucy O'Brien? She's a reporter for one of Florida's biggest newspapers. Or John Friedman? Isn't he a millionaire?"

"Don't be so modest. You're perfect for the job." She taps

the side of my arm. "Skip is a millionaire, but we wouldn't ask him to be emcee." She tee-hees behind her hand. "Can you see Skip talking in front of a mike?"

I make a face. "Skip who? Skip Warner?"

She smiles and holds up her ring hand. "Yes, I'm Joley Mc-Gowan Warner now. We've been married for two years."

"Really. Well, congratulations." Good grief. Joley Mc-Gowan and grease-under-his-nails Skip Warner? Is no one's life turning out as I'd planned?

Joley and Skip Warner. Wow. Hold it. Did she just use the words *millionaire* and *Skip* in the same sentence? I covertly give her the once-over again. Her Sunday dress is pretty, but simple. Her shoes? Go-with-everything taupe pumps. I peek at her left hand again and see a simple gold band coupled with a modest diamond. Skip, a millionaire? Is she sure?

She's still talking. "John Friedman is a fuddy-duddy. Come on, be our emcee." She smiles her perfect smile. "You'll be great."

"Let me think about it." I can't promise more than that, really I can't. I grit my teeth to keep from blurting out the truth right then and there, confessing in front of the entire Sizzler congregation that Macy Moore is not a success after all, but a failure.

I can't emcee our high school reunion when my life is on a carousel. I can't. I won't.

"I saw you talking to Joley Warner." Dad eyes me from the other end of the table.

"She wants me to emcee the class reunion."

"Wonderful. You should do it." He sips his iced tea.

I lean his way. "You never told me she married Skip Warner and that he's a millionaire."

"You never asked." He spears a piece of steak with his fork.

"Are you going to tell me how he's a millionaire or do I have to ask twenty questions?"

"Oh, for goodness' sake, Macy. He's into cars." Mom flutters like a mad hen. She hates this kind of table talk. "He owns a fancy, imported car dealership. Lots of rich clients."

I shove my salad around on my plate. He asked me out once in our senior year, but I turned him down. Not my type, I told Lucy.

More and more I want to run home, crawl into a hole and surface sometime after a nuclear attack.

I gather my wits and look at my salad plate. Apparently I wasn't paying attention. Two leaves of lettuce, a smattering of shaved carrots, and a mountain of bean sprouts. This won't do.

I hop up, get back in line and add tomatoes and cucumbers to my plate with some ham bits, grated cheese and a ladle of dressing.

Back at the table, Suzanne is telling Mom about her current class schedule. Across from me, Dad and Cole are in an intense discussion about an upcoming NASCAR race.

"Jeff Gordon."

"No, Dale Junior."

NASCAR is not my kind of Sunday-lunch chatter. I join Mom and Suzanne's discussion, desperate to focus on something besides me. My whine is getting a little sour.

"Ten years of part-time school and finally I see the light at the end of the tunnel," Suzanne says fervently, her chestnut bangs falling across her Sandra Bullock-like face. "I can't wait."

"I'm proud of you, Suz," I say, meaning it.

She presses her hand on my arm, squeezes up her shoulders and wrinkles her nose. "Thank you. I'm so excited and relieved. Now I can get a real job, like you, Macy."

I smile. "Hopefully better than me."

By two o'clock the family waddles out to the parking lot discussing the insanity of all-you-can eat food bars. I catch sight of Skip and Joley climbing into a shiny silver Hummer.

Figures.

I face the family. "I'd better get going. I don't want to miss my flight. Can't change my ticket again."

Chapter Seven

As I fiddle with the gas nozzle at the 7-11 near Sizzler, I console myself. So I'm not married to a millionaire. Okay, I'm not married at all, nor do I have any prospects. Forget the fact that I'm temporarily a failure.

I top off the tank, put the gas nozzle back in the thingy and screw on the gas cap. I head inside to pay.

From the corner of my eye I catch a flash of red. I turn. Lo and behold, Dylan Braun is at the pump across the way. Propped against the side of his red Dodge Ram, arms folded across his chest, his white shirt collar open, his dark tie loose, he looks like an image from the cover of *GQ*. And he's looking at me.

Zing!

I wave as I stroll, gliding like a runway model. "That thing got a hemi?" I call out. Light, airy, cute.

I don't see the next pump island rising out of the pavement. My toes jam into the concrete and I fall face-first into the trash bin. My right hand and face are buried in greasy paper, half-full soda cups and candy wrappers. I knock an "oomph!" out of me as I spin and hit the ground.

Oh, please, say this isn't happening.

"Macy! Are you okay?" Dylan runs to my rescue.

I bounce around, rubbing my knees and flinging soda from my hand. "I'm all right." I make an effort to gather my cool while my voice squeaks up an octave or two.

"You went down face-first." His eyes never leave my face.

"Any other way and you're a coward."

He laughs. A good, hearty, that's-funny laugh.

My right knee is throbbing and my pride stinging. I prop my hand on my hip, then drop it by my side, then on my hip again. I'm not sure what to do with my hands.

Worse, I'm not sure what to do with myself. Dylan's blue-green eyes watch me. Oh no, please tell me I plucked that one dark hair from my chin this morning.

"You're looking good, Macy," Dylan finally says.

Yes, I yanked it. I borrowed Mom's tweezers. "Thanks."

Hard to imagine I once loathed Dylan. In fourth grade he wrote a haiku about me that the class chanted for a month. In those days I was a little pudgy due to my affinity for peanut butter and jelly sandwiches, and vanilla ice cream smothered in chocolate syrup.

I can still hear him read his stupid little ditty before the entire class.

I went out to play
And I saw Macy Moore
She's fat.

The class howled. I slid under my desk and despised him.

I carried a small grudge—okay, a huge grudge—until junior high. By then, Dylan was incredibly popular, athletic and handsome. He breezed through puberty unscathed. All the girls liked him. I, however, couldn't get beyond "she's fat."

But during church camp the summer after seventh grade, I forgave his dumb haiku when our counselor described the crucifixion of Jesus for *my* sins. It had me in tears and I could no longer justify seething over Dylan's poetry.

I stole a peek at him during the closing prayer and caught him wiping his eyes with the back of his hand. My heart melted a little.

By the time we started high school, I fell face-first in love—pure, unrequited love. Any other way and you're a coward. But he never knew.

"I think you'll live," Dylan says, reaching for my hand to examine the scrapes. He brushes away the dirt and gravel. I feel light-headed. For a man built like a Mack truck, his touch is tender.

"And not die of embarrassment? Please, give a girl her due." Perhaps a swoon is coming on. This is definitely a swoon moment.

"Never let it be said I kept a girl from her due." He laughs low and peers deep into my eyes.

Well, well. Dylan Braun. "I thought you would be fat and bald by now." My senses start to solidify and my composure returns.

"That was the plan, but some things just don't turn out." His grin is still his best feature—rakishly Clark Gable.

"Married?" I flirt, knowing he's not. His mother, Margaret Braun, and my mother are birds of a feather, descendants of blue-blood Europeans with dukes and duchesses in their lineage. If Dylan married, I'd hear about it.

"Not yet. You?"

"Not yet."

"Haven't met Mr. Right?"

I laugh. "Oh, sure I did. Turned out to be Mr. Wrong."

He stares at me for a long second. "I saw you talking to Joley in Sizzler."

He was in Sizzler? "She wants me to emcee the class reunion."

"Will you? I told her to ask you."

"You?"

"I'm reunion coordinator this time. Don't ask me how I got roped into it. Did you get Alisa's flyer?"

"Yeah, as a matter of fact." I regard him for a moment, seeing a new side to him. "Why me as emcee? And don't say because I was voted most likely to succeed."

He slips his hands into his pockets, rolls his big shoulders forward and looks away. "I wanted to have the prettiest and the smartest, that's all."

The prettiest? Did he just say prettiest? Is there room

to swoon? Can I swoon without it looking like another pratfall?

"We're proud of you." He regards me openly.

We? We who? We as in the plural of Dylan, we?

"I wasn't the smartest, Dylan."

"No, but the smartest *and* the prettiest."

That's it. I'm swooning. I glance around, but can't find a place to light. "When is the reunion again? I may have a business trip scheduled."

"Fourth of July weekend. Surely you're not booked then."

Surely I'm not, but I just can't say yes when my life is sagging. If I could get a new job, I could emcee with dignity, but who knows what the next few months will bring. "I just don't know, Dylan."

"Say yes." He grips my hand again and peers right into my eyes.

I blurt out, "Yes. Yes, I'll do it." I'm an idiot.

"Good. And by the way—" he nods toward his truck "— it has a hemi." He winks.

Meltdown complete.

Monday morning I stride toward my sunny corner office with my confidence reservoir up a fraction. My trip to Miller Glassware was a moderate success, I had a nice weekend in Beauty and—blow the trumpets—Dylan Braun called me pretty.

I dock my laptop and boot up, carefully store my bag in the bottom desk drawer and flop into my chair. Despite recent upsets, being in my office gives me a sense of normalcy, as if the world is right side up again.

Wearing a pair of rustic red capris, I feel light and breezy. This is the feeling I wanted yesterday when Dylan watched me tumble into a pile of trash. I wince at the mental instant replay. Bless Dylan for not letting loose with a knee-slapping belly laugh.

Attila the Hun pops her giant blond head around my door. "Hello, Macy."

"Roni." Her presence makes me queasy.

"Be sure to file a report on your Miller trip, and we need your input on the Holloway proposal." She waits for my okay.

"Sure," I say without looking up. I'm feeling very passive-aggressive today. Sure, I'll do it. Next week. Maybe.

Once Roni is out of earshot, I autodial Lucy. One ring and she picks up. "Lucy O'Brien."

"Hey."

"How was Beauty?"

"Believe it or not, great." I peruse work e-mail, reading and deleting.

Holloway Proposal. Delete.

"Wonders never cease."

"Oh, you of little faith."

I click on the Delete folder and retrieve the Holloway proposal. So Roni is a self-promoting shrew—it doesn't mean I should stoop to her level. I do *not* want to be like her when I grow up.

"I never understood why you were so desperate to leave home. Beauty is a wonderful, cozy little town," Lucy says.

"I talked to Joley McGowan at Sizzler." I smile, knowing she's going to die when I tell her the news.

"What'd she want?" Lucy, sweet Lucy who loves everyone, never cared much for Joley on account of my crush on Dylan and the fact that Joley dated him.

"She wants me to emcee the class reunion." I recline back in my desk chair and gaze out the window. I see nothing but blue skies and the tops of green palms.

"Are you going to do it?"

"I told her maybe." Never mind what I told Dylan. I attended reunions five and ten strutting around like a proud peacock over my Casper career. The girl most likely to succeed *did*.

The fifth reunion came right after my trips to Madrid and London, and right before my trip to Florence. Not South Carolina either—Italy.

I bragged and gloated. Snubbed those stay-at-home moms with their two-year-olds. I regaled the room with my "travel abroad" stories.

The tenth reunion came right after I'd been promoted to team leader. Two years later I made manager.

Serves me right. Pride goes before a fall. Now look.

"Macy, be the emcee," Lucy says with resolve. "You're perfect for the job." While she is no way as alluring as Dylan, she is my best friend and that has to count for something.

"Maybe," I say. "But never mind that. Guess who's a millionaire?"

Open bomb-bay doors.

"Besides John Friedman?" She's dying to know, I can tell.

"Skip Warner. And he's married to Joley McGowan." Bombs away!

"What? I knew that. Tell me something I don't know, Macy."

"You knew?" I shoot out of my chair. "Then why don't I know? What kind of friend are you?"

"Oops, I meant to tell you. I guess I forgot." She sounds sheepish and repentant, but I'm not letting her off that easily.

"Then I guess I forget to tell you what Dylan said to me yesterday."

"What? You can't keep Dylan news a secret. Details, details." She's yipping like my aunt May's toy poodle.

"Nope, too bad. You'll have to wait."

"Fine, but I want all the details, every last tidbit, right down to the brand of his T-shirt." Her normal voice, thank heaven, returns.

I laugh at her desperation. "Okay, details it is." I'm actually dying to tell her.

I stretch and walk over to the window. The day is so gorgeous. Procrastination is beckoning. I look out at my car in the parking lot, wondering if I can escape. Um, hey, there's Roni getting into her car with Mike.

"Lucy." I whisper.

"What?" She whispers back.

"Attila is leaving with Mike Perkins."

"Really?"

"Do you think—"

"Stop. Don't go there, Macy. It'll only pollute your mind. You don't know and you can't assume."

I watch Attila's burgundy car exit the Casper campus and head south. "You're right."

"Doesn't help your feelings, though, does it?" Lucy says softly.

"Not really. But you know, I hope it's not true. Mike is married with little kids."

I feel burdened. Not only for me, but for Mike Perkins and Roni Karpinski. She lives one sad life, but she believes she has it all. One day she'll be forced to retire, and Casper & Company won't care that she sits alone in her house on the river with no one to visit.

Fear of being another lonely Roni blinded me somewhat about Chris Wright, along with the incessant ringing of my bio clock.

Lucy breaks in to my thoughts. "Mace, I have a phone interview in a few minutes."

"Yeah, I need to get to work." I glance at my desk. "See you tonight? I feel like shopping."

"Old Navy's having a sale."

"Now you're talking. What time? Six-thirty?"

"Better make it seven. I've got a lot to do."

Without manager duties plaguing me, I don't have a reason to stay late anymore. "I'll be there already. Look for me."

"Don't forget tomorrow night, either."

I think for a second. Ah, yes. "Tuesday. The infamous gathering of the Single Saved Sisters."

"We miss you."

The Single Saved Sisters, well, well. I haven't met with the Sisters since my third month with Chris. "Same time, same place?"

"Of course."

"Thank goodness some things never change." I hang up, grab a soda from my mini fridge and double click on the Holloway proposal.

Chapter Eight

❧

Tuesday at eight the Single Saved Sisters gather at House of Joe's for coffee, consolation and consultation.

The club emerged two years ago when Tamara Clayton and I had an epiphany in the church parking lot.

"Where are all the good Christian men?" Tamara asked. We stood by my old car.

"Married." I unlocked my door and tossed my purse and Bible onto the passenger seat.

Tamara laughed. "So what are women like us supposed to do?" Tamara raised her arms toward heaven. "Please, Lord, where are all the good, available men?"

That's when I suggested we get Lucy and several others to meet at House of Joe's for coffee to discuss the gravity of the situation.

The first meeting of the Single Saved Sisters consisted of me; Lucy; Tamara, a gorgeous, intelligent, fiery black woman; Adriane Fox, a writer, muse and introspective philosopher; and last but not least, Beka Roth, a preppy, Rory Gilmore–type lawyer.

Two years later the crowd is the same except Beka, who recently joined the Happily Ever After club by marrying a colleague, Rick Gainer.

I abandoned them briefly, but I am back with a clear head and renewed commitment to getting it right. When I arrive at the coffeehouse Tuesday night, Lucy, Tamara and Adriane are already seated on two of the love seats.

"It's about time you showed up." Tamara lunges at me with her arms wide. "Hiding out with Chris is no excuse."

"I was hoping he would rescue me from this excuse of a girls' club," I retort, giving Tamara a tight squeeze.

I drop my handbag on the coffee table, kiss Adriane on the cheek and fish out my wallet to buy a large fat-free latte.

Adriane leans forward and examines my bag with her fingertips. "A Hermès Birkin?" She regards me with her angular chin in the air, her wrist poised as if she held a cigarette. She quit smoking four years ago, but her hand has never forgotten. "Did you rob a bank?"

"No," I say, proud of my signature handbag. "eBay."

"How much?" Adriane picks up the purse for closer scrutiny.

If I tell her, she'll never let me hear the end of it. She'll lecture me on the needs of the world's poor and homeless.

But I didn't take money designated for the poor to buy this expensive accessory. No, I bought the bag when I thought my career was on the rise and perhaps I would become the wife of a successful financier.

"She's not saying." Tamara takes the bag from Adriane. "Must be bad."

"Two thousand," I blurt. "And change."

Lucy's mouth drops open. "I thought it was a knockoff. Are you telling me you bought a real Birkin?"

I twist my lips into a halfhearted smile and squeak out a yes.

"How much change?" Tamara pinches the purse handles between her thumb and forefinger. "Don't want to smudge the leather."

I mutter. "Five hundred dollars of change."

"Oh, Macy!" All three speak at once. Twenty-five hundred dollars for a handbag? Of all things…

I cover my ears and foot it over to the coffee bar. I order my latte and go to the ladies' room while Zach whips it together.

I don't feel guilty for buying a Birkin. I've wanted a designer bag since my first trip to Manhattan in '97. But the Single Saved Sisters' brutal honesty causes me to question my priorities.

According to my recent tax return, I spent less than the cost of that purse on my charitable giving last year. Way less. Sure, I didn't spend funds designated for the poor to buy that luxury item because I didn't designate any money for the poor. I curl my lip at my reflection in the ladies' room mirror. Not a thrilling revelation about myself.

I pick up my latte and decide to make a foxhole confession to my comrades that I'll be more charitable this year despite my recent career setback.

But the conversation at the table is no longer about my expenditures. They are arguing about the reality show *Average Joe*.

"No way would a handsome man choose an Average Jane. Would not happen," Lucy argues, her cheeks as red as her hair.

"Oh, no way," I agree, taking my place on the couch as if I'd never missed a Tuesday.

"Let's see them create the Average Jane series." Tamara gives Lucy a high five. "One hunky man choosing among twenty very average women."

"No one would watch," Adriane drones, her hand still waiting for that cigarette. "No one, not even women, want to watch or read about a homely girl. She has to be beautiful."

"Oh, come on, Adriane, you're kidding?" Lucy digs through her shoulder bag for something. "What kind of message does that communicate to teens and young women?" Lucy slaps the table with her notebook.

I sense a story in the making.

Adriane looks right at her and says, "If you aren't beautiful, you'd better be smart. And if you aren't smart, you'd better be funny."

"And if I'm none of those?" Lucy challenges. She flips open the pad and jots a few notes with a House of Joe's pen.

"What do you mean? You're all of those," I interject. Lucy is sickening. She's beautiful in a Julianne Moore kind of way. She's smart, funny and logical. I feel like sticking my tongue out at her.

She looks at me as if I'm an idiot. "I don't mean me. I mean women in general." She jots a note. I stick out my tongue.

"What is it about the human race that makes us desperate for beauty?" Adriane waxes philosophical. It's what we love about her. Yet what annoys us. Who can answer that question? But there she sits, waiting for one.

"I think God made us to desire beauty. But I'm learning we have to first find our beauty in God." Lucy sips her coffee, glancing around at each of us.

I nod, feeling far away from that reality. I chew on my stir stick, meditating on her words.

Tamara bobs her head at me. "All right, out with it. What happened with Chris?" Her lips are puckered with attitude and her brown eyes are wide. As a corporate accountant, she likes details.

"He fell in love with someone else." I meet her gaze and am happy to say the words didn't sting at all.

"Just like that?" Tamara snaps her fingers over her head.

"Just like that." I mimic her snap. "I didn't know there was someone else until two weeks ago."

"How could you be so naive?" Adriane clicks her tongue in disgust.

"Right," I retort. "Who here had a gay boyfriend?"

"Hmm-hmm, that's right." Tamara points at Adriane.

We stifle our laughs behind our mugs. We can't help it. The expression on Adriane's face is comical, yet oddly disturbing.

"I wasn't a Christian then." Adriane defends herself. "I had absolutely no discernment."

"So what's your excuse, Macy? Why didn't you know what was going on with Chris?" Lucy pokes me in the side with her finger. How annoying. I frown at her. How can someone so beautiful, so smart and funny be so annoying?

"The ringing," I say, sipping my latte.

"The ringing?" Tamara echoes, looking at Lucy and Adriane.

I nod. "My biological alarm clock was going crazy. Ringing and ringing."

Tamara slaps her knee. Lucy laughs and Adriane smirks. They know.

"Anybody know how to turn that thing off?" I glance at each of them.

"No," says Adriane, the oldest among us at thirty-four. "Best you can do is hit the snooze button."

"There's a snooze?"

Tamara asks, "Well, I for one would like to find the Men-of-God tree. I'm tired of waiting." She's only thirty-one, but anything over thirty feels like the Terrain of the Desperate.

Adriane turns to Tamara. "Haven't you found it yet?"

"No, but at least I'm looking. Not pining away for four years like this one." Tamara jerks her thumb toward Adriane.

"Don't drag me into this. I'm focusing on my writing and my relationship with God. I don't have time for men."

Lucy takes this opportunity to reveal secrets from our Monday-night shopping spree where I downloaded the Dylan details. "Macy knows someone she could pluck from the Men-of-God tree."

"Hold it!" Tamara holds up her hand. "I'll be right back. More coffee."

I eye Lucy as Tamara scoots over to the coffee bar. "What are you talking about? There's nothing to tell."

She makes a face. "Please, there's plenty to tell."

Tamara returns, breathless, sloshing coffee on the table. "Okay, now tell me. Who?"

"Dylan Braun," Lucy reveals like she's announcing the Oscar for best actor.

Tamara curls her lip. "Dylan? That guy from your high school?"

I give Lucy an I-told-you-so face. "Yes, my sisters, Dylan from high school. Move on, there's nothing to see here."

"He told her she was pretty."

I laugh. "Lucy, can you *be* any more junior high?"

Adriane has a faraway look on her face. "All my best love stories begin with the hero calling the heroine beautiful, or pretty."

"Well, fine and dandy, but this is my life, not a romance novel. He said *was* pretty, past tense."

"Bite your tongue." Adriane wags her finger at me. "Besides, truth is stranger than fiction."

"You are stranger than fiction, Adriane. The queen of skepticism. You can write it, but you can't live it," Tamara challenges.

"And what about you?" Adriane returns the challenge. "I don't see you blazing a dating trail."

"I've been on a few dates," Tamara confesses with a heavy sigh. "Dweebs. All of them."

We raise our mugs and clink them again.

"Lucy's the only one here who manages to date decent men on a regular basis." I won't let her escape this conversation.

"Hey, that's right." Tamara pokes Lucy's leg with her pointy fingernail. "Where are you hiding them?"

Lucy evades the inquiry. "Macy is also going to emcee our class reunion." She is just full of Macy Moore news tonight.

"Gee whiz, Lucy. Maybe, I said maybe," I protest a bit too loudly. "I'm not sure I'm even going this year."

"I thought you loved going to your high school reunions."
Does Tamara remember everything about me?

"Well," I begin, "I used to before my life went belly-up."

"Belly-up? What are you talking about?" Adriane asks.

"Work woes," Lucy blurts. I eye her again. She's hiding
something about her own life by blabbing about mine—I
just know it.

Now I have to tell them about my job fiasco. But first,
more latte.

Chapter Nine

I hum to myself on the way home from the Single Saved Sisters java jam, turning into the supermarket parking lot, tired of my refrigerator with its sodas, a loaf of moldy bread and an occasional half-eaten apple.

I've thrown away enough food to feed a small Guatemalan village. Never mind how much food I could buy with the twenty-five hundred I spent on a designer leather handbag.

Now that the Sisters have pointed it out, I feel silly walking around with a purse that is intended for the rich and the famous. Of which I'm neither.

I wouldn't feel quite so bad if I'd done more for others this past year. But I haven't. Lavishing time and money on myself netted me nothing.

Funny how a crisis can put life into perspective, fine-tune

the eye of the heart, like laser surgery. In less than a minute everything comes into a twenty-twenty view.

I regard the Hermès, riding like a kid in the shopping cart. I stop my cart in the middle of the aisle and peer inside the bag.

There's the weathered wallet I paid fifty bucks for ten years ago when I started at Casper. I ate ramen noodles for a week so I could afford it. There's my beat-up makeup bag with assorted lipsticks and powders I bought on QVC from Lisa Robertson. Eyedrops, an assortment of pens I think I'll use but never do, my cell phone and my keys.

Did I think owning this bag would make me happy? Define me? *Look at Macy Moore. She's successful.*

"Excuse me!"

I look around to see a large angry man. I scoot my cart out of the way.

"Sorry." I smile sweetly, but he snarls as he pushes past.

In the checkout line I tear off one of the coupons at the cash register and donate ten dollars toward food for the needy. The old put-your-money-where-your-mouth-is routine.

Now only $2,490 to go.

When the rude guy gets in line after me, I flash him a big grin. "Have a nice night."

He grunts.

At five to eleven I pull into my garage and unload groceries. I string all the plastic bags on my arms—seventy-five dollars and I can carry it all inside with one trip.

I close the trunk with my elbows.

"Macy?" A small voice calls me.

"Yes?" It's dark, but I catch Mrs. Woodward's silhouette in the low glow of the streetlights.

"It's me, Elaine."

"Hi, Mrs. Woodward. Is everything okay?"

"Yes, thank you." She shuffles into the garage wearing her robe and slippers. Despite my bags, I give her a neighborly hug and breathe in the scent of lemon drops.

"Would you like to come in?" I motion toward the door. I'm sort of tired, but I get the sense she wants company.

"That would be lovely."

Mrs. Woodward offers to help me with my packages, but I ask her to push the garage-door button instead. It glides shut as we go inside. I drop my purchases on the kitchen counter and tell my neighbor to make herself comfortable.

"Would you like some tea?" I peer into the living room from the pass-through window. Mrs. Woodward sits on the edge of the couch with her hands folded and legs crossed at the ankles. She's as regal as any queen.

"Oh, I don't want to be a bother."

"It's no bother." Ducking back into the kitchen, I put on the kettle. I can't imagine what has Mrs. Woodward up and visiting at this late hour, but I'm captured by her gentility and elegance.

"Here we go." I carry in the tea tray with my grandmother's china rose teapot, matching cups and saucers, sugar bowl and creamer. It's rare for me to break out the antique set, but Mrs. Woodward deserves it. I open a new bag of gingersnaps and arrange them on one of the saucers.

"Oh, how lovely."

"My grandmother gave me the tea set several years ago. It belonged to her grandmother, a true Englishwoman." I pour and pass.

"I adored my grandmother." She holds her tea and gazes absently across the room into her past.

I let her reminisce in silence for a moment. "Do you have grandchildren?"

She shakes her head. "No, just one son. He's been married several times, but no children." She spoons sugar into her tea.

"Does he visit? I've never seen him around." I hold out the plate of gingersnaps.

"He and his father argued over money. When I sided with my husband, Walter—" she takes a cookie "—James became very angry and left."

"I'm so sorry."

"He accused Walter of hoarding cash and he wanted some of it to start a business. But I assured him we did not have a secret bankroll." She sighs. Even her sigh is elegant. "We raised James the best we could, but he turned out spoiled and selfish."

"Time mends relationships, Mrs. Woodward. Don't worry."

"It's been too many years to worry now." She presses her hand on mine as if to comfort me.

We lapse into casual talk for the next fifteen minutes or so, sipping tea and munching cookies. I tell her about my work in Atlanta and the weekend in Beauty.

She tells me the news of our community, The Gables, and assures me she's had no more stomach episodes.

"Nevertheless, you need to see your doctor." I pop the last cookie into my mouth. I'm worried about her. Regal and lovely, she also seems fragile and frail.

"Perhaps, dear. We shall see."

Did I say fragile and frail? Forget it. She's stubborn and feisty.

At eleven-thirty she thanks me for the tea and announces she must go.

"Thank you for coming over." I escort her to the door, realizing that in the three years I've lived here, I've never invited her inside until tonight.

"Your home is lovely, Macy." I notice she shakes slightly when she speaks.

(Mental note 4: be a better neighbor, get Mrs. Woodward to the doctor, second reminder to rejoin the gym, find a place to write down dumb mental notes.)

I watch her walk home, making sure she's safe before locking my front door and flipping off the porch light. Such an odd visit—no purpose, no reason. Just for company.

My heart is content as I wash my face, slip into my nightshirt and crawl into bed. Thinking of the Single Saved Sisters, my grocery-aisle epiphany and Mrs. Woodward's visit, I'm reminded of the good things in life. I've been missing them for too long. I poured everything I had into Chris and Casper. Now I'm emotionally and spiritually bankrupt.

Clicking on my bedside lamp, I reach for my Bible. It's covered in dust, an embarrassing discovery. I run for a damp cloth.

Has it been that long since I read my Bible? That's like Christianity 101. I hop back into bed and flip to the verse Pastor Gary used Sunday morning at Beauty Community Church.

Isaiah 61:3. "To console those who mourn in Zion, to give them beauty for ashes."

I close my eyes and slip down under the covers. Change is in the wind. What, when, where, why and how? I'm not sure. But I'm ready for the path of beauty. I set my Bible aside and click out the light.

"Thanks, Lord, for Your love and patience, and that I still have a job. Thanks for my home and car." I close my eyes, fading. "For the Single Saved Sisters, for Mrs. Woodward and for simple things like food—"

I bolt up in the darkness. Food. Supermarket. I scramble out of bed and tumble to the floor, my foot caught in the sheets. My groceries are still in the bags on the counter. And I bought ice cream!

Mike pops his head around my office door. "S-o-o-o, Macy…"

I eye him over my laptop. Nothing that starts out "S-o-o-o, Macy" is ever good.

Several weeks have passed since my Atlanta trip and I've adjusted well, if I say so myself, to my new role at Casper.

Not much has changed, really, other than that I report to Mike and he reports to Roni. Since he's so clueless about how to manage anything but his TiVo machine, much less a customer service team, I graciously assist. I could be pig-headed about it—he and Roni deserve it—but in the end that will only make me look bad and there is enough of that going on already.

People stop talking when I pass by in the hall. Sometimes they meet my gaze and smile with sympathy. I hate that expression the most. I'd rather be the target of their gossip.

But seeing Mike in my office makes me churn with suspicion. I haven't seen him ride off with Roni again and I'm glad I don't have any more of those scenes added to my arsenal.

"What can I do for you?" I ask in my most professional tone.

"I put a couple of trips on your schedule. Suddenly the sales team is frantic for W-Book installations."

"We knew it'd be a hit."

"It'll put Casper & Company on the map."

"Kyle Casper gets what he wants." I finish the e-mail I was typing and click Send.

Kyle, a contemporary of Bill Gates, seethes to this day that Bill beat him to the market with his everyman's computer company. Then he invested a chunk of change in search-engine technology and spent a night in hospital with heart palpitations when the Google guys launched their search engine six months before the Casper engine was ready. He had to scrap the whole project.

"Check your schedule. Let me know if you have questions." Mike pounds his palm with his pen.

I double click on the shortcut to the company Intranet to check our schedule.

"I might need some vacation days." There's Dad's launch party, and the reunion, though I haven't decided if I'm going to either yet.

"Oh?"

I glare up at him. "I still get vacation, don't I?"

"Um, well, I can check with Roni, but I'm sure you do."

I feel a little sick to my stomach as the schedule opens. I find my name and check out my assignments. Lovely. Just lovely. Two weeks in Smallville, Kansas, another two in Podunk, Mississippi, and a week in Desert Town, Nevada.

I snap my head up. Mike continues to stand in the doorway. "And I get all the small towns because…"

"Just worked out that way."

Yeah, right, it just worked out that way. Who's he kidding? I see New York, L.A., Portland, Dallas, Seattle, St. Louis on the schedules of less senior people. Don't I get some credit for hanging around for ten years?

If I didn't know better, I'd say Mike—or Roni—was trying to get rid of me. Do they know I saw them out the window that day?

No. Besides, it's all innocent, right? Roni promoted Mike because she wants someone to control. He's got more loops for puppet strings than Pinocchio.

After Mike walks away, I study the schedule for a swap possibility. Aleta is going to New York City when I'm going to Desert Town, Nevada.

I dial her office. "Aleta, have I got a deal for you."

"What?" She sounds skeptical.

I'm hoping my rank as her former boss holds clout. "How about you take Nevada, I'll take New York?" Decisive. Bold. One would think I'm still in charge.

She laughs in my ear. "Are you kidding me? I have tickets to a Broadway show."

"Come on." I'm not above begging. "Do your old boss a favor."

"Okay."

My heart lightens. "Great."

"But you have to give me your BMW."

I slap the receiver to the cradle. I dial Mick next. His Portland trip fits my schedule just perfectly. He answers, "I'll do it for your Beemer. And you have to have dinner with me."

"Not in a million years."

Mick was my last option. I'm stuck. I exit the schedule. Life on the road is bad enough, but life in one-horse towns is pure torture.

I have the urge to vent. I check the time. Five-thirty. The Single Saved Sisters are gathering tonight and I'm ready to unload.

Chapter Ten

With the workday technically over, I launch Monster.com and create an account. No harm in posting my résumé, right? And where's Peyton Danner's card? I dig in my laptop bag for her card.

A light knock outside my door interrupts my Monster mission. "Yes?" I look up, dropping Peyton's card next to my laptop.

A handsome phone guy stands in my doorway. I sit up straight, minimize the Web page and toss my hair over my shoulder. I hope I look beautiful despite feeling rather obtuse.

"Excuse me, but I need to check your phone." He steps into my office.

"Please, do." I shove my phone to the edge of the desk. He's really handsome. A manly man. Like a young Viggo Mortensen.

I go back to my computer and launch the Monster page, create an account and watch Phone Guy in my peripheral vision. He looks familiar. Wouldn't that be the corniest line of all time? *Haven't I seen you somewhere before?*

With a click of this and switch of that, he finishes whatever business he had with my phone. "All set."

Already? Macy, hurry. Think of something to say. "Have we met?" I blurt out. Blah! Not cool. Too desperate.

"You were at Beka and Rick Gainer's wedding." He shifts his attention from the phone to me for a second.

Of course. "We ran into each other in the buffet line." I recall. "I spilled punch on your meatballs." I laugh.

He flashes a shy smile before turning to his toolbox. "I suppose you did."

"Right." Not how I want him to remember me. The punch slosher.

"It was nice seeing you again." He lingers for a moment. Is he waiting for me to do something, say something?

"So, the phone's all set?"

"All set."

"Are you sure?"

He chuckles. "Positive."

Okay, so I insult the man's integrity and work ethic. That's not worse than dousing his food with red punch, is it? Of course it is.

"Can I go?"

I sink down to my chair. "Sure. Thanks for…fixing my phone.

He disappears into the hall. I slap my hand to my forehead. Brilliant, Mace.

* * *

An hour later the phone rings.

"Macy Moore."

"Macy, it's Beka Gainer." Her voice is airy and sweet, like always.

I sit forward. "Beka, hello." Odd that she's calling so soon after Phone Guy left my office. "How are things at the law offices of Gainer & Gainer?"

"Pretty good for newlyweds going into practice together."

I grin. "As long as you don't kill each other."

"That's the goal. He keeps to his tax law, I keep to corporate. And we never bring work home."

"Sounds like a plan." I know she did not call to discuss her law practice, so I wait.

"I had an interesting call a few minutes ago from Austin Ramirez."

Ah! Austin Ramirez. "What did he say?" I drop my head against the back of the chair.

"Apparently you made quite an impression on him," she says in a singsong, I-know-something-you-don't-know voice.

"Yeah, we had a nice...chat."

"He was asking me all about you. He asked for your number, but I wanted to check with you first. Are you still dating that guy?"

That guy. I lift my head. "No, I'm not dating Chris anymore. Austin wants my number?"

"He doesn't date much, Macy, so you must have really made an impression on him. He's very particular."

We verify home, office and cell, then say goodbye, promising to get together for lunch soon. We know we won't, but it makes us feel good to pretend.

I work until six forty-five on the Holloway proposal. It required a second review after Mike added his recommendations.

Tonight the Single Saved Sisters are meeting in the mall at seven for dinner. Adriane had a hankering for Barney's Coffee and Asian Chow.

I shut down my laptop. So Austin wanted my number. I wonder if he's called already. With my heart fluttering, I check my home answering machine. No messages. I double-check to make sure my cell phone is on and that the battery is charged.

Sigh. I grab my bag and click off my office light. I'm sure he'll call. Right. Later. He's probably busy.

Of course he's busy. I like my men to be busy. He'll call. I'm sure he will.

In the food court Tamara spots me and points to our saved table. She and Adriane are in line at Asian Chow buying our dinners and Lucy is at the Barney's window.

I stand in line for a large Diet Coke to go with my garlic chicken and fried rice.

Once we are all seated and Tamara has offered thanks for our food, I lightly clap my hands to get their attention.

"I have news."

"Good or bad?" This from Adriane. "It's been mostly bad from you lately."

Snarl, she's right. "Good news. Austin Ramirez called Beka for my number."

"Girl, no way. He's gorgeous."

"When did you see him? Have you been holding out on me?"

"Who's Austin Ramirez?"

Lucy, Tamara and I gawk at Adriane. Tamara snaps her hands in front of Adriane's face. "On the count of three, wake up and behold, life."

Adriane spears a teeny miniature piece of chicken. She's convinced there are fewer calories in smaller chunks. "Your sarcasm is really getting to me, Tamara."

Lucy takes over. "Austin is that hunky Latino from Beka and Chuck's wedding, A. You remember him. All the girls wanted to sit with him, but he picked the bachelor's table."

"So, he called you?" Adriane looks at me.

"Well, no, not exactly. But Beka said he wants to call me."

Adriane lifts her chin. "Ah, so there's really nothing to be excited over."

"Well, no, not really." And her point is?

Tamara hooks an arm around our friend's shoulders. "I'm sorry for, you know, the sarcasm."

Adriane looks over at her with a small smile. "I know. Look, you guys, I want to *behold* life again, but I can't seem to get past the hurt of Travis." Adriane reaches across for my napkin and dabs under her eyes.

"You'll get past it." Tamara brushes Adriane's bangs away from her eyes. "Take all the time you need. And when I get too mouthy, just slap me or something. Gently."

We laugh the laugh of relief. I get up for a fresh stack of napkins. We seem to be going through ours tonight.

"I know what your problem is, Adriane," I say, plopping down the napkins.

"What?" She peels a napkin from the pile.

"You just haven't met the right man."

Tamara jabs her fork in my direction. "You're right, Macy."

"How's meeting the right man going to fix my trust problem?" Adriane wads up her napkin and reaches for another.

I glance at Lucy before explaining. "Look, Luce and I have a friend back home, Emily. Beautiful girl. The kind with porcelain skin and sky-blue eyes."

"Lovely person," Lucy interjects.

I go on. "Guys flocked around her in high school and college. She'd go out with them one time, then dump 'em, breaking their hearts. When they passed her in the hall or across campus, she'd turn up her nose."

Lucy takes up the tale. "Then she met Greg. One date and she knew."

Adriane smiles. "She met the right one."

"Exactly." I pound the mall table. "They were engaged five months later and now they have three of the cutest little kids ever."

"When you meet the man God has for you, the trust issue won't *be* an issue," Lucy says.

Adriane shoves the tiny cuts of chicken around her plate. "There's no Emily, is there?"

Lucy and I gape at her. "Of course there's an Emily."

Adriane looks directly into Lucy's eyes. "Emily who?"

Lucy, for all her reporter savvy, stammers, "Ah, Em-Emily Finkenstadt."

I laugh, which blows the last lid on our cover. I flick Lucy in the arm. "Finkenstadt? That's the best you could do?"

"I read it on a police blotter today. Adriane tricked me."

I confess. "So we made it up, Addy. You think you're the only storyteller in the group?"

"Yeah." Lucy hoists her nose in the air. "We can make stuff up, too."

Adriane shakes her head and laughs softly. "I guess you can." She looks at us with gratitude. "Thank you, though. I hear what you're saying. I just need trust in God, not myself."

"Now you're getting it," Tamara says. "But, I gotta tell you what's bothering me, ladies."

We lean to listen. I anticipate one of Tamara's esoteric conclusions about life and love, some sage snippet that I can ponder for the next few days.

"Why is it when I gain a pound or two it goes straight to my inner thighs?" Tamara smacks her hand on the top of her leg. "My jeans rub together—zip, zip, zip—when I walk."

She is dead serious. Her confession and expression are so comical we burst out laughing.

"You think I'm joking?" Tamara hops up and walks around our table. Sure enough, her thighs rub together with a zip, zip, zip sound.

"Whatever you do, don't buy corduroy," Lucy advises with a cackle.

Tamara hasn't let me down. I will ponder that sage snippet for the rest of the week, and laugh. We may be a sad lot of single, desperate sisters, but we can laugh.

Just as we settle down a bit and start talking about dessert, my cell phone chirps. I spill the contents of my bag trying to get to it before voice mail picks up.

"Macy Moore."

"Is it him?" Tamara asks in a very loud whisper. I shush her with a finger to my lips.

"Macy, hi, it's Austin Ramirez." He sounds nervous, but I like the resonance of his voice.

"How are you?" I walk away from the group, since they are about to explode with squeals. Good grief. You'd think I was the ugly duckling getting a call from the prince.

"It was good to see you today," he starts.

"Yes, good to see you, too."

Pause. Hollow silence. Finally, "I—I was wondering if you'd like to have dinner."

"Yes. Yes, I would."

"Saturday at six?" Decisive. How refreshing.

"Great."

"I'll call you Friday to confirm and get directions."

"Perfect. Talk to you then."

"Have a nice evening."

"You, too."

I push End and turn to the Single Saved Sisters ready for their squeals and yelps. Instead, they glare at me with sour faces.

"What was that? A business deal?" Tamara curls her lip in disgust.

"What? No. We were making a date."

"Sounded like a sales call to me," Lucy observes.

"If that's dating, I'm content to stay out of the game," Adriane laments.

"You guys. Come on. It's our first real conversation. He was clear, decisive and courteous. What did you expect?"

"*Amor,*" Adriane breathes.

"Shiny eyes," Lucy concludes.

"Blushing cheeks," Tamara adds.

I shake my head. Lousy dreamers.

Chapter Eleven

I wake up Saturday with two words on my brain. Date day.
Macy Moore has a *day-ate*. It's a beautiful Saturday and only
five short weeks since my devastating dump by Chris. He's
well on his way to becoming a distant memory.

Maybe tonight's date is the beginning of something beau-
tiful, I don't know. But God does and I'm leaving it up to
Him. If I've learned anything this spring, it's to lean on Jesus.
I've lived the results of my handiwork. Not so pleasant.

I decide it's just too gorgeous a day to stay inside. Standing
on my screened porch, I gaze out toward the complex pool.

I haven't sat by the pool and soaked up rays in years.
Wouldn't that be fun and relaxing? Nothing like a little kiss
from the sun to make me look radiant.

I hurry inside to get ready, but my trip is delayed when I
can't find my bathing suit.

I call Lucy. "Where's my bathing suit?"

"How should I know?" She sounds sleepy.

"Are you just waking up?" I look at the clock. Ten-thirty.

"I stayed up until two reading."

"Ooh, pass it to me when you're done." Anything that keeps Lucy awake that late must be spectacular.

"Why are you looking for your bathing suit?" Her question is punctuated by a big yawn.

"I'm going to the pool."

"What? Macy, don't. You'll get burned."

"Get burned," I echo. "Hello, I'm not twelve."

"Whatever. Did you look under that pile of stuff in your laundry room?"

I check the "to be dealt with later" pile and find my suit under a stack of wrinkled clothes. Fortunately, it's clean.

"Are you excited about tonight?" Lucy asks.

"Actually, I am." I anchor the phone between my chin and shoulder and wriggle into my suit.

"I'm coming over to help you get ready."

I laugh. "You just want to check him out."

"Well, I don't have a date tonight."

"First time in what, forever?"

"Please. I didn't have a date last weekend either."

"Okay, forget this weekend and last. How many dates have you had since January first?" I run upstairs for my beach towel and flip-flops.

She evades my question with one of her own. "What time shall I come over? Four-thirty?"

"If you insist." I let her off without an answer, but I know she's been on at least five or six dates this year.

I grab the novel I've been reading, which by no means keeps me awake until 2:00 a.m., my journal and a pen just in case inspiration hits.

I jerk my minicooler from under the sink and stock it with water, Diet Coke and grapes. At ten forty-five I head for the pool.

By eleven o'clock I'm slathered in coconut-scented oil with an SPF of four. I plan to be out here only an hour or so. The low SPF should get me a nice glow while protecting me from those nasty UV rays.

I recline, slip my shades into my hair and welcome the warm sun and cool breeze on my face. This is the life.

Two minutes later I sit up. Now I remember why I never sunbathe. It's mind-numbing.

I pick up the novel, drop my sunglasses over my eyes and start to read. One sentence later I trade the book for my journal and pen. I am not in the mood for other people's words.

Opening to a blank page, I wait for inspiration to hit, though it's all around me. Blue skies, golden sun, thriving oaks and green palms. The breeze carries the scent of orange blossoms, the song of the birds and the laughter of children. I realize how blessed I am, even in light of recent events.

I open my journal and scribble at the top of the page, "Things I want in a husband."

Thumping my pen against the paper, I ponder just what exactly makes a man husband material. What qualities did Chris have that made me consider him for a lifetime commitment?

Well, he's handsome, intelligent and has money. Shame on me for not digging deeper. I write my first requirement.

"Committed to Jesus." I underline it for emphasis. Deaf,

dumb and blind by the ringing of my biological clock, I overlooked that aspect with Chris. But I won't the next time.

Good-looking (at least to me.)
Sense of humor
Sense of seriousness
Kind
~~Rich~~
~~Poor~~
Somewhere in between rich and poor
Love fast food
Love my family
Nice teeth (I have a thing about teeth. Ever since junior high hygiene class.)
Loyal (Chris was not)
Smart; common sense
My best friend

I pause and review. While Chris fit most of the requirements I jotted, I've learned to go deeper and ask the hard questions. Sometimes we can want something so badly we refuse to look at what we see.

I'm in a list mood, so I turn to a new page.

Things I want in a job
Attila-free zone
Mike-free zone
Respect
Respect (worth repeating)
Opportunity for growth

Challenging and creative environment
More money
Good money (as long as the work is satisfying)
Cozy office
Decision maker
God first, work second

There. Straight from my heart. I like my lists. They make me feel content and focused. I settle back and close my eyes. The sun is warm and the breeze refreshing. In a few minutes I'll take a dip in the pool....

I wake with a start. Something's not right. Why is the sun on the other side of the pool? I snatch up my watch.

Two o'clock. I scramble to my feet. Oh. My. Word. I've been out here for three hours. And the spring sun is the worst—I am *so* burned.

I slip my feet into my flip-flops and stoop to gather my unread book, unopened cooler and unused towel when Drag strolls by in his wet suit, surfboard tucked under his arm.

"Whoa, Macy. You *are* fried." He falls against the pool gate and I see pity in his eyes. "You really should use sunblock."

"No kidding." I grimace. "I didn't mean to be out here so long."

"You look like a candy cane." Drag points out, laughing like Goofy. "The red is red, and man, the white is white." He shakes his head and pushes his sunglasses down over his eyes.

I offer a crushing retort. "Har, har!" and I shuffle home

in pain, the cooler banging against my burned thigh. When I fumble through my front door, the air-conditioning in the condo hits me like an arctic blast. I drop my stuff in the foyer and run to the downstairs bathroom mirror. Oh, no.

I look like a slice of red velvet cake. Worse yet, I fell asleep with my sunglasses on and white rings circle my blue eyes. Everything else is red. Lucy will never let me live this down.

I go upstairs, hop into the shower hoping to wash away the redness. But after toweling off, smearing on what's left of a two-year-old bottle of aloe lotion, I am redder than ever. And freezing. I turn the air up to eighty.

I slip into my pink robe and, catching my reflection in the dresser mirror, I can't tell where the robe ends and my skin begins. I hope Austin likes this color, because he's going out with Pinky Moore tonight.

By four-thirty when Lucy rings my doorbell, I've put the pool gear away, eaten a light lunch and paid a few bills.

She falls against the door, laughing. "Oh, Macy, I don't want to say I told you so!"

"Then don't."

"I told you so!" She just couldn't leave well enough alone. "You're brighter than Rudolph's nose." She makes no effort to contain her merriment, which only irritates me more.

"I'll have you know, I'm in pain." I ease down to the couch, wincing.

"I'll bet. What happened?" She kicks off her sneakers and goes to the kitchen. I hear the fridge door open and close.

"I fell asleep."

"Classic move."

"But I did accomplish something today."

"Besides that brilliant sunburn?" She collapses on the couch next to me sipping bottled water.

"I made a couple of lists."

"What kind of lists? *The* list?"

"One list for my dream job. And yes, *the* list." I wriggle my eyebrows at her.

She made her list years ago, but I refused. How unromantic is it to look for a man the way one shops for groceries? But today somehow it seemed like a fun idea.

"Well, I'm impressed. Let me see it." She holds out her hand.

"Forget it. It's between me and God."

"What? You've seen my list!"

"Whose fault is that?"

She looks shocked. "I'm your best friend."

I offer to show her my job list, which she reviews begrudgingly. She's sure I can find a better boss, but doubts I have the guts to do it.

"Why not?" I demand.

We banter back and forth until Lucy happens to notice the time. "Macy, it's five-thirty."

"Rats." Now I'm scrambling to get ready. Fortunately my hair is thick and straight, so it's easy to style.

I lose the robe to the bedroom floor and stand in front of the closet. Lucy is calling out the time from the living room, where she's flipping through TV channels. "Five forty-five."

I skim through my wardrobe. Ah-ha, just as I suspected. "I have nothing to wear," I yell out my bedroom door and down the stairs.

"Are you insane?" Lucy yells back. "Your closet is so stuffed you can't push the clothes aside to see what they look like."

"I'm telling you, I have nothing."

She stomps up the steps to help me, laughing again when she walks into the room. "I can't help it." She motions to my face. "It's so red."

Since I'm so burned, we decide I should dress warm to combat frigid restaurant temperatures.

"Here, try this." Lucy jerks a white top out of the closet, one with three-quarter-inch sleeves and a scoop neck.

"I forgot I had that." I slip it on and decide it looks fabulous against my red skin.

"And this."

Lucy tosses me a soft purple sweater, and a pair of jeans with the tags still on them.

Last but not least, she pulls out my pair of vintage red Mary Janes.

"Ooh, I love those shoes." I slip gingerly into the jeans and I try to button them. Hmm, a little snug. I suck in my breath and try again.

"Didn't you try them on?" Lucy asks, hands on her hips, head tilted in disbelief.

"Well, I was in a hurry. Normally this size fits me fine."

"Oh, they must be sizing down these days." She's so sarcastic.

"I'm sure of it." I squat and walk duck-style around the room. The material rubs against my burned legs.

"Or maybe all those large fries have come home to roost on your backside."

I duck-walk from the bed to the bathroom hoping to relax the gripping threads. But when I stand, a tiny roll of flab pooches over the waistband.

Lucy gives it a pinch. "No way. You can't go out in those. They are too tight."

I unbutton with a loud exhale. "They were killing my legs, anyway." The jeans slide to the floor.

"Wear this skirt." Lucy hands me a cotton flared skirt with a purple pattern that matches the sweater. "And these mules."

The skirt does not irritate my sunburn and is the perfect look for a spring date. Now I feel pretty and skinny.

"Hurry with your makeup. I'll go downstairs and wait for Austin."

I smack Luce's cheek with a kiss. "Thank you."

Austin rings the bell at 6:02. Lucy hides in the kitchen while I open the door and invite him in. He declines, saying he'd rather get going.

"Fine." I peek at Lucy as I grab my bag. She gives me the he's-gorgeous expression and I'm off on a date with Austin Ramirez.

Chapter Twelve

The date starts slowly and awkwardly, but that's to be expected. He opens the car door for me, bumping my shin with the door's edge. The metal end scrapes across my sunburn and I breathe through my teeth, wincing. "Ow."

Austin apologizes. Of course he didn't mean it.

On the way to dinner, he compliments me without even glancing my way. "You look nice. I love your cologne. What is it?" He sniffs.

"My *perfume* is Chanel number five."

"Very nice."

His words flow like memorized lines from *Dating for Dummies* and do not give me the warm fuzzies. My sunburn feels cozier. But I chalk it up to first-date jitters.

In a nice turn of events, he chooses a place for dinner

without taking a ride on the where-do-you-want-to-eat merry-go-round, and I'm adequately impressed when he drives to Bella's in downtown Melbourne. How did he know I am in the mood for scrumptious Italian food?

We exchange the expected small talk as we walk in—the weather, what he did today, what I did. Which is not hard to guess, since I'm still as red as Bella's tomato sauce.

We are seated at a cozy table for two by the window. The waitress takes our drink order, but when she walks away, so does our ability to converse.

He stares out the window at the street. I stare at the dessert menu. The cannoli look great. After a few minutes I remember a tidbit Beka told me.

"Beka tells me you like to fish."

"Yes." He looks at me for a nanosecond, then back to the street.

"Interesting. I know nothing about fishing other than that it requires hooks and worms. Ha, ha."

He doesn't laugh or say another word until the waitress returns with our drinks and a basket of garlic knots and we order our main course.

"So, Austin Ramirez," I say after ordering stuffed shells. "Where is your family from?" I sip my Shirley Temple and reach for a garlic knot.

"Around here."

I study him for a sec. Well, of course. "I mean originally, Spain, Mexico?"

He shrugs. "My dad and mom were born in Puerto Rico."

"I hear Puerto Rico is beautiful."

He nods with a shy smile. "Yeah."

We fall back into an awkward silence. I get nosy and probe some more. Do you know your grandparents? Have you traveled to other Latin American countries? Et cetera, et cetera. As it turns out, my boy Austin, thirty-two years old, has never traveled outside Florida besides Puerto Rico. He lives with his parents and from what I can tell, always will.

His mom does his laundry and cooks his meals. Marriage, he claims, is a mystery and children are a quandary.

"Don't you have any goals or aspirations?" I am so frustrated. What kind of thirtysomething lives at home and lets his mom do his washing?

"Sure. Fish, work on my boat, go to the gym."

"What about your job? Do you want to advance? Earn more money?"

He shrugs. "Not really, unless I want to buy a bigger boat."

When the food arrives, I'm relieved. Now I can use my mouth for something besides this incessant questioning. I have absolutely no response to his last answer—a bigger boat. Wow. I never dreamed.

Nevertheless, dinner smells marvelous and I'm starved. Asking a bazillion questions does that to me.

While I'm shoveling in the creamy cheese-covered shells, Austin barely touches his dinner.

"Aren't you hungry?" I ask.

"I've had a stomachache for several days." He wrinkles his nose and rubs his belly. "I almost called to cancel, but my parents insisted I go."

I fall against the back of my chair and set my fork down. "Are you okay?" I can't believe it. Going on a date with me has made a man ill.

He eyes his car just outside the window and claims, "I'll be fine."

This is a new low. The Single Saved Sisters will not believe it. As a collective group we've had our share of awful blind dates, no-show dates and he-tried-to-grope-me-all-night dates, but this is a whole new category. How could Beka and Rick not warn me?

Our waitress breezes by with a smile and I motion for the check. Might as well release Austin from his misery. Since tonight barely qualifies as a date, I offer to go Dutch.

"What?" He furrows his brow in confusion. "Go Dutch?"

Ooh, I hope he's not insulted. "I know it's not what the night started out to be, but...?"

"What do you mean, 'go Dutch'?"

I'm shocked. I shouldn't be, but I am. "It means we each pay for our own dinner."

"Oh, no, I can't do that." He insists on paying the bill. Seems his father coached him in the fine art of bill paying and tipping. At least the waitress is one girl Austin took care of tonight.

With his food boxed up, the two of us standing on the street corner, Austin asks, "Where to now?"

I can tell he's in pain—if not physical, mental.

"Listen, I love hanging around downtown. Why don't you go on home? I'll talk to you later, okay?"

"Are you sure?" He smiles with relief, a beautiful, sweet, empty smile. What a waste.

"I'm sure." I back away, indicating he doesn't have to kiss me good-night or tell me he'll call sometime. I want this night over, cut clean. Done.

"How will you get home?"

"Cab, friend. Don't worry, I'll find a way." I shoo him with my hands. How I'm getting home is a good question. Not sure I thought this one through. Call Lucy, I guess. Oh, man, she's going to love this.

As he drives away, I chat with the Lord. "Take care of that one. He's going to need it."

At the Sun Shoppe Café, I order a large latte and sit outside. It's a chilly but enchanting night, despite my bomb of a date. I pull my sweater close and sip the hot latte.

The moon is bright and beautiful and all the stars are plugged in and twinkling. All around me the old downtown shops are illuminated with strings of tiny white lights.

Sigh. A night made for lovers and here I sit, kissing a coffee cup.

In the chronicle of bad dates, tonight has to rank among the worst. An inductee into the Hall of Fame of Worst Dates Ever. And it happened to me, Macy Moore. I decide to dial up the sisters.

First Lucy. "I'm at the Sun Shoppe."

"How's it going?"

"Not."

"What?"

"Austin went home to his mommy."

"No-o-o." She almost hyperventilates begging for details.

"Meet me down here. I'll give you every last juicy tidbit."

She hesitates. "I'm sorta in the middle of something."

"The middle of what?" Is it me or has she been acting strange lately?

"I'll tell you later."

"Don't use my line on me. What are you in the middle of?"

"I guess I could come down there if you really need me."

"Your enthusiasm overwhelms me."

"Macy, I—"

"Never mind. Do whatever it is you're doing. I'll catch a cab home."

"A cab. No, I'll come get you."

"Lucy, I'm fine."

"Are you sure? Call if you need me."

I just did. Look where it got me. "Talk to you tomorrow."

I tap my phone against my palm, deciding what to do next. I dial Adriane. "Darling, I'm up to my eyeballs in edits. They are due next week and my heroine took a wrong turn in the jungle on page 102."

"Well, then, better rescue her."

"How'd the date go?" she asks, hurried.

"I'll tell you tomorrow."

"Yes, lunch after church. Pray I wake up in time for services."

I grin. "Will do."

She hangs up without a goodbye. Next I call Tamara, to find she's at work.

"On a Saturday night?" I make a face.

"IT upgraded the computers and I want to make sure everything is working before Monday morning. We're near the quarter's end."

Well, aren't we a pitiful lot. Two of the SSS are working, one is recovering from a bad date and the other…who knows—up to something dubious.

"Macy? Hello."

I look around. Oh crud, it's handsome Dan emerging from the shadows with Perfect Woman. Another sophisticated-looking couple follows them.

"Hi, Dan." I stand to shake his hand.

"You remember Delia." He motions to Perfect Woman.

"Certainly." I give a little half wave and a nod. "Nice to see you."

She smiles. "And you." I squint at her in the glow of the Sun Shoppe's lights. Nope, still no visible imperfections.

Dan introduces the other couple. "This is my boss, Quentin Harper, and his wife, Kelly."

"Boss? You're a partner now, Dan," Quentin Harper corrects in a deep voice, stepping toward me with a meticulous smile, hand extended.

To me, Dan explains, "I made partner at the firm this week."

"Congratulations."

Perfect Woman links her arm with his and purrs. "We had a lovely dinner at that new little French restaurant."

"Wonderful," I say. I didn't even know there was a new French restaurant.

"So," Dan says, eyeing me. "What brings you to downtown Melbourne on a Saturday night?"

I fiddle with my latte cup. No use lying. "A date. He felt ill and went home."

Dan looks startled. "Went home?"

I nod and sit down before I fall down. Why does honesty have to be so embarrassing?

"Do you need a ride home?" Perfect Woman asks.

"Oh, no, no. I can call a cab." A cab? Why didn't I say

friend? A friend. I can call a friend. Cab sounds so lonely and desperate.

"Nonsense. We're on our way home now. Ride with us," Dan insists.

I wave them off as if sitting downtown, alone, is actually fun for me. "No, I'm fine. Thank you."

"We insist," Perfect Woman says.

Refusing now would just look stupid. "Okay, thank you."

The Harpers go their way while I follow Dan and Perf— I mean Delia to Dan's white Mercedes.

I didn't think this night could get any worse. I'm grateful for the ride home, but did it have to be with Mr. Success and Miss Perfect?

Dan takes the scenic route to the Gables, driving along the river. Moonbeams sparkle like diamonds on the water. He and Delia talk quietly for a few minutes, so I make myself at home in the backseat, nestled against the cool posh leather, and think thoughts to God. I decide not to fret anymore about my crash-and-burn date.

By the time we drive home, my disappointment over Austin Ramirez has gone the way of moondust.

Chapter Thirteen

I search my purse for my keys.

"Can you get inside?" Dan calls.

I wave. "Yes, thanks again." Go on, now—I've had enough humiliation for one night. The white Mercedes disappears into Dan's garage.

I find my keys, unlock the door and step inside to hear the house phone ringing. Probably Lucy. I check the clock on the stove as I answer. Eight-fifteen. And date day is over.

"Hello?"

"Macy, it's Dylan Braun."

My bag drops to the floor. "H-hi."

"Are you up for some company?"

"Who?"

He laughs low. "Me."

Yowza. My heart starts the tango. "Um, sure."

"It'll take me about an hour to get there. I'm in Daytona."

"G-great." We talk directions for a few minutes before we hang up.

With the portable dangling from my hand and my feet bolted to the kitchen floor, I figure I must be dreaming. Dylan Braun is coming to visit me. I slap the side of my face lightly. *Wake up, Macy.* The sting of my burned skin tells me I'm awake. Very awake.

The next hour is a blur. I remember checking the downstairs bathroom for clean hand towels and switching on a few ambient lights, but after that, I'm not sure what I did.

Suddenly I'm opening my door to Dylan Braun. "Hello."

He's propped against the wall, hands in the pockets of his leather jacket. "Hi."

"Come in, please." I stand aside for him to pass, breathing in sandalwood and spices as he walks through the door. I feel light-headed. Sandalwood and spices. My new favorite scent.

"This is beautiful, Macy," he says, observing my home.

"Thank you. So what brought you to Daytona?" I move to the couch.

His blue-green eyes smile at me. "Dad and I came down for Bike Week."

"Bike week?"

He sits next to me. "We started making custom motorcycles last year. Braun Bikes. Bike Week is a good place to advertise."

"Custom bikes. Wow."

We fall silent and stare at each other for a few seconds.

But not at all like the silence between Austin and me during dinner.

"Coffee?" I ask, breathing in his presence.

"Sure. As long as it's no trouble."

"No trouble," I say, getting up. Unless I don't have any coffee—then it would be trouble.

From the kitchen pass-through I look out at him. He's watching me, so I move away. His gaze makes me feel exposed and vulnerable as if he can discover all my private thoughts.

He's such a curiosity to me. He's a man's man, but the kind who smiles easily and helps elderly ladies across the street. He's athletic and competitive, yet compassionate and caring.

I look out again. He winks. I duck back into the kitchen with a shiver. Must be the sunburn. Has to be.

I reach for the coffee filters, absorbing the reality of Dylan Braun driving down from Daytona to see me. This is the perfect ending to my rotten day.

"I hope I'm not imposing on your evening, Macy," I hear him say.

"Oh, not at all." I peek around the door. He's standing, shedding his jacket, moving toward the kitchen.

My knees wobble. "Good. I thought you might be on a date or something." He boldly enters the kitchen and straddles one of the chairs as if he's been to my house a hundred times.

"Well, I *was* on a date," I admit with a laugh, reaching for the mugs that dangle from the mug tree. Dripping coffee fills the kitchen with the aroma of hazelnuts.

He stiffens. "Oh?"

I make a face. "The night ended early. He didn't feel well."

He relaxes with a grin. "Lucky for me." His comments feel deep and personal.

"Let's have coffee in the living room," I suggest when the pot is perked. I pour the coffee, offer Dylan the remains of toffee-flavored creamer and shove the sugar bowl his way.

While we doctor our coffee, my mind swirls. Dylan, in my home. I've known him most of my life, but we've never really *hung out*.

Once in a while, when our moms got the families together, we played table tennis in the Braun basement or watched a movie in the Moore living room. But our high school and college social circles rarely intersected. This is a monumental moment in the life of Macy Moore. Earth-shattering. Should I call NBC, maybe Oprah?

Following me to the living room, Dylan asks, "Do you mind if I light a fire?" He motions toward the fireplace. "I'm a little cold from the ride down."

"Not at all." I smile and set my coffee on the end table. Frankly, Dylan Braun is all the warmth I need, but I'll keep that as my little secret.

Dylan sets his mug next to mine, then lights the fire as if he spent every Saturday night in my living room. Whew, it's warm in here. I fan my face with my fingers.

"So," Dylan says when he joins me on the couch.

"So," I echo, smiling. My gaze catches his and for a long moment it's as if we're the only two people on earth.

"Are you still with Casper?" Dylan asks.

I nod. "Yep, and you? Still torturing Beauty High students with math and science? Didn't you coach track and football, too?"

He laughs, cupping his mug between his hands, elbows resting on his knees. "I gave up *torturing* last year."

"Really? The bike business is that good?"

He grins. "It's getting there, but I'm also doing some bronze and pewter sculpting. I have a few large sculpture commissions this year."

I'm shocked. I'd always pictured Dylan as the steady job, Toyota or Honda kind of man. Leaving teaching for the elusive world of art shows guts and belief in himself. If possible, he's soared even higher in my admiration stratosphere. At this rate, I'll never reach his heights. "It must feel great to follow your dreams."

He leans my way. "I learned it from you."

"Me?"

"Yes, you."

The phone rings before I can think of a snappy reply. I step to the kitchen, where I left the cordless.

"You made it home." It's Lucy.

"I did."

"Did you call a cab?"

"No." I peek at Dylan from the kitchen. He smiles and nods. I duck behind the wall and lower my voice.

"Someone's here. I can't talk now." I hang up before she can say another word. I don't want to tell her about tonight over the phone. Besides, she's got a secret—so do I.

Back to the sofa and Dylan. When I sit, my leg touches his. Did he move? Am I in the right spot? All my nerve endings are snapping and firing at once.

"I like your sunburn," he says, his voice reminding me of melted chocolate.

"Th-thank you." I giggle with an awkward quiver. "It was an accident."

"Usually is." He slides a little closer.

I can't breathe. Is he going to kiss me? I think he might kiss me. Why are all the colors in the room fading to purple?

His hand lands on mine. His thumb strokes my fingers and I'm sure the tingle in my right arm is indicative of the heart attack I'm about to have.

I want him to kiss me, I think. Ever since eighth grade I've wanted him to kiss me.

But oh, please, don't kiss me. I don't know if I'll survive. What kind of kiss would it be? Just for fun? Just for friends? A kiss to begin? A kiss to end? Dylan's visit can't mean anything, really it can't. He lives in Beauty. I live here.

I can't believe this. I want a dissertation before a simple stupid kiss. No, no! It's not a simple stupid kiss. It's a kiss from *him*—Dylan.

His eyes search mine. Is he asking for permission? How do I make my eyes give him an answer? Right eye say yes, left eye say no.

"Macy…" he starts.

Yes. No. Yes. No.

"Dylan," I say, grabbing his hand. "I—"

The phone rings and I pop up off my seat like a jack-in-the-box. "Excuse me. Ph-phone."

"So I hear." Dylan eases against the back of the couch, his shirt unable to hide his muscular frame. He has a come-hither look on his face.

My knees buckle when I try to walk and I have half a mind not to answer. Let the machine get it. No! What if it's Lucy? What if she starts talking about Austin? Better answer.

I bark, "Hello?" I'm half out of my mind with indecision.

"Hello, Macy, it's Elaine."

I soften my tone and come to my senses in an instant. "Mrs. Woodward? Are you okay?"

"The pain is real bad this time. Can you come over?"

I look at Dylan. Her timing is incredible. "Sure, I'll be there."

She moans and hangs up. Elaine Woodward, like it or not, just shot a dose of reality into my heart's fantasy.

I tell Dylan, "My neighbor isn't feeling well and wants me to come over. She lives alone." I slip on my flip-flops.

He stands, his brow furrowed in genuine concern. "What's wrong?"

"Not sure, but she's going to the doctor next week if I have to throw her over my shoulder and haul her there myself."

"Can I help?" He stands close, regarding me.

"I don't think so, but thanks. I'm sorry we got interrupted."

"Me, too." He runs his hand over his blond hair. Is it possible he's more handsome than he was a few weeks ago?

I smile. "I'm glad you came."

"You're still planning to emcee our reunion, aren't you?"

A brick of disappointment hits me. Is that why he came down? Is that why he leaned my way? I'm waiting for "can I kiss you" and he's thinking "are you still the emcee?"

Figures. There will never be a Macy Moore-Dylan Braun romance. Never.

"I said I would, so I will," I hear myself say.

"Good." He smiles, hesitates, then steps toward the door.

I grab my house keys and walk out with Dylan.

"Which way you heading?"

I motion. "Right there. One door down and over."

"I'll walk with you."

"Thanks again for coming down," I say when we stop at the edge of Mrs. Woodward's walkway.

"Thanks for having me." He reaches for my hand. I'm trembling from the cold, or perhaps his touch, but either way if I speak my teeth will clatter like old bones. He hugs me for a good long second, kisses my forehead and says, "I'll see you soon."

I nod and say something clever like "Mmm-hmm." Does he realize the power he has over me?

He steps off the sidewalk and disappears into the darkness.

"Mrs. Woodward, please let me take you to the emergency room or call 911."

"No, sweetie. No."

"All right, but listen to me, woman…" I wag my finger. "I'm calling your doctor Monday morning, making an appointment and carting you there myself."

She chuckles at me. "All right. My doctor's number is on that notepad by the phone." She reclines against the back of the couch, breathing deeply between each word. I can tell she is in pain.

I'm at a loss here. I've huffed and puffed and stuck out my chinny-chin-chin, but she refuses to go to the E.R.

"Do you want some aspirin or Tylenol?" I have to do something.

She shakes her head. Her face is pale and lined and her hand is pressed between her ribs.

With nothing else to do, I sit next to her and whisper prayers. I know God heals, so I ask Him to do that for Mrs. Woodward. Finally she rises and excuses herself to the bathroom. "I need to vomit."

I wrinkle my nose. "Really?"

She nods. "It helps."

I aid her to the bathroom. "Do you need me to stay in here with you?"

She shuts the door on me, which I take as a no. I sit on the edge of her bed and wait. A few minutes later she emerges.

"Do you feel better?"

"Yes," she says. "I think I'll curl up here, on my bed."

"Good idea." I fold back the covers and she climbs under, snuggling against her pillow.

I position myself next to her, propping my head against the old headboard, and slip my hand under hers. It's warm and soft, like my grandma's. She exhales without moaning, so I know she's feeling better. After a few minutes she's snoring.

I make sure she's tucked in and click off the light. Gently I kiss her cheek. "Sweet dreams."

Chapter Fourteen

Walking home, I am tired and drained. The sunburn is making me both hot and cold. I want a shower and my bed. I want to lie there and remember Dylan's visit.

I'm almost to my front walk when I hear, "Psst, Macy."

Who is pssting me? Shivers creep down my legs.

"Psst, Macy."

I jump into the overgrown palmetto bushes and squint in the darkness. I have *got* to tell the condo board about all these late-night visitors.

The voice calls, "Where'd you go?"

I recognize the intonation this time and relax. "Drag, is that you?"

"Yeah, it's me."

I climb out of hiding. The pointy ends of the palm fronds scrape my burned arms and snag my skirt.

Drag is lying flat on his back, smack in the middle of the condo's guest parking slots.

"For crying out loud, what are you doing?"

"Shhh, get down." He karate chops the back of my knee (not the sunburned side, thank you) and I collapse to the pavement. "Lie flat," he whispers.

I laugh as I tuck my skirt under my backside, draw my sweater closer and lie down. This is nuts.

"What are we doing?" I whisper back. If he tells me we're about to be invaded by alien creatures, I'm outa here.

"Gazing."

Gazing? I can do gazing. I *gaze* at him for a second, wondering if he's all right. Maybe he's smoked some funny grass? I sniff. He smells like Irish Spring, and unless deodorant soap is more potent than I realize, Drag is lying on the pavement at midnight with a sane mind, and has managed to get me to do the same.

After a second Drag waves his arms toward the expanse. "Look at all the stars."

"They're beautiful." I've seen the stars tonight, but not through Drag's eyes. I'm captivated by his ability to see meaning in simplicity. Who in their right mind would make their bed on pavement and be in awe?

"Makes you wonder who's out there," he whispers, as if he's afraid "they" might hear.

"God's out there. Actually, He's everywhere," I say with confidence and conviction.

"You've seen Him?" Drag asks right in my ear.

"Not with my eyes, but with my heart." I tap my chest. "The Bible says, 'Christ in you, the hope of glory.'"

"Then how can He be out there?" Drag points to the stars. "And live in you?"

I laugh. He's a twentysomething with the heart of a six-year-old.

"Like I said, He's everywhere." I remember part of a Psalm. "'If I ascend to the heavens, make my bed in Sheol, You are there. If I take the wings of the morning, or dwell in the uttermost part of the sea, Your hand will lead me.'"

"Awesome. Shakespeare?" Drag asks.

"No, King David." Quoting the verse bolsters my own faith.

"Sounds like Shakespeare."

"Perhaps Shakespeare sounds like King David."

"Where do I read King David?"

"The Bible," I say. "The Psalms."

"I'll check it out."

I bite back a laugh, contemplating how strange it is to be stretched out on the pavement with Drag talking about God and King David.

"Drag, do you ever feel like a failure?" It's a personal question, but it seems to fit the moment.

"I'm a surfer, Macy." He chuckles with an endearing *yuck-yuck*.

I look over at him. Moonlight shines on his scratchy brown beard. "What does that mean?"

"I don't worry about failure. Or success—just catching the next wave." He weaves his hand up and down over my face.

I laugh. "You must be joking."

"Nope. Life is about the wave." He sighs, content.

"Drag, you have to teach me to surf."

"You worry about failure?" he asks.

"No," I say, then confess. "Yes."

"Like what?"

Is he serious? Like Everything.

"Career, relationships, love, money, life in general."

"Sounds like my old man. Gave himself a heart attack try-ing not to fail."

"Do you see your parents much?" I'm not sure if this question is over the line or not. Drag doesn't talk much about himself.

"They live in New York."

That's all he offers and I figure that's all I'm going to get. So I change the subject.

"You *did* check on Mrs. Woodward while I was gone, didn't you?" It's been weeks, but I never thought to ask.

"Sure I did." He doesn't sound defensive, as I would if someone questioned my integrity. "She's a nice, sweet lady."

After that, Drag and I let time pass without a word. The wind blows softly and I pull my sweater tighter. It's get-ting colder.

I'm about to call it a night when out of nowhere a police cruiser rounds the corner and stops just shy of my big toe. Drag and I leap to our feet synchronously. My heart flies out of my chest and splats onto the pavement.

Two of Melbourne's finest slip slowly out of the squad car wielding two gigantic light-saber flashlights.

"It's Andy and Barney," Drag whispers to me.

I clap my hand over my mouth to block the laugh.

"Sir, step away from the lady and put your hands behind your head."

What in the world?

Drag clasps his hands behind his head. His face is contorted in a frightened expression and I think he regrets his Andy and Barney comment. He circles behind me. "I didn't do it."

"Do what?" I ask out the corner of my mouth.

He steps away with a shrug. "Don't know, but whatever it is, I didn't do it."

The chubby officer—I'll call him Andy—moves around to the front of the car and pulls Drag away. The skinny officer—I'll call him Barney—addresses me.

"Macy Moore?"

Wow, his voice is loud. For a skinny guy he's got large lungs. "I—I'm Macy Moore." I dust pavement pebbles from my shirt and sweater, and tuck my hair into place.

"Step toward the car, ma'am." Barney spotlights my face with the flashlight. I consider breaking into a show tune. *There's No Business Like Show Business.* Do a little soft shoe—anything to keep myself together as I stroll his way. But I reckon he wouldn't find it funny.

"What's this about?" I ask, peeking to see if the lights are on at Dan Montgomery's place. They're not. Where's a good lawyer when you need one?

The officer lowers his flashlight. I blink away spots. "Are you all right?"

That's the question he asks me. *Are you all right?*

"Of course I'm all right!" It's snarky, and I mean it to be. What's the big idea, scaring us half to death? Asking Drag to "step away" with his hands behind his head?

"Can I have your name, sir?" Barney shines his gargantuan light on Drag's face. Drag blinks and squints. I hope he'll do his Goofy laugh.

"Name's Drag. I'm a friend of Macy's." His jaw is clenched, and he says his name like Clint Eastwood in *Hang 'Em High*.

Name's Drag. I look over at him. That's it. Name's Drag.

"Is he a friend of yours?" Andy asks me.

"Yes, he is. He's weird, but my friend."

"What are you two doing out here on the pavement?" Barney asks.

"Looking at the stars." My nerves settle a bit. I pick my heart up off the pavement.

Barney glances up. "It is a lovely night."

"Why did you come here?" I demand.

"Someone called, a mutual friend. Asked us to drive by." Barney hems and haws.

"Mutual friend? Who?" As if on cue, Lucy's yellow car squeals around the corner and screeches to a halt in front of my condo.

Lucy! She called the police? Lucy O'Brien, investigative reporter, who's paranoid about danger, destruction and devastation. It's her one endearing flaw. She's insane about it.

Personally, I never watch the news, unless it's *Extra* or *Entertainment Tonight*. Nor do I read the paper unless Lucy tells me about one of her exclusives. If I want despair and destruction, I can read the last chapter of my own life.

If World War Three begins or if Madison Avenue resurrects whalebone corsets and hoopskirts, I'm sure I'll hear soon enough.

Lucy-the-Loon stumbles out of her car wearing an oversize T-shirt and a pair of cutoff jeans. Her flip-flops slap against her heels as she strides my way with her red ponytail swinging back and forth, back and forth.

"You called the police?" My adrenaline rush ebbs and I start to shake. Drag moves next to me.

"You hung up on me. You didn't answer your phone for over an hour. Cell or house." She faces me, hands on her hips as if I owe her an explanation. "And you were alone with someone."

"So you call the police?"

"Well…"

Hands on my hips, I dip my head Ricky Ricardo-style. "Lucy, you got some splainin' to do."

"I didn't think it would hurt for a squad car to drive by," she confesses. "Just to check on you."

Drag laughs. *Now* he decides to do his Goofy impression.

I scowl at Luce and motion to Andy and Barney. "I think you owe these two an apology."

Drag nods. "Yeah."

"Guess I let my imagination get away from me, but seriously, Macy, you know the kind of stories I've done. It's always the nice, single, unsuspecting female who gets caught off guard."

"Give me some credit, please."

Lucy starts to say something, but I raise my hands.

"It's over. Let's go inside." I motion to my place. She doesn't follow. I stop, and for some reason it registers for the first time that she's standing mighty close to Deputy Fife, *and* wearing a Florida Gators T-shirt. "Why are you wearing a Gators T-shirt?"

She's a Georgia Bulldog. The Gators are our rivals. I don't see the humor here. First she calls the police, then she shows up wearing a Gator T. I wouldn't use one for a dust rag.

"Oh, that." She looks down at her shirt, then at me. "Macy, I've met somebody."

I lean her way. "Come again?"

As if on cue, Barney puts his arm around Lucy. She smiles at him. Oh-oh. Do I see sparks? I've never, ever seen her look at a man the way she's looking at Deputy Fife.

Barney Fife. My best friend is dating Barney Fife. Lucy introduces me to him—real name Jack Westin—before he leaves with his partner, real name Brett Stuart.

"I can't believe you held out on me." We're inside my house now. Lucy kissed Barney, er, Jack Westin goodbye and Drag arranged to teach Officer Brett to surf.

Nuking two mugs of coffee, I prod her to spill the beans.

"You've been through so much lately, I didn't want to make matters worse. Besides, we really didn't know how we felt until today. We talked before his shift."

We sit at the kitchen table. "Lucy, I always want to hear this sort of news." Is my life so rotten my best friend can't tell me she's in love?

She crosses her heart. "I won't hide it from you again."

The short version of their love story is they met last year while investigating a Melbourne Beach white-collar crime. He called her a few weeks ago and they went to a musical.

Lucy and I talk until after two. I tell her about Austin, Dan and Delia, the surprise visit by Dylan, Mrs. Woodward and then lying on the pavement, quoting a Psalm to Drag, which boosted my faith.

After Lucy leaves, I take a quick, hot shower, washing away the good, the bad and the ugly of the day. I fall into bed and picture Dylan's face as he nears me for a kiss. (Okay, maybe he wasn't going to kiss me, but I can dream, can't I?) I linger there for a nanosecond, then move on before my mind throws a gutter ball and I end up in a place I don't want to be.

I jot a mental note to make a doctor's appointment for Mrs. Woodward, wish I were more like Drag, laid-back and gazing at stars, and smile for Lucy and Jack. Why is it that in these quiet moments all of my emotions and thoughts surface and demand attention?

Please, Lord, don't let my gravestone read "Here lies Macy Ilene Moore. Second fiddle to a man obsessed with Xena, the ex-girlfriend of a rogue financier and Beauty High's most successful failure."

I want the life of the beautiful, not the life of the overwhelmed.

I slip under the covers as if hiding from the life I lead. I shouldn't try to make sense of it all now, when I'm tired and my brain is sunburned. Yet underneath the layer of self-pity, I know the Lord is with me, and there's beauty in my ashes.

Chapter Fifteen

❧

Monday morning I arrive at Casper with renewed vigor. Pastor Ted's Sunday-morning sermon about trusting the Lord for our future knocked me out of my weekend doldrums.

I settle in my office and get busy planning my next Casper excursion with a sense of destiny. Yeah, God and me. He's in control.

But by 1:00 p.m. the details for my trip remain at large. My sense of purpose is deflating a little. My destination is a Kansas town so small that even Jillian couldn't find it on the map when booking my flight.

Somewhere in no-man's-land there is a thriving e-business in need of new Web tools and one W-Book application. Enter Macy Moore, the tool lady.

Around two, I decide to break for lunch. Lucy's comment

about too many French fries coming home to roost on my backside leaps to mind, so I order a to-go grilled chicken salad from Pop's.

In thirty minutes I'm back at my desk, eating and reviewing the new W-Book installation manual, when a dark shadow falls across my desk. I glance up. Roni.

"Hello." I square my shoulders. She's wearing a new Armani suit. Bonuses must have been good this quarter.

"Do you have a moment?" she asks, walking back to shut my door.

"Sure." Heat surges through me and I can feel the salad croutons melding in my stomach into tiny lead balls.

She perches on the edge of the desk with her arms folded, looking down her nose at me. She exudes the warmth of an iceberg.

"I need to know where you're at, Macy."

"Where I'm at?" *I'm right here.*

"I'm wondering about your commitment to Casper." She stands and paces, arms still crossed.

"My commitment to Casper?" I slip on my sweater. Where is she going with this? Didn't she see my renewed vigor this morning? I practically cartwheeled into the office.

"Is your heart with us? Are you sure this is where you want to be?"

What is she talking about? I pinch my lips to keep from calling her the first thing that comes to mind.

"Roni, what's going on?" I strain to modulate my voice.

"You tell me. I just don't see the energy and commitment in you I want to see. Where's the old Macy Moore?"

"Well, excuse me if I'm a little deflated after you took my job away." There, I said it.

"It's more than that, Macy."

"What exactly is *that*, Roni?" I glare at her because she's glaring at me. It's uncomfortable, but if this is a shoot-out, I want my eye on her trigger hand.

She bends down close to my face. "Don't be coy with me. I'm watching you." Without another word, she turns and sashays out of my office.

I sit there with my mouth open. It's not my best look—a dangling jaw—but I'm dumbfounded. What is she talking about? Watching me?

"Lord, what's going on?" Sigh.

I take a deep breath and sense a little shower of peace, so I go back to work, shoving aside the exchange with Roni. I see Jillian flutter past my door, then a second later she bops into my office.

"Was the Hun just in here?" she whispers.

"Yes." I focus on my computer screen.

"Was she mad?" She stoops over to catch my attention.

"Do you have a point here, Jillian?" I click on an unread e-mail about the Holloway proposal. Please not another revision. The hourglass cursor appears, so I wait.

"Well…" She shuffles nervously. "Maybe a little bird sent your résumé to Danner Limited."

I stand. "What?"

"A little bird sent your résumé to Peyton Danner."

"A little bird named Jillian."

"Depends."

"On what?"

"If you're mad or not." Wincing, she ducks behind a manila folder.

"Why would you do such a thing without telling me?" I shove the folder away from her face.

"I saw her card on your desk. I think you deserve better than the way Kyle and Roni are treating you."

"Where did you even get my résumé?" I tuck the tips of my fingers into the pockets of my chinos.

"Roni has all the résumés in the personnel files. I found your old one and updated it." She hides behind the folder again.

I'm confounded. I don't know whether to hug her or berate her. Her resourcefulness is impressive, while her audacity is galling. I regard her for a moment or two, thinking.

"How did the Hun find out?"

"She overheard me talking to Peyton when she called for you."

"Peyton called?"

Jillian nods. "While you were at lunch. I didn't know Roni was listening." She's still excusing her actions, crunching the manila folder and its contents between her hands.

I wave off her worry. "Is Peyton going to call back?"

The little busybody smiles for the first time since this conversation started. She hands me a folded pink message slip with Peyton's office number.

I bite back a grin and give my pesky admin a hug. "If this works out, those Gucci boots are yours."

Friday morning I pull up to Mrs. Woodward's and help her into my car.

"I can't believe I'm letting you do this to me," she says.

"Someone has to be reasonable." I remind her to buckle up as I gently close the passenger door. "We're lucky the doctor had a cancellation this week."

"Lucky? It's misfortune, I tell you."

She's a riot. Feigning a fuss about this trip to the doctor's, but deep down, I know she's happy to go.

I'm sorry I haven't spent more time with her before. Sorry I turned down all her soup invitations. She's spunky and brave.

God put Mrs. Woodward in my life exactly when I needed her. She's a lifeguard of sorts, blowing the whistle when I dip too many times in the pool of pity.

I took the morning off from work so I could take her to the doctor. I told her not to make me regret it. She chuckled. "Don't make *me* regret it."

As we pull away from Mrs. Woodward's place, Dan Montgomery fires out of his garage and speeds away. I toot-toot my horn and wave, but he doesn't look back. In contrast, Drag lollygags out his front door, long board under his arm.

Mrs. Woodward and I chitchat about the weather, the beautiful day and the new Gables condo manager. When I make a left at the light into Wuesthoff Medical Center, Mrs. Woodward sighs heavily.

"It'll be all right." I reach for her hand.

"I miss Walter," she says, her hand trembling under mine.

"I know." I park, slip the keys out of the ignition and open my door.

Her face is white. "You think I'm dying, Macy?"

Ah, so this is the source of her fear. "No, I don't."

"Could be my heart, you know." The lines fanning out from her wise blue eyes are not crinkled into a smile. She's scared.

"And it could be nothing. Something simple. Either way, there are wonderful medications and procedures today. You'll live to be a hundred."

She squeezes my fingers. "Not without my Walter. I'm ready to see him."

Oh, my heart hurts for her. I'm angry at her son for ignoring her so she has to face old age without his love, without the comfort of family. I may be chasing my own career rainbow, but I love my family.

I slip out and go over to her side of the car. It occurs to me that I should pray for her.

But here, in the parking lot?

Mrs. Woodward slides her pocketbook over her arm and links her elbow with mine. "Better go before I change my mind."

We take a few steps. I can't shake the idea of prayer, so I gently grab Mrs. W's elbow and say, "Can I pray with you?"

It felt good to get the words out. I wonder if she'll protest, but she bows her head. "All right."

"Lord..." I pause, not sure where to go next. Starting over. "Comfort Mrs. Woodward, Father. Assure her that You are with her and that You love her."

Her eyes are brimming with tears when she looks at me. "Thank you."

"Let's go hear some good news."

Two hours later, we know the source of her ills. It's her gallbladder. Oh, the gall! We had fun with that one on the ride home.

"See, you're not dying." I had to bring it up, but didn't rub it in.

"It sure felt like it at times." Mrs. W's voice is fresh and chipper. Relieved.

"The doctor's office will call with a surgery appointment and you'll be good as new." I pull into our complex and up to her driveway.

"You'll go with me, won't you?" Her voice cracks with uncertainty.

The doctor assured her about a hundred times what a simple and painless procedure it is to remove a stone-filled gallbladder, but I don't think she's buying it.

"Wouldn't miss it," I say. "But remember I leave Monday for a week. It has to be after that, okay?"

"Thank you, Macy."

I help her to her door. She reaches up, grabs my neck and pulls me down for a tender kiss on the cheek. With tears in my eyes, I hurry off to work.

Smallville, Kansas, turns out to be more like Dot In The Dirt, Kansas. How the Casper sales staff finds these out-of-the-way companies I'll never know. Locating this town had to require a Lewis and Clark expedition.

There's no Wal-Mart, no McDonald's, no sub shops and no cell service. Tuesday morning I head west out of the motel parking lot, down Main Street, the *only* main street, to Carrington's Western Warehouse.

The sunny day is cold and windy, but the sun is shining. My stomach rumbles as I look for a place to grab a quick bite. I pass *the* drugstore, *the* grocery store/diner, but by the number of cars out front, I figure the diner would take too long. Next is *the* hardware store, then Carrington's Western Warehouse. It's last on the tour.

I'd pay fifty bucks right now for an Egg McMuffin and large Diet Coke. How can they not have a McDonald's? Fighting fast-food panic, I grip my cell phone in my hand. I can't even call Lucy to complain.

Being without cell service also means I won't hear from headhunter extraordinaire Peyton Danner. We played phone tag all last week. As curious as I am to hear what she has to say, I am kind of glad we haven't connected. Being stranded in Kansas gives me time to think and pray. If God has a new job opportunity for me, I'll be glad to take it, but if there is a lesson to be learned at Casper, I want to learn it.

I park my rented car in the visitor slot by Carrington's front door. I check my watch—8:05. Perfect.

"Amos Carrington," I say to the receptionist.

"Shore thang. What's your name, honey?" She's a cowgirl behind a desk, wrangling e-mails, phones and faxes. I like her.

"Macy Moore, Casper & Company."

Within seconds a lanky rancher wearing pointed-toe boots and a string tie comes out with a Kansas-size grin. He pumps my hand. "Little lady, welcome. We start work at 7:00 a.m. around here."

I grin. "Yes, sir."

Chapter Sixteen

It's a Monday in mid-April when I head for my Casper office, having survived a week at Carrington's Western Warehouse.

Amos gave me a parting gift—a pair of luscious deep red leather boots. He said, "Macy, I trust the good Lord knew what He was doing when He gave you brown hair, but if you ask me, you're a redhead at the roots."

So this morning I felt a little feisty as I jerked on my Carrington boots. How do you like me now, Attila the Hun?

Humming a chorus I heard on the radio, I thump around the corner to my office, thinking ahead to tonight's dinner with Lucy and Jack.

Suddenly Jillian jumps in front of me.

I bang into the wall trying to get out of her way. "Jillian!"

"Sorry to scare you, Macy." As always, she's hiding behind a manila folder. I take a deep breath and start walking again.

Jillian walks backward in front of me. "Welcome back. How was Kansas?"

I stop. "It was a one-horse town, and the horse recently died."

She tee-hees. Something's up. "Little bird, what have you been up to now?"

"Me? Nothing." Her expression is strained and out of shape. "Gorgeous boots, Macy! Did you get those at Carrington?"

"Yes, and you're not getting these." I step around her. "You get the Guccis."

"Sure, whatever." She shuffles in front of me, blocking my path again.

"Okay, out with it." I stare down at her.

"There's something you should know."

"Obviously. Did Roni fire me?"

"Oh, no," she says with a giggle. "She's not that crazy. Just paranoid."

"Then what?" I push past her.

"Your office has been moved." There, she said it.

"What?" I ask, as if I really need her to repeat it. I heard her loud and clear the first time. "Where?"

"Over…there." She motions with her pen to a black hole beyond her shoulder.

I peer around her. "Can you be more specific?"

She twists her arm back and points down the hall. "Down there. At the end."

"I didn't even know we had offices in this part of the building." I'm trying to be cool about this. I am, but to what Borg cube have they banished me? I have Carrington red boots. I refuse to be assimilated.

"We do now," she says.

"Lead on." I motion to the "wherever" of my office.

We walk and we walk and we walk. This is like the opposite end of the universe. I resist the idea that I'm the unwanted stepchild and try to maintain professional dignity in front of Jillian, but I admit, my bottom lip quivers.

"Did Mike move into my office?"

"Mmm-hmm." Jillian stops in front of the janitor's closet. "Here you go." She steps aside for me to pass.

"The janitor's closet?" I shriek.

"No, there." She points to a second door.

The door creaks when I shove it open. Sure enough, my stuff is crammed into this hole-in-the-wall. Literally.

"This was the only office available," Jillian explains, hiding half of her mouth behind the folder.

"This pillbox qualifies as an office? There are no overhead lights!"

"I'll call maintenance." She dashes away.

Light from the hall filters into the tiny room. I step inside with caution. I let my laptop case slip from my shoulder to the floor and drop my purse on the desk. It plops onto a big pile of loose papers and topples to the floor, taking half the stack with it.

Great. Just great.

My too-large desk is wedged into a too-small office. My floor lamp is tucked into a corner and my retro '60s chairs sit on either side of the filing cabinet—which I don't need anymore.

There's barely enough room to turn around, let alone work. Ten years of pictures, mugs, travel souvenirs and knickknacks are strung all over the office floor, along the wall and in the chairs.

What a mess. Should've dropped most of it off in the room next door.

I inch around to the minifridge. What this moment needs is a nice cold Diet Coke. I crack my knee against the desk's edge and yelp. Since I'm in outer space, I figure no one can hear me. So I yelp again.

I pop open the little door with the toe of my red boot. Warm air floats up and water sloshes all over my fine-leathered toe.

"Ah, no!" The smooth, beautiful top of my boot is awash with defrosted ice. "Drat." Do what you will to me, but do not harm my new red leather boots.

I stare at the fridge with my hands on my hips. When they moved it, they forgot to plug it in. Imbeciles. The iceberg wrapped around the minifreezer melted. I drop to my hands and knees, looking for a plug.

"Welcome back, Macy."

I lift my head to see over the mountain of junk on my desk and hit the edge. I don't yell this time, but grit my teeth and press my palm against the pain.

Mike Perkins stands in the doorway. "Hi, Mike." I crawl into my chair. My morning confidence and cheeriness are deflated.

"Veronica wanted my old office for a small conference room, so…" He steps inside, trying to act casual, unsure what to do with his hands.

"Can't ever have too many conference rooms," I murmur. I dig around under the pile on my desk for the tissues. I need to dab the water from my boot.

"How was your trip?"

"Grand." I wipe my boot dry, wad up the tissue and toss it to my trash basket—which is not there, so the blob falls to the ground. My head throbs from the desk banging and I desperately need my wake-up Diet Coke.

"We haven't had time to reroute your phone number yet."

"Okay." It's all I have heart to say. I feel nervous, as if I might cry.

Mike motions to the piles of stuff on my desk, on the floor and along the wall. "I guess I'll leave you to this."

"Thanks." Ten years of my life with Casper & Company piled into a cubicle next to the janitor's closet.

By midmorning I'm squared away. Maybe it is out of spite, maybe out of discouragement, perhaps out of weariness, but I shove the pile on my desk to the bottom of the trash bag I grabbed from next door. Copies of personnel reports, old documents, customer records, five-year-old tech notes, outline of my plans for the department in the New Year, all trash.

I don't need it. Don't want it. I know full well why I'm in this dinky, dank room. Roni is mad, threatened over Peyton Danner's call. Well, sticking me in the Borg cube isn't going to discourage me.

Getting rid of stuff is liberating. Should have done it long ago. When all the junk is cleared away, I find the laptop's docking station and pop my computer in and boot up.

I discover my new office has no network connection. How am I supposed to work without a network?

I pick up the phone to call IT, but of course there is no dial tone. I have no phone. I have no network.

Laugh or cry, laugh or cry. Laugh. I should laugh. Suddenly a brilliant idea hits me. Pray, Macy. Pray for grace, for wisdom, for peace.

I close my eyes and put my lips into silent motion. I pray to stay focused on the beauty in my ashes—Jesus. I pray for grace. I have a feeling I'm going to need it. I open my eyes, and I admit I'm slightly disappointed to see my prayers didn't shatter the Casper walls.

Then Mike appears at my door again. "Call for you in my office."

"Thanks."

In my old office I pick up the blinking phone line. It's Lucy.

"Macy, was that Mike?"

"Yes. It's his phone now."

"No-o-o-o!" she says in a deep voice.

"I'll tell you about it later." It's creepy to be in my office, my old home, now permeated with Mike's presence. "He's got a framed picture of Lucy Lawless as Xena."

Lucy laughs. "His poor wife."

"Yes, on many levels."

"Lunch at Steve's Hoagies? One o'clock?"

"Oh, yes, absolutely." As I hang up, Mike comes in and shuts the door. My heart lurches. Too many doors are shutting behind me, in front of me, all around me these days.

"Got a second?" He motions for me to sit.

"Sure." An adrenaline surge causes my heart to race. I fold my hands in my lap so tight the ring on my right hand bites into my flesh.

Mike smiles as he searches his desk drawer for something.

This does not feel like a smiley moment. It's awkward and weird. My gut is telling me, "Beware."

Ooh, what if he's heard all my rude comments about his Xena obsession?

(Mental note 1,001: keep mouth shut.)

My feisty, red-boot confidence from this morning and the peace I had from my prayer is gone.

"I have your review." He pulls a paper from a legal-size envelope.

Ah, I *am* wrong. This *is* a big smiley moment. Now you're talking, Mike. I'd forgotten it was review time. Well, isn't this a nice boon to my day.

"As you know, things have changed around here."

"Obviously," I reply. I click my red heels together, thinking there's nothing like a raise.

"Kyle, Roni and Dave Weiss feel that since your job change, your position does not warrant any more salary at this time."

I'm on my feet. "What?" Hands on his desk, I glare down like a hungry vulture. "This raise isn't about my supposedly *new* position. It's about my last year's performance. My overtime alone is worth a six-percent raise."

Dave Weiss, our CFO, is supposed to be a friend of mine. I expected this from Roni, but not Dave. Not even Kyle. I gave him credit for having more integrity.

Mike hems and haws. I shouldn't berate him—he's simply following marching orders. How could Roni be so indignant about the headhunter when she knew this was coming?

He clears his throat and parrots the rehearsed answer. "You are a salaried employee. Overtime is part of the job."

"Corporate baloney, Mike. Merit raises are also a part of the job. Salaried employee doesn't mean abused employee."

"Your current position doesn't warrant any more money. You make one and a half times the highest-paid tech."

Mike's song and dance to the company tune resounds like a bad vaudeville routine.

I pound the desk. "Roni shoved me into this position. My raise should not reflect where I am now, but what I've done."

"I hear you—"

"Do you, Mike? Do you really?"

"It is what it is, Macy." He shuffles papers around.

It is what it is? "What kind of answer is that?" I crack the heel of my boot against the floor.

Mike silently slips my performance evaluation across the desk and asks me to sign.

I burn a hole in the thing with a single glance. I can see it's all filled out, without any of my input, and signed by the powers that be. A sticky yellow arrow reads "Sign Here" and points to my signature line at the bottom of the page.

I stab my finger on the cheesy arrow and say to Mike with a pound of conviction, "I'm not signing anywhere."

"I can't believe you." Lucy shakes her head as we slide into a booth at Steve's. We've ordered and paid. Now we wait for them to call our name.

"Lucy, the form was already filled out and signed. Like a prison sentence without trial."

"They are your bosses."

I make a face. "Bosses, not slave masters."

"I guess that doesn't excuse them from not doing it right."

"My point exactly. I don't have to sign if I don't agree. And I don't agree." While ranting, I check my cell phone for messages. In the Borg cube I didn't have cell reception, but I really want Peyton to call. Today of all days, I want Peyton to call.

"What are you going to do?" Lucy asks.

"Connect with Peyton Danner." There are no messages or missed calls on my cell. "Right after lunch."

"Do you feel right about that?"

I get Lucy's subtle nudge. Is this where God is leading me? "Remember when I moved down here after college?"

She nods.

"I prayed and prayed, then finally a door opened and I leaped. Isn't that the essence of faith?" I sound wiser than I feel.

"I suppose." She smiles to remind me she's for me. "It's just sad to realize that this job search could change our lives forever."

Lucy's comment is sobering. "I know. But this situation at Casper is not working."

"I agree. You've been at Casper too long already, but I don't want you to move."

"I wouldn't be surprised if Casper lets me go." I make air quotes around *lets me go*.

"Then be faithful until they do."

"It's awful to feel this way about my job. After ten years, it boils down to this."

"Let God defend you. He'll take care of you."

I smile. "I'm counting on it."

"Macy!" The Steve's Hoagies guy calls my name and tosses my chicken sandwich basket up on the counter.

"Lucy!" he belts out.

"I'll get them," I say.

When I return to the table we bow for a quick prayer before digging in.

Ignoring her sandwich, Lucy gushes, "Enough about you—let's talk about me." She's beaming.

"All right. Talk." I feel like eating instead of talking anyway. I brace for a flood of Jack this and Jack that to wash away the mire of my life's trials. It's good to see Jack Westin's light in Lucy's eyes.

"Macy," she starts, "you're looking at the new news desk assistant editor."

I look up, my teeth buried in my chicken sandwich. She's glowing and it isn't even about Jack. "What?" I ask with my mouth full.

"I interviewed for the position before you went to Kansas. Remember? I competed against that *New York Post* reporter who just moved to Cocoa Beach."

I nod, remembering. Between chews and swallows, I congratulate her. "Fabulous! Good for you."

"I'm, like, dumbfounded. I can't believe I got the job. I start next week. But brace yourself for this...."

If she says Jack asked her to marry him, I'll scream. Right here. Right now. Promise. They've been dating for what— three, four weeks?

"I'm braced," I say after fortifying myself with a slurp from my soda.

"The job is in a new salary category. I'm getting an eight-percent pay raise."

I choke. "Eight percent. That's incredible."

"I'm in awe of what God is doing in my life. The publisher told me the salary on my way out the door to meet you for lunch."

"Good for you." I shove my half-eaten sandwich aside and fall against the back of the booth.

I hate my life.

Chapter Seventeen

After lunch and Lucy's good news, I sulk in my dank office. Where is the beauty for my ashes, Lord?

I drop my forehead to the desk with a sigh. I'm depressed.

"Macy." I lift my head to find Attila the Hun, in person, filling the doorway. She points to her forehead. "You have a pink slip stuck to your head."

I reach up and yank off the While You Were Out sticky. Peyton Danner's number is embossed with an oily stain.

"Are you available to meet at five?" She smiles, but there's an arctic nuance in her voice.

"Do you want to tell me what this is about?"

"A continuation of your discussion with Mike." She flips her hand in my direction as if it's no big deal.

A chill tightens my scalp and runs down my spine. Bunch

of malarkey. She's up to something. Probably going to force me to sign that stupid performance review. Well, I won't.

"Sure, see you at five." When she's gone, I snatch up the pink slip. Stop sulking. Call Peyton.

I pick up my phone. No dial tone, still. Not to be deterred, I scurry out of my hole and down to the lunchroom, where I know my cell gets reception. When I arrive, the room is empty. Perfect.

I dial Peyton with determination. While the New York City number rings, I rehearse my greeting.

Good afternoon. Macy Moore for Peyton Danner.

Peyton Danner, please. Macy Moore calling.

"Danner Limited," the receptionist answers.

I jump to attention. "Um, hello, yes, this is Macy Moore. Can I speak to Peyton Danner, please?" Unbelievable. Ten years as a businesswoman and I come off like a second grader asking for her mommy.

A few seconds later I hear "Peyton Danner." Now, that's the voice of a woman who owns her world.

"Peyton, this is Macy Moore."

"Well, at last. It's easier to run into you in the Atlanta airport than get you on the phone." She laughs, low and friendly. I exhale and relax. "Your résumé is stellar, Macy."

"Thank you." I wonder if I should tell her the truth about how my credentials got cyberspaced into her e-mail box. I decide against. Only if she asks.

"What's going on at Casper?" Peyton asks.

"I'm glad you asked." I stall while formulating an intelligent answer. How do I tell the truth without sounding like a kid who can't play hardball with the big boys? "I've been at Casper for ten years. It's time to expand my horizons."

She laughs. "Listen, I know Veronica Karpinski. You should have left Casper years ago."

"No time like the present." Nice, safe answer.

"Casper doesn't have you locked in with a noncompete clause, do they?" I can hear Peyton flipping through papers.

"No, actually, they don't." Excitement hits me.

"I'm sure you're aware of a company called Myers-Smith Webware?"

"I'm very aware." In the bottom of those red boots my toes tingle.

"They are looking for a director of customer service to work in the New York or Chicago office. They haven't decided, but I faxed over your résumé."

I sit in the nearest chair. "Fascinating," I croak.

"That's what they said about you, Macy. Can you interview in two weeks?"

What did Jillian write on my résumé? "Name the day and time." I can ask Mike for a couple more vacation days.

"You'll interview at the New York office."

I slap my hand to my forehead and mouth a silent thank-you toward heaven. Director. Interview in New York.

Peyton rattles off some details, none of which I remember, but I say yes and mumble mmm-hmm to all of them.

"Tell you what—I'll confirm it all in an e-mail."

"That'd be great."

Walking back to my office, I realize the dark clouds of gloom, despair and agony are gone. The sun has broken over my life. Perhaps everything that happened the past few months is God's way of kicking me out of my comfort zone. Do I *know* New York is it? No, but I'm at peace with the journey.

"Knock, knock," I say outside Roni's office. It's a minute after five o'clock. Her head is bent near Mike's, and she jumps away at the sound of my voice.

"Macy, come in." Roni pulls out a chair for me and closes the door. Sigh. Another closed door. She remains standing, hands clasped together. Mike sits like a puppet in the corner.

"Macy, as you know, employee and employer relationships don't always work out as we intend." Roni pauses, waiting for me to respond, but I keep my mouth closed.

"We—" she motions to Mike "—don't feel you are a fit with our company direction."

"What do you mean?" My stomach knots.

She clasps her hands at her waist. "We simply feel you'd be happier elsewhere. Casper is just not a fit for you anymore." She tilts her head to one side as if to show sympathy.

"That little office you crammed me into seems like a nice fit, don't you think?" Sarcasm—it becomes me.

Roni shakes her head. "I'm sorry, Macy."

"No, you're not, Roni. Two months ago I'm manager of customer service and today I'd be happier somewhere else? How do you know what is best for me, what would make me happy?"

"Sometimes things don't work out." Mike jumps in, clicking the push button of his pen over and over.

I protest. "You've got to give me more than this. What's going on?"

"It's like I said—we feel you'd be happier somewhere else."

"This doesn't have anything to do with Peyton Danner, does it?"

"No, no," they say in unison, a well-rehearsed chorus.

For a half a minute I regard her and eyeball him. I'm speechless. "I'll get my things." I stand and to my surprise, feel amazing relief.

Mike hands me a folder as I hit the doorway. "Your severance."

Twenty minutes later I walk out of Casper & Company for the final time. The day is ending, but I think my life is just beginning.

Tossing the box of knickknacks, pictures and souvenirs into the trunk of the Beemer, I smile, pop the top and head for the beach.

Six-thirty Tuesday evening Lucy calls. "You're coming, right?"

"Of course," I say, then ask, "To what?"

"House of Joe's. Tuesday. Single Saved Sisters."

Ah! It is Tuesday? "Right. I'll be there."

"What have you been doing all day?"

"Relaxing." More like lamenting, but she doesn't need to know. I may have felt relief yesterday when leaving Casper, but reality hit me today. I'm unemployed. Axed. Fired.

Guess that's why I'm still in my pajamas and the verticals are closed. I've spent five hundred dollars on QVC—and that's with practicing restraint. But when Leslie from Bare Escentuals showed up with her new spring beauty line, my day found its destiny.

At 6:45, I go upstairs to get ready for the SSS meeting. I boycott showering—there's really no time. So I do the surface stuff—brush my teeth, wash my face, dust it with powder and pull my hair into a ponytail. (How did it get so greasy sitting around the house?)

The pièce de résistance is an old pair of jeans and a sweatshirt that's seen better days. Feeling quite comfy and only slightly grungy, I head out.

I'm the first one at House of Joe's. I drop my Hermès on a tabletop away from the stage—looks as if they've got a singer tonight—and go to the coffee bar to order.

"Hi, Zach. Can I get a latte with all the fat?"

"Sure." He gives me the once-over. "Taking a day off?"

"In a manner of speaking." Nosy.

Adriane is next to arrive. Tamara and Lucy walk in two minutes later.

"Oh, Macy, really."

"I hear the baggy look is coming back."

"Doing something new with your hair?"

I shoot back. "Please, I just got fired."

"Fired?" Zach echoes. He hands me my latte with a smirk.

I hand him a five. "Keep the change." Hint—mind your own business.

"What'd you do today?" Adriane wonders, dumping sugar into her mocha.

"Nothing." I can tell all points of conversation will revolve around me.

"Did you post your résumé on Monster? Job hunt at all?" Lucy eyes me over her gargantuan coffee mug.

"No."

"Why not?" Tamara pokes me in the arm with one of her swordlike fingernails.

"Because I've got Peyton Danner in my corner. Let me see how this New York interview turns out."

"Yes, by all means, put all your eggs in that basket." Lucy is ripe with acrimony tonight.

"Don't you have a boyfriend to pester?" I ask, slouching down in my chair, cradling my latte.

"He's working." She beams.

"Somebody's in la-hove." Tamara sings.

"Yeah, let's talk about tha-hat." I join the song.

"Let's not." Lucy sets her mug down on the table with a loud clank. "Tonight is about you, Macy."

I glance at Adriane, who is watching, amused, her hand in the air, bent at the wrist, holding that phantom cigarette. "Are you going to help me?"

"You're doing just fine." She smirks at me.

"Okay, you want to know what I did today? I watched QVC, spent five hundred of my severance dollars and for lunch I ate M&M's on the front stoop waiting for the mailman."

They laugh. "The mailman? Were you waiting for your Publishers Clearing House brochure?"

"Ha, ha. No. But guess what did come in the mail?"

"What?" Lucy asks.

"Another flyer for our class reunion. 'Emcee and host, Macy Moore, Most Likely To Succeed,' in big bold letters right across the bottom."

"Fabulous."

"Yes, how fabulous for the 'Most Likely To Succeed' to sit

on her front steps in the middle of the day, in the middle of the week with M&M's-stained fingers."

Tamara giggles and waves the idea off with a flick of her hand. "Temporary, only temporary."

"Do you think Dylan would ask you to emcee if you were a failure?" Lucy asks, angling over the table to make sure she has my attention.

I curl my lip. "He doesn't know I've been fired."

Tamara waves her chocolate-covered biscotti at Adriane. "Are you taking notes for your next novel?"

"No, this story is too sad." Adriane shakes her head in pity, but there's mirth in her tone.

"Girl, you can say that again." Tamara bites off the tip of her Italian cookie.

"Hello, I'm sitting right here." I refuse to admit my life is too tragic for one of Adriane's romance novels.

"What are you wearing to your New York interview?" Lucy asks, wisely moving the conversation in a different direction.

"My black travel Chico's suit, pants and jacket, with a blue top."

"Perfect." Lucy reaches for Tamara's biscotti. "Wad and wear. Can't go wrong."

"That's what I'm thinking. Peyton said not to dress like an eighties yuppie. Chico's should be a nice outfit."

"Are you going to eat that biscotti or sing into it?" Tamara asks, holding out her hand for her cookie.

Lucy bites from the uneaten end and hands it back to Tamara. I smile to myself. As rotten as the past few days have been, these women brighten my life. Faithful friends, a reminder of God's goodness to me.

On the other side of the coffeehouse a young woman takes the stage with her guitar.

"Hi, everyone," she says softly into the microphone in a quiet voice.

The din in the room fades a little.

"My name is Claire—" she smiles shyly at us "—and I'm going to play a few songs for you. Hope you like them."

As she starts to strum, the conversational buzz in the room rises a notch. Tamara whispers something to us, but I am tuned in to the song. I like Claire's sound—Jewel meets Bethany Dillon.

I sink into the cushiony chair and close my eyes. Her words are simple and pure, yet profound. She's not overtly singing about God, but I can tell she's singing with a power greater than herself.

"She's good," I hear myself say with a sense of rightness. First bit of that I've had all day. Even shopping QVC didn't remedy my despondency the way I'd hoped.

"I think I've heard her before," Adriane whispers. "Maybe a concert up at the big Baptist church in Merritt Island."

"She can sing to me any day," Tamara intones to the rhythm of Claire's song.

The entire House of Joe's crowd is now quiet, being drawn and transported by the petite blonde's glassy vocals and staccato beat.

Grungy and all, I'm glad I came tonight. "I love you guys," I say mushily.

"Love you back," they say.

"Friday-night movie at my place?" I offer, feeling cozy and warm with the residuals of the song.

"I'll bring Chinese," Lucy volunteers, holding up her slender hand.

"Oh, girl, have you tried that new place off Wickham?" Tamara mm-mm-mms while we beg her for details.

Chapter Eighteen

The Sunday night before I fly to New York, I pack with a steady, growing excitement. I hope it's not too cold in New York for open toes.

It's been a long two-week wait, but I'm ready for this interview. Peyton e-mailed me about a megabyte of Myers-Smith data and I've memorized a few choice pieces like the company's brief history, names of their current officers and the branding of their main products.

I zip up my bag and hang it over my bedroom door just as the phone rings. It's Dad. In a sentimental moment I confess my whole job mess to him. He's not surprised, as I expected, and very supportive.

"I've always seen the Lord's favor on your life, Macy," he confesses, which bring tears to my eyes. "I am confident He's working all of this for your good."

"I have to believe that or go crazy."

He chuckles and passes the phone to Mom, blabbing the news to her before she takes over the conversation. She fires off one question after another, drilling me about this New York company, asking what I plan to wear, advising me on hair and makeup.

"Don't wear too much makeup, Macy. It makes you look cheap." She whispers *cheap* as if it's a four-letter word.

"Gotcha, Mom. I'm a little familiar with the business world." I head downstairs to double-check my e-ticket and itinerary.

"Right. Right," she says, a birdlike chortle chasing her words. "Guess you know more than I."

"All your advice is right on, Mom. Thank you." Kitty Moore will always want her little girl to need her.

"What does Chris think about this New York trip?"

Chris. Ah, yes, that news I haven't broken yet. "Actually, he doesn't know, Mom."

"Why not?"

"We broke up." There, now all my laundry is on the line, flapping in the breeze.

"Oh, Macy, when?"

"Couple of months ago." Has it been that long?

"Why didn't you say something?" Mom's tone resonates with compassion.

"I just did. Chris and I broke up." I find the e-ticket and itinerary in my purse safe and sound. Good.

"Be serious. Tell me what happened."

"Simple. He met someone else." Getting over Chris was probably one of the easiest things I've done in my life. I don't know if that proves my fortitude or exposes my shallowness.

Mom fires questions like a seasoned Washington reporter. I flop on the couch, stare at the ceiling and answer like a seasoned Washington politician.

Around nine I wind up the conversation, slip into my pajamas and piddle around the condo.

I pause at the printed pile of Myers-Smith data lying on the dining-room table. Should I review it again? I flip through a few pages, but decide against. I don't want to sound rehearsed.

As I wander to the kitchen for a little dinner Lucy calls on her way home from a movie with Jack. She gives me the "go get 'em" speech, then segues into a short, sincere prayer.

"Call me when you get there," she says.

"Will do. Say hi to Jack for me."

I browse the refrigerator for something to eat. Looks as if leftover Chinese is my only choice. I'm about to pop a plate of beef and dried-up fried rice into the micro when I hear a light knock on my kitchen window.

I yelp, then see Adriane's heart-shaped face peering at me through the glass. I smile as she holds up two bags bearing the Carraba's Italian Grill logo.

Say no more. I toss the fried rice and beef into the waste can and meet Adriane at the front door.

"What a pleasant surprise."

"I felt like some company," Adriane says, setting bags of food on my coffee table. "I hope you're hungry."

I catch a sound of sadness in her voice. Hmm. "I'm starved," I say with a little too much cheer. "I'll get some plates."

"Are you ready for New York?" Addy asks, coming into the kitchen behind me and opening the cabinet for glasses.

"The question is, are they ready for me?" I grin at her over my shoulder.

She laughs. "Now you're talking. Myers-Smith won't know what hit them."

"Well, let's not go too far. I do want them to hire me."

"Oh, yes, right."

I grab a tapered candle from the mantel before we settle on the couch for dinner.

"Nice touch," Adriane says as I light the candle. She pulls open the first food bag and amazing aromas waft through the house.

"Oh, yum, yum, yum. This is a great New York send-off." I choose the mushroom-smothered sirloin from one of the cartons.

"Can you imagine that in a month or two you could be living in New York or Chicago?" Adriane spears a chicken breast and drops it onto her plate.

"No, I can't, but living in a big metropolitan city would be fabulous."

She nods, cutting her chicken into small bites. "I loved growing up near New York City, but now you couldn't drag me away from the beach."

I laugh. "I never got into the beach." I notice Adriane is shoving her food around the plate without eating.

I set my fork and knife down. "Okay, what's going on?"

She peers up at me and with a wobbly sigh, puts her plate on the coffee table and covers her face with her hands.

"Adriane, what's wrong?" For a moment I feel her sadness. I scoot over next to her.

She weeps without a word for several minutes. I hug her shoulders.

When she sits up and wipes her face with her napkin, she tells me with a half laugh, "Sorry. I didn't mean to spoil your evening with my tears."

"Please, you've endured my whining lately. Did you get a book rejection or something?"

She blows her nose and crashes against the back of the couch. "Of course not. For that, you'd be driving me to the E.R."

I smile. "A thousand pardons, then."

"You know my story, right?"

"Which one? Fact or fiction?"

She lifts her hands to her head and squeezes the short ends of her hair between her fingers. "Fact. My family."

"Uh-oh." Adriane's family picture is in the dictionary under dysfunctional. "What'd they do this time? And who?" I ask.

"My brother."

I nod. "The one who works at Kennedy Space Center?"

"Yes. We were supposed to meet at Carraba's for his birthday dinner. My treat." Her voice quivers and she bats away tears.

"He didn't show, did he?"

She pinches her lips, sniffles and shakes her head.

"Sugar, I'm sorry. How rude."

Through her tears she explains, "You and I think so, but when I called him to see where he was, he got mad and defensive. Said he didn't feel like a sermon on his birthday."

I grimace. "What does that mean?"

"That he's paranoid." She laughs. "He's so defensive if I even mention God or church. He claims I'm shoving it down his throat. But believe me, I'm very careful what I say around him."

I hand her another napkin-tissue. "Sometimes the silent sermons are the worst."

She blows her nose again, nodding. "I guess so. For all the grief I'm getting I might as well say the words."

I grab her hands. "Let's pray, give the situation over to Jesus and eat this great food before it gets cold."

She looks at me, the whites of her big brown eyes streaked with red. "Thank you, Macy."

"Any time, friend, any time."

We pray and take a moment to wait on God. Adriane's breathing slows and I can tell she's being filled with His peace. After a few minutes she retrieves her plate, smiles at me and picks up a big bite of chicken.

I grin and return to my steak. With pleasure.

Midchew, Adriane absently reaches for the Beauty High reunion flyer dangling from under a pile of mail on the end table. "'Emcee and host, Macy Moore, Most Likely To Succeed.'"

"Please, don't torment me. I'm enjoying my dinner."

"Who's Joley?" She points to one of the contact names on the bottom of the flyer. "I like that name. It'd be great for a heroine."

"She's a classmate and on the reunion committee. Back in the day, she was Dylan's girlfriend."

"Ah, the competition."

"Not even in the same league," I confess.

Adriane peers at me with her head tipped sideways. "Gorgeous?"

"Very. Plus she's nice and sweet—you know, altogether sickening. She's married now."

"Really?"

"To a millionaire car dealer."

Adriane laughs. "It's always the way, isn't it?"

"Not in my life."

Adriane digs in the Carraba's bag and retrieves a capped cup of butter. "For our bread," she says, pointing to the other bag.

I peer in to find a warm loaf of bread and a carton of alfredo noodles.

As we fix ourselves up with the sides, Adriane ventures, "Tell me, why do you like Dylan?"

"Like him?" I tear at the slice of thick bread. "He's just a friend."

"Really?"

Clearly Adriane is over her brother's neglect and probing into my life.

"You know, your eyes glaze over at the mention of his name and I bet your heart goes pitter-patter."

I make a face. "I beg your pardon—my heart never pitter-pats."

She laughs. "Oh, I think it does. Dylan, Dylan, Dylan."

"Stop," I say, trying not to laugh. My mouth is full of bread.

With a shake of her head, Adriane concludes, "He must be fabulous."

"In a word—" I sigh dreamily "—yes." I don't confess my next thought out loud because Adriane will reprimand me, but truthfully the Good Ship Dylan Braun has sailed. He lives in Beauty, I live here—maybe soon Chicago or New York.

Adriane twirls noodles on the end of her fork. "Don't you find it more than coincidence that he's still single and you're still single—"

"No, I don't. What are you implying?" I know what she's implying, but I want to hear her silly little words.

"That maybe there's really something between you two."

Whoo, now that's a load of silly words. I fidget, reaching for the Diet Coke bottle to refresh our glasses. Then I have a thought. "Remember that Oprah show?"

Adriane furrows her brow. "Which Oprah show?"

"The one with the authors of the book *He's Just Not That Into You*."

"Right, yes. I met those authors at a book party in New York during my last visit."

"Very nice. Here's my point. If Dylan wanted to pursue a relationship with me, he would."

"Hasn't he?" She regards me and I sense another cocka-mamie theory brewing behind her beady little eyes. "He did come to visit you. That's gotta mean something. Perhaps he's waiting for you to give him the green light."

"There's no light, Adriane. We aren't even in the same city, let alone on the same street, the same block, looking at the same traffic light."

"Don't be literal when I'm speaking symbolically. Just because you're not in the same town doesn't mean you should let love pass you by."

I smirk. "Oh, look who's talking. Eat your dinner."

She shrugs. "I'm just saying."

"I know. Eat your dinner."

We finish eating and clean up, chatting about her next

book, chatting about all the great things to see and do in Chicago, which reminds Adriane of a great shopping spree she had once at the St. Louis station, which then leads us to sing "Meet me in St. Louis," which leads to watching the DVD.

Curled up in my lounger, I try to shove all thoughts of Dylan from my pea brain while the opening credits of the movie flash across the screen. My attention needs to be on my career, not chasing down a high school crush.

Meanwhile, Adriane stretches out on the couch, boldly singing along with Judy Garland, off-key. She makes me laugh.

Midway through the movie Lucy calls to check in, and stresses her jealousy over the mini girls' night.

I tease her. "You can come over any time. Just be sure to let Jack know you picked us over him."

"It's not fair. I want both."

I relay the conversation to Adriane who, as I suspected, expresses no sympathy. "You go on with your man. Leave us Single Saved Sisters alone."

Before she hangs up, Lucy demands, "Next time, call me."

"Whatever."

"And call me when you get to the city."

"Yes, Mother."

"Don't be smart. Bye."

I laugh. "Bye."

At midnight Adriane crawls off the couch with a yawn and carries her glass and plate to the kitchen. "You have to get up in a few hours, don't you?"

I follow with my own dishes. "Yeah, but I can sleep on the plane." I hug her. "I'm so glad you came over."

She kisses my cheek. "Me, too. I had a great time. Thank you so much. This was much better than being with my grumpy brother." She slings her purse over her shoulder. "Good luck in New York."

"I'll take Manhattan."

She smiles. "You're a shining star in my life, Macy. Maybe I *will* write a book about you."

"Oh, please. You want to stay published, don't you?"

When she opens the door, the April night seems atypically cold and has me rethinking the strappy sandals I packed. Maybe I should go with heels.

"I can't find my keys," Adriane says, searching her bag. "I must have dropped them on the counter." She runs inside to see.

I wait for her by the door, shivering, but I'm amazingly content. Content in body, content in soul and spirit. What a great way to end the weekend and start the week.

When the phone rings, I holler for Adriane to pick it up, fully expecting it to be Lucy demanding an update on our evening.

Adriane hands me the cordless with a puzzled expression. "I don't know who it is," she whispers.

I take the phone. "Hello."

"Macy, it's Elaine."

Chapter Nineteen

❦

"What's wrong?"

"I'm in so much pain." I hear her wheezing and moaning.

"I'll be right there."

Adriane insists on going with me, and as we scurry toward Mrs. Woodward's walk, I update Adriane on my neighbor's recurring condition. "She was supposed to have gallbladder surgery, but for some reason it never got scheduled."

I suspect Mrs. W. avoided confirming the date and time. The front door is unlocked, so we let ourselves in. Elaine Woodward is curled up on the couch, sweating and pale.

I make a command decision. "You're going to the E.R."

She's in so much pain she can't lift her head, but she has the moxie to protest. "No, no, it'll pass. Just stay with me." Mrs. Woodward's hand trembles as she touches my arm. Her skin is hot on mine.

"Could be rupturing," Adriane whispers in my ear.

"I concur, Doctor."

She grins at me, then kneels in front of Mrs. Woodward, brushing a gray curl away from the older woman's face, and speaks with extraordinary tenderness. This is a rare side of the wounded, pessimistic Adriane Fox. "Hi, Mrs. Woodward. I'm a friend of Macy's. Your gallbladder could be rupturing. You need to go to the hospital."

"Macy?" Mrs. Woodward strains to open her eyes. Her dull eyes search the room until she sees me.

"We're taking you to the E.R. No questions," I say.

She gives me a slight nod. "No ambulance. Macy, you drive me."

"Fine." I run home to get my car while Adriane helps Mrs. Woodward off with her slippers and on with her shoes. I'm so glad she is here to help. I've known Addy for many years, but never felt this close to her. I'm grateful for tonight. Amazing how the tragedies in our lives bind us together with cords of camaraderie.

They're walking out as I pull up. Adriane holds Mrs. Woodward steady as she eases down into the passenger seat. She groans and gasps.

As I shut the door, Adriane whispers in my ear. "Let me take her. You've got the interview. I just turned in a manuscript and for once don't have a looming deadline. Let me help."

I slip behind the wheel and check the car clock. Twelve-fifteen. By the time I get Mrs. Woodward checked in and wait around, it's going to be the wee hours of the morning. My flight is in six hours. Suddenly I don't feel so good.

I smooth my hand on Mrs. Woodward's arm. She feels so

thin and frail under my palm. "I'm supposed to fly to New York in a few hours. Would it be all right if Adriane takes you? She's one of my best friends. She'll take great care of you."

She presses her hands to her cheeks and shakes her head.

Adriane kneels and offers, "It's not a problem, Mrs. Woodward. I can stay as long as you need me."

Mrs. Woodward shakes her head again. I'm about to make another command decision, since she's sort of done this to herself. New York is the biggest opportunity of my life. I'm sorry she can't have what she wants, but at least she'll be taken care of in the hospital. And Adriane will be with her. It's not as if I'm leaving her alone.

"Look, Mrs. Woodward, I have an important job interview—"

She touches my hand with hers. I'm shocked to find it wet with her tears. Suddenly I'm hit with how overwhelmed she is, how scared and lonely. I can't do it. I can't leave her. For once, it's not about me.

"I'll take her." I start the engine.

"Macy, are you sure?" Adriane asks. "You'll miss your flight, your big opportunity."

I tip my head toward Mrs. Woodward. "No, *this* is my big opportunity."

All the traffic lights are green and I make it to the hospital in record time. The E.R. staff tend to Mrs. Woodward with an uncanny swiftness and wheel her into surgery within an hour of our arrival. Adriane calls my cell for an update as I doze in the waiting room.

"She's in surgery." I yawn between each word.

"Do you need anything?" In contrast to me, Adriane is wide-awake.

"No, I'm good. I'll just sleep in the waiting room until they tell me she's okay and in her room."

"Let me know what I can do. Really, Macy, I don't have anything else scheduled and Mrs. Woodward is such a darling."

"She is, isn't she? I'll call you later."

By midmorning I drive home, exhausted and sore, as if I'd run into a brick wall. My hair is oily and stinky, my face grimy and my breath hideous.

My sweet, darling neighbor came through the operation without complication and is tucked away in a private room until tomorrow. She looked pale and weak when I said goodbye, but the shadow of the Grim Reaper no longer tainted her round cheeks.

"Thank you so much, Macy." She warmed my heart with a kiss on my hand. "You missed your flight."

"Not a problem. I'm just glad you're all right."

Being with her in a time of crisis reminds me what life is supposed to be about. It takes the edge off recent events and trumpets, "It's *not* all about you, Macy Moore." Mrs. Woodward is one of the precious diamonds I've found in the rubble.

"Can you take a flight tonight?"

"I could," I said with a nod, "if you don't need me."

"I can manage. Perhaps Dan Montgomery can come by if I need, or that dear boy Drag."

"I'd like my friend Adriane to pick you up tomorrow. Would that be okay with you?"

She closed her eyes and nodded. "Yes, she's lovely."

"She thinks you're pretty special, too."

I pull into my garage. Exhausted, I prop myself against the kitchen counter and dial the airlines, hoping I can change my flight to the 7:00 p.m.

Fortunately, I can. With a stopover, I'll arrive in New York in the early-morning hours, but I'll make the interview.

With the excitement of emergency surgery waning, sleep beckons me. But there's no time for a nap. I drag myself up to the shower, debating about calling a cab or leaving my car at the airport.

I condition my hair, which is in desperate need of a cut. Though I have plenty of time to drive to Orlando to get one of Michele's masterpieces, I can't justify spending the money these days.

I slip into a clean pair of shorts and a T-shirt, and run down to Drag's.

I knock three times, loudly. Once again he answers looking the way I feel.

"Macy…s'up?"

"I took Mrs. Woodward to the E.R. last night."

"Dude, what happened?"

"Gallbladder."

"Whoa, is she okay?" His uncombed, bleached-by-the-sun blond locks swing freely as he bobs his head.

"She's fine, but I'm going out of town tonight. Can you look in on Mrs. Woodward again?" Waves of sleep surf over me.

"Absolutely."

"My friend Adriane will pick her up from the hospital tomorrow, but you'll need to look in on her until Wednesday when I get back."

"No prob, Macy. I'll watch out for the old lady."

"Thanks, Drag."

"Hey." He leans against the door frame. "I've been reading about that dude King David."

His declaration catches me off guard. "Really?"

"He was one bad dude, raiding and pillaging. Wrote a lot about God, though."

"The Bible says he loved the Lord with all his heart."

"He had a funny way of showing it."

"Keep reading." I'm curious how and when he picked up a Bible, but I don't ask. It's strange to think our pavement conversation had such an impact on him.

Back at my place, I call Adriane. "You're on to pick up Mrs. Woodward from the hospital tomorrow."

"Good. I've been praying for her all morning. I don't think I'll ever forget her tears when she was sitting in your car."

"I know I won't. Broke my heart. She called you lovely, by the way."

"Isn't she sweet? What about your flight?"

"I leave tonight." I collapse on the couch. Maybe I have time for a quick nap.

"Good for you."

"Yeah, good for me." I say goodbye and drop the phone to the floor. Close…my…eyes…for…just…a…minute.

I wake up to the serenade of my cell phone. The condo is shadowy with the light of late afternoon.

I scramble to my feet. "What time is it?" I dash to the kitchen. Five-fifteen.

I dig my ringing cell from the bottom of my purse. "Hello." I dash up to my bedroom, peeling off clothes.

"I thought you were going to call me?" It's Lucy. "How's New York?"

"I'm not there. I'm here." I stuff myself into a pair of jeans and a T-shirt.

"What?"

I bust into the bathroom to brush my teeth. "Hold on, Lucy." Seconds later I toss my toothbrush and paste into my waiting toiletries bag.

"Why are you still here?" Lucy asks, wailing a little.

"I had to take Mrs. Woodward to the hospital. Emergency gallbladder surgery."

"Oh, Macy, is she okay?"

"She is now." I grab my purple sweater and thunder downstairs. Pick up my purse, click on a living-room light to low and with one last glance around, I'm out the front door.

"What about your interview?"

"I'm taking the seven-o'clock flight out of Melbourne."

"You'd better hurry."

"Can you meet me there with some dinner? I'm starved." I toss my toiletries bag and my purse onto the passenger seat and speed away to the airport. I'm a dimwit. How could I let myself fall asleep?

Lucy and I polish off our sandwiches while I keep an eye on the time. Melbourne's airport is small, but I don't want to risk getting tangled up with security and miss my flight.

"Isn't it amazing how emergencies come at night, or when you're on your way out of town?" Lucy stands and takes our wadded-up sandwich paper.

"I'm just glad we were able to convince her to go to the E.R." I sling my purse over my shoulder. I don't want to miss this flight. "Thanks for the sandwich, Luce."

"Any time." She walks with me to security, then waves goodbye, smiling her best cheerleader smile. She won cheerleader of the year three years running when we were in high school, so she has the expression mastered. "You're good to go, right? Got your chic Chico's outfit…"

I whirl around to face her from the other side of security. "Lucy." Oh, I feel sick. "No, I don't have my chic Chico's. I left my bag at home."

Chapter Twenty

Three days after the Myers-Smith debacle, I drive to Beauty for Dad's *Food Connection* launch party. The New York interview runs on a repetitive loop in my head.

The Myers-Smith human resource manager shook my hand and said, "You take business casual to a whole new level."

I explained my dilemma in as few words as possible without sounding like a complete imbecile. I do want them to hire me.

He nodded and muttered that he understood as he walked me to my first interviewer. There were six interviews in all and Bob-the-HR-manager, as I came to know him, explained to each one why this candidate for director interviews in her street clothes.

It made for great first impressions.

Flying home on Wednesday, vacillating between relief and disappointment, I pondered the day while the stewardess poured me a Diet Coke and tossed over a third pack of peanuts.

Two months ago I was Macy Moore, savvy and smart in Anne Klein and Ann Taylor. Today I'm a dimwit in jeans and a T-shirt.

I concluded all I can do is hang on and enjoy the ride. If the Lord had a plan for me before I showed up to a New York City interview in my country-girl clothes, then He has a plan for me now. I just hope I didn't botch it up too much.

But let me just say I am now a woman with a mission: float my résumé to every possible company. Get a job. Pure and simple. Lucy was right—I shouldn't have put all my eggs in the Myers-Smith basket. I've lost two weeks of valuable job-hunting time.

I left Peyton Danner a message Thursday morning, hoping she didn't hear about my Myers-Smith mishap until I talked to her.

Thursday evening, the SSS called a midweek meeting and we met at House of Joe's for a Macy comforting.

Then, Friday morning I got up, packed, remembered my suitcase this time and drove to Beauty.

It's late afternoon when I arrive home. As I pull into the driveway, I remember Mom's affinity for napping. No sense waking her. I back out and head for the Moore Gourmet Sauces office.

I find Dad in the front office with his admin assistant, Sharon Lee.

"Macy, you're here." He holds out his arms to me. "I'm glad you came."

"Hi, Daddy." I fall into his embrace.

"How'd the interview go?"

I reach for Sharon's chocolate candy jar. "I showed up in jeans and a T-shirt."

"Now, that's a new approach," he says.

I give him the whole, drawn-out story.

It takes me about three hours to tell it all, because Dad's dealing with customers, his five-person staff and the event coordinator for Saturday's launch party.

While he's working with his new IT-network guy on a Web order entry problem, I sneak onto a computer and log on as the administrator. I check out the network and the local hard drives to make sure this new guy is keeping up with maintenance and security procedures I outlined for Dad when he started this e-venture.

Sure enough, he is. Good for him.

"How's it feel to be back at Moore Gourmet Sauces?" Dad claps his hand on my shoulder when the busyness dies down.

"Weird. It's been so long."

"So, bottom line on the New York job?" He starts toward his office.

"I survived. End of story." I step in time with his leisurely Georgia gait, hands in my hip pockets.

"You might have impressed them with your courage, confidence and ability to face difficult circumstances."

I chuckle. "Too bad you're not hiring me."

"That can be arranged."

I furrow my brows and pass on responding. "You know what's really ironic?"

"No, what?" Dad opens his office door and moseys to his desk chair. I fall backward onto the old leather couch.

"I remembered my toiletries bag. From the neck up, I looked fantastic."

"Now, there's your silver lining."

Staring at the slow-moving ceiling fan, I reminisce out loud. "I debated the whole flight up if I should even have gotten on the plane, knowing I didn't have business clothes. I debated canceling the interview, or running through Bloomingdale's and showing up late."

Dad shakes his head. "That would be worse than showing up in jeans."

"Exactly."

Saturday morning, Dad and Mom run around the house, frantic, calling to each other up the stairs, down the stairs and I think even once out the window. "Earl, where are the gift bags?"

"Kitty, the country club's on the phone. Did you order shrimp?"

I bury my head under my pillow and will myself to go back to sleep. The launch festivities, which include an all-out barbecue, don't start until 2:00 p.m. I have time. Plenty of time.

"Earl, where's my dress?" Mom bellows down the hall, her voice creeping under my closed door.

"I don't know, Kitty. Did you pick it up from the dry cleaner?"

"Oh, land sakes. The dry cleaner."

Right then, my door bursts open and I peer out from

under my pillow to see Mom standing there, legs apart, robe askew, head wrapped in a towel turban.

"You've got to run to the dry cleaner and get my dress."

I sit up, shoving my hair from my eyes. "Now?"

She waves her hands frantically. "Yes, now. They close at noon."

I move slowly out of bed. "There's plenty of time."

"It's almost noon now."

"Really?" I didn't sleep well. I dreamed I met with a boardroom full of Myers-Smith executives while wearing a pair of cutoffs. Ooh, shudder.

"Please, Macy, will you go?"

"Yes." I brush my teeth and put in my contacts wondering what the big deal is. It's a launch, I know, but at the core, it's a good ol' Georgia barbecue.

I ask Dad about it on my way through the kitchen for a slice of coffee cake. "*The Food Connection* is sending a camera crew for a live remote. Wherever Rhine Flagstone goes, so do the cameras."

A live remote? I brought a nice pair of shorts and flip-flops, but not television nice. More like it's-okay-if-I-get-barbecue-sauce-on-them nice. Now I'm going to have to run into Wal-Mart to get something to wear.

And all my recent QVC purchases sit at home. Considering my life lately, this does not surprise me.

Before I leave the house I dial the dry cleaner so they know I'm coming.

"Mr. Pong?" I say, starting to feel a little frantic myself. Live remote? Rhine Flagstone? Shopping at Wal-Mart?

"Yes," he says, clipped.

"It's Macy Moore. My mom left her dress at your store. She desperately needs it for Dad's business party. Can I please pick it up?" I hold my breath, scrunch up my eyes and brace for a brisk "No."

"Be here in five minutes."

I exhale and smile. "I'm on my way." I buzz across town on a stunning May day. Golden sun, white, wispy clouds and a breeze scented with freshly cut grass and pine.

Mr. Pong meets me at the front door with the dress in hand, lips pursed, brow creased. "Here are the dresses. Have your father pay me next week."

"Um, okay." Why are there two dresses?

"Next week." He shoves the dresses at me again.

"All right, all right." I slip my hand under the hangers and examine the dresses through the cellophane wrap. "Mr. Pong, there's two here."

He sighs. I know I'm irritating, but I can't leave with someone else's dress.

"Two Moore dresses—see the tag." He raises the tip of the tag with his forefinger. "One for the mother, one for the daughter. See?"

I check the tags. One reads Kitty, the other Macy.

"My wife hemmed the dresses and I pressed them. These are the ones." He regards me with his hands on his hips. He may be only five foot four, but he's towering over me right now.

I gawk at him with my mouth dangling. He waits less than a nanosecond, then shoves me out the door. "Have to go home and get ready for the party myself."

"Well, okay. Thanks for your help. See you there." I think Dad invited all of Beauty to this barbecue hoedown.

At my car I pop the trunk and lay the dresses flat. They are beautiful midnight-blue poplin summer dresses. I slip behind the wheel, whip out my cell and autodial Mom.

When she answers, I ask, "Why are there two dresses? Exactly alike."

"Oh, right, yes. Surprise!" Uh-oh. She sounds a little too English.

"Surprise?" Dread washes over me. I have a feeling I won't be visiting Wal-Mart after all, but wishing I was.

"I wanted us to look smashing," she says nervously. Occasionally English expressions fire out of her mouth and bewilder us all.

"So we're going as twins?" Why do I keep having these *Twilight* experiences? I'm working my way through life and next thing I know, I'm on *The Food Connection* dressed as Mini-Me.

"Oh, I thought it would be fun. I found two Marc Jacobs dresses on sale, you see. I had your hem dropped a little, because you're so tall, you know—" yes, I'm aware "—and mine taken up a smidge."

Is she serious? Does she really want to show up at a Moore Gourmet Sauces whoop-de-do dressed like Barbie and Skipper? I don't think she's thought this through.

"Mom, I appreciate you thinking of me and all, but—"

"You're welcome. And, oh, I forgot. You have a manicure appointment with Ling at one, so don't dillydally."

I glance at my watch. "At one? And the party starts at two?"

"Yes, but bring the dresses home first."

"Mom, there's not enough time."

"Oh, quit your bellyaching and get moving." *Now* she sounds like a true Georgian.

* * *

It's well after two when I slip through the polished oak doors of Beauty's country club wearing the blue poplin Mom bought. The dress is actually fabulous, but I'm terrified of being caught standing next to her.

Dad catches my eye and waves me over to where he's standing with *The Food Connection* crew and Rhine Flagstone.

"Rhine, this is my daughter, Macy."

"Very nice to meet you," Rhine says. He's pleasant enough, with incredible blue eyes and an overly white capped smile, but not as egotistical as I thought.

"She's the one I was telling you about," Dad says.

I eye my father. "Telling him what?"

"How charming you are," Rhine answers, a sneaky twinkle in his eye.

So help me, if Dad is trying to fix me up with Rhine… No, he wouldn't dare. Rhine's married. I've heard him talk about his wife and kids.

(Mental note 1,123: find out what Dad's up to.)

"Macy." My sister-in-law, Suzanne, touches my forearm. "I'm so glad you're here. I know how busy you are, but no Moore party is the same without you."

Is she the sweetest thing, or what? "I wouldn't miss it." I squeeze her hand. Never mind that my days are freer than a roaring river—it's good to be here. For Dad. For the family. For the free barbecue.

"You and your mom look adorable dressed alike," she says just as her husband—and my brother—Cole joins us.

"How's it going, Skipper?"

I swat his shoulder. "Stop. Go ahead and call Mom Barbie and see what happens to you."

He laughs. "I can't believe she got you to wear the same dress she's wearing."

"Quit it, Cole," Suzanne nudges him. "I think it's sweet. Not many women have the ability to wear the same dress yet seem so completely unique."

"Forget him, Suz—he's just jealous."

Cole scoffs. "Yeah, that's it, Macy. I'm jealous."

By now Rhine has moved into position, the camera and crew rolling around him, Dad smiling augustly at his side.

"Welcome everyone," Rhine begins, a swashbuckling air about him that draws people in. Digital camera flashes snap and buzz.

"We're here in Beauty, Georgia, with *The Food Connection's* latest partner, Moore Gourmet Sauces."

I fade out and watch Dad, whose grin is so wide I think his face might get stuck. He's worked hard for this. I know there were dark days when he wanted to quit and work a nine-to-fiver like everyone else.

I like the fact that Rhine is treating him with respect. He's putting his arm around Daddy now.

Very cool. You go, Rhine. Mom strolls over to me with two glasses of punch.

"Look at your Dad. He's beaming."

I take a step away. "So are you." I sip some very spunky sherry.

"He's achieved his goal with this business. It's a sound, solid company."

"You guys make a great team, Mom. Dad's ingenuity. Your recipes."

She turns to me with misty eyes. "Two silly kids meeting at Woodstock, of all places, led to this. The blessing of God overwhelms me."

Caught up in the sentiment of the moment, I hug Mom. She's worked as hard as Dad.

"Here's Earl's wife, Kitty, with their daughter, Macy."

Mom and I jerk away from each other. Rhine and the entire *Food Connection* camera crew are coming right for us.

I smile and half wave, and giggle, I think. I hope not. Mom stands there with a deer-in-the-headlights look.

"Relax," I whisper out the corner of my mouth.

"I didn't know I was going to be on national TV dressed like you."

I knew she didn't think this thing through.

"Kitty Moore," Rhine says in his TV-man voice, slipping his arm around Mom's shoulder.

"Good afternoon, Rhine." Mom tilts her head and smiles at the camera, then politely, forcibly, shoves me out of the shot.

Chapter Twenty-One

All afternoon the three hundred or so guests roam the country club's beautiful grounds, talking and taking shade under the magnolias. The breeze is heady with the scent of grilling meat and barbecue sauce.

Rhine is broadcasting from one of the stainless steel grills, eating a chicken wing, grinning and holding up a bottle of my family's sauce.

"Have Moore sauce," he says, chuckling.

I find a secluded spot in one of the tents, watching and enjoying the show, proud of my parents' success.

Across the way I see Cole and Suzanne sharing a table with her folks, Regis and Connie Gellar, eating ribs and potato salad. Cole has a brown dab of sauce on the side of his face, as always.

People who see our family snapshots for the first time always ask, "Cole, did you have this mole on the side of your face removed?"

Yep, with a bar of soap and a washcloth.

Mom dashes up to me. "Macy, please put this in your car. It's a gift from *The Food Connection* and I don't want to lose it." She shoves a wrapped box into my hands. "I don't know where your father parked our car, so please, be a love." She squeezes my shoulders and scurries away.

I go inside to find my purse and keys, then exit the side door and walk slowly to my car, enjoying the breeze and beauty of the day. Springtime in Beauty is gorgeous and fun. I admit I always loved this time of year in my hometown.

There was the Spring Festival. Beauty Days with Saturday In The Park. The art show. Cruising Jasmine Street in Lucy's car under the blooming magnolias. Waiting for the May day when the public pool opened.

As I near the BMW, I press the unlock button on the remote. Other than my youthful restlessness and zeal to see the world, life in Beauty wasn't so bad. My memories are pleasant.

"Nice ride."

I turn to see Dylan striding across the country club's manicured lawn, a root beer can dangling from his hand. My eyes send messages to my heart—beat faster, beat faster!

"What are you doing out here?" I open the passenger door and drop the gift onto the seat.

"Eating barbecue." He approaches, motioning to my car, eyeing it as if it's a rare impressionist painting. "Who'd you steal this from?"

"Kid on the corner. He wanted to sell it to buy a bike."

He laughs. "Casper & Company is treating you well." He walks around the Beemer again, chin jutted out.

"They did."

"This is quite a big deal for your dad and mom," he says, leaning against the passenger door, his legs crossed casually, regarding me with his blue-green eyes and an expression I can't describe. Interest? Curiosity? Something stuck between my teeth? I run my tongue over them just in case.

"Yes, it is."

"Your dad is quite the businessman."

"Yes, he is," I answer robotically, an odd quiver in my voice. My heart swirls with surreal images of the night he visited my place, the night he almost kissed me. (I think.)

Stop, Macy. Don't get your heart in a wad over a guy you'll never have.

"You look beautiful," he says. "Was it your idea to dress like your mom?" He gives me a coy look and sips from his can.

"What do you think?" I laugh. He's looking *right* at me! My insides shimmy. Is my green light on or something?

"Probably not, but only you could pull it off, Macy."

His compliments so confuse me. I know he's sincere, but where is it all going?

"I got the second reunion flyer," I say, changing my stance, putting some distance between us.

"Alisa said she mailed them out. How'd you like it?"

"It's weird seeing my name in such large print. Macy Moore." I talk too loud and too fast.

He shakes his head, laughing. "I don't know why you discredit yourself, Macy. You're a star, don't you know?"

A falling star. I'm on a confidence merry-go-round and right now the horse is sinking down.

"Why'd you come to visit me that night?" I blurt out.

He looks into my eyes. "I wanted to see you."

I tip my chin up. "Any particular reason?" I ask without considering where this conversation might end up.

He coughs. "Anything wrong with a friend visiting a friend?" He taps the heel of his shoe against the pavement.

"No, I guess not." I feel disappointed, a little. Maybe I didn't know where my questions would lead, but I suppose I wanted more than a friendship answer.

Why? I can't say. I'm acutely aware that Dylan lives in Beauty. Always has, always will. And I'm bound for some northern city. Better make sure the green light is off.

Propped against my car, we slip into a gentle conversation, talking about anything and everything. He really is amazing to be around.

When the sun begins to slip behind the trees, haloing them in gold and red, I say, "I'd better get back to the party." I'm leery of losing my heart to the fairy-tale magic of this moment.

He glances skyward. "Me, too."

Silence. Staring in opposite directions, neither one of us moving. It's as if all these unspoken words linger between us, yearning to be said.

My heartbeat picks up the pace to a light jog. This causes me to draw a deep breath, and while I don't mean it to, the air whispers out of my lungs in a perfect Marilyn Monroe impression.

He snaps his head around. I jump to life. "Gotta go." I beep the car locked and stride toward the country club.

He runs up behind me. "Wait, I'll walk with you."

I look back at him. "Dad has a bluegrass band lined up for the evening," I say for no reason other than to fill the air. Otherwise, I might blurt something like, "Why don't you love me?"

"Should be fun. I need to get going, but will I see you at church in the morning?" he asks.

My heart thuds. I glance at him. "Yes, and then Sizzler."

He laughs. "Yes, Sizzler. It's a Beauty Community Church tradition."

"Who am I to buck tradition?"

He laughs with a deep, resonant cadence. "You're all about bucking tradition, Macy Moore."

At the clubhouse he goes in one direction, I go in another. I find my purse, drop my keys inside and tell my heart to stop dreaming.

Mid-May. Where have the days gone? Still no word from Myers-Smith. I expected more from them, but at the same time, expected nothing at all.

What's so hard about dashing off a letter on corporate letterhead, letting a girl know she didn't get the job? Use a lot of corporate buzzwords about how you found a candidate more tailored to their corporate needs and yadda, yadda, blah, blah, the deed is done.

On a positive note, Peyton Danner returned my call. No, she had not heard about my interview in jeans, but she dismissed it with "I've heard worse, much worse."

She's talking with other companies about their need for

a person of my substantial (her word, not mine) qualities, but these things take time.

So I go about my daily, unemployed routine. Up around eight, power walk three miles (cancel all mental notes to rejoin the gym), shower and dress, then sit down for prayer and Bible reading.

I try not to let my mind drift and wander down dark mental trails during the quiet moments of my devotional time. I try not to dwell on the fact that I'm both jobless and husbandless at thirty-three.

It's *The Apprentice* meets *The Bachelorette*. Maybe I should write Mark Burnett.

But I've come to grips with the fact that "finding myself" lies not in the soul of Macy Moore, but in the heart of God. Easier said than done? Yes.

After prayer, I hop on the Internet looking for jobs. I've posted my résumé with about ten companies, but so far, no nibbles.

Sometime during the day I check my bank balance to see if it's miraculously multiplied. It hasn't. Around the middle of August my well of severance and vacation pay runs dry and I'll be broke unless I dip into my 401K or land a fabulous job.

At noon I break for lunch. Habit, I guess. I make a sandwich or run out for fast food, which totally negates my three-mile power walk, but for the moment I'm keeping life in precarious balance. Lost my job, lost my man, I'm hanging on to my deep fried potatoes.

Around three I visit Mrs. Woodward, who is completely recovered from gallbladder surgery. The past few days, Drag has joined us for a rousing game of Scrabble. His dumb surfer dude shtick is a phony and a fake. He's crazy intelligent.

Tuesday night I meet the Single Saved Sisters at House of Joe's, sans Lucy. She has to work. Something about an early deadline for the local news pages.

At eight o'clock Tamara and I are the only ones here. We sip lattes and chew the fat, wondering what happened to Adriane. Her empty chair is like the calm before the storm. Something is up.

"Where do you think she is?" I ask Tamara with a quick glance toward the door.

"Maybe she's on deadline?"

"No, she turned in her latest manuscript the week I went to New York."

"You think she forgot?" Tamara looks at me as if she knows it's a wild idea, but she's reaching.

"Has she missed a meeting since we started this ridiculous club?" I check the door again.

By eight-thirty she's still missing, not answering her home or cell phone. Tamara is contemplating a call to the hospital when Adriane Fox finally waltzes in and floats over to our table.

"What *is* up with you?" Tamara demands, sheathing her cell phone with vigor.

"Nothing," Adriane says, but the singsong in her voice and the sparkle in her eye tells a different story.

She orders her coffee and rejoins us, going on and on about inane stuff like how the driver next to her at a red light looked like the hero in her first book, *Hearts & Roses,* and

how she thinks we should all go shopping at the Viera out-
lets on Saturday, and has anyone seen the new Lexus? It's *gorgeous.*

Tamara rallies with a wicked cross-examination, but Adriane maneuvers around her. Me? I observe, saying nothing.

Then it hits me. "You met somebody."

She snaps, "What makes you say that?"

Now Tamara's caught on. "You did. You met someone. I
wondered why you were yapping so much."

She crumbles easily. "Okay, what if I did? You've been pes-
tering me for years to—"

"Date?" Tamara interjects.

"If that's the word you choose."

Tamara and I woo-hoo right in the middle of House of
Joe's. This is fantastic news. Out of the corner of my eye I
see Claire is about to take the stage. I'm glad she's singing
again tonight, glad we didn't interrupt her set.

"Why the cloak-and-dagger?" I want to know.

"We recently realized how we felt and I'm not sure
where things are going." Adriane scrunches up her shoulders, and shades of her usual pessimistic self shadow the
conversation.

"Hold it," I say, standing, palms up, "until I order another round."

"Let me buy," Adriane insists. "You're unemployed,
Macy."

"Thanks. I forgot." Women in love are so arrogant. "Just
tell everyone in earshot I don't have a job, that I'm a failure."

"You're not a failure. Get over yourself." Adriane scoots
away to order lattes.

"A pessimist in love," Tamara says. "Not sure I can handle it."

Come to find out, Adriane's new man is an editor with her publishing house. While e-mailing and IMing over one of her manuscripts, they became friends.

"He's a Christian?" Tamara asks. "Don't be walking the line like our girl Macy."

"Hey!" It's a primitive defense, but the best I can do on short notice.

"Please, I've been that route. Yes, he's a Christian," Adriane says. "Talking about our faith is how we became friends."

I recognize the expression on her face. The same one I've seen on my sister-in-law Suzanne's face. The one Lucy now wears. The look of love.

Eric Gurden, Adriane's new love, was in Orlando on business and drove over to see Adriane Sunday afternoon. The rest, as they say, is history.

We hear how Eric hung the moon and lit the stars, and set Adriane's heart in motion. It's good to see her touched by love. Not once during the evening does she poise her hand as if waiting for a cigarette.

"You know," I say suddenly, sort of thinking out loud, "when and if I decide to get married, I'm going against the grain."

"Oh, yes, same here," Adriane echoes.

"Not me," Tamara counters with a shake of her head. "Tradition, tradition, tradition. Stained-glass-window church, wedding march, big reception. The works."

"I want a wedding under the stars," I begin, "with me in a white, flowing cotton dress. No flowers or unity candle. I'll walk down the aisle to the music of a violin. I'll curl my bare toes in the grass and make a covenant with God and my man to never give up on love."

"Oh, Macy, how lovely," Adriane says, exhaling. "I might have to steal that scene for a book."

"And I want chocolate, lots of chocolate," I conclude.

Tamara slaps the table. "Now you're talking." Then she stands. "I hate to go, but I have an early-morning meeting."

"It's only nine-thirty," I protest.

"I know, I know, but I was falling asleep at my desk today."

She takes a last gulp from her mug. From the corner of my eye I see a man passing by our table, staring at Tamara. He stops, then backtracks. "Tamara Clayton?"

"Yes." She turns around.

"I can't believe it. It's me, Sam Peterson from Live Oak."

"Well, Sam Peterson." She hugs him, then looks at us. "He was my brother Phil's best friend."

"I just moved into town. Came in with a new project at Rockwell-Collins."

"Well, welcome." Tamara flirts. Right out in the open. No shame. I don't blame her, though. Sam is very fine.

"Maybe we could get together, talk about old times," Sam suggests, his gaze glued to her face. "You know, growing up, I always had a crush on you. Phil's little sister."

Tamara chortles. Oh, brother.

"Why don't I take you on a tour of the town?"

Sam's big white smile brightens his entire being. "That would be wonderful."

Before our very eyes, Tamara makes a date. Then they leave House of Joe's, her arm linked with his, gabbing ninety miles an hour as if Adriane and I don't even exist.

"How do you like that?" I muse.

"Don't be bitter, Macy," Adriane says.

"What? Bitter? I'm not bitter."

"Well, life has thrown you a few curves—"

"But I'm still in the game, Adriane."

"That's my girl. Keep that positive attitude," she says, like *pip, pip, cheerio.*

Who does she think she's talking to? Keep a positive attitude, huh! I'm about to say something when her cell phone jingles. By the way she answers and the flush on her cheeks, I know it's Eric. She grabs her stuff, waves goodbye and I'm left to walk out alone.

Chapter Twenty-Two

❧

Memorial Day weekend I have a brain freeze. I don't know what happens, but I let the Single Saved Sisters talk me into attending the church singles function.

"Will there be more than ten people there?" I ask during a late-afternoon visit with Lucy. Bored, I drop by the paper to see what morbid news story she's working on.

"Of course. Stop this ridiculous phobia. You're in crowds of more than ten people all the time."

"Ridiculous phobia? Please, it's self-defense."

"You ride on airplanes with hundreds of people and it never bothers you."

"I read where Robert Mitchum had a crowd phobia."

"And he's your role model? A fifties actor?"

"I'm just saying."

"Say you'll be there."

"Okay," I say, but call her bluff. "I'll go if you fry a hamburger in a skillet on the stove."

She fades to green. "Gross."

"As I thought." Feeling puffed up, I sit back. We all have our phobias.

Lucy leans my way. "Macy, you have no boyfriend, no job and all you do is sit home in those ratty shorts, conduct phone interviews and surf cable channels."

I make a face. Cheater. "Okay, I'll go."

So here it is, Memorial Day, and I'm going to a singles shindig.

I get ready for the Bash on the Beach, packing my tote with a towel and my cooler with shrimp salad.

The silver lining to this cloud is that Lucy is off the market and perhaps, oh, if I can dream, the one or two cool guys will gravitate my way. Just for the day, that's all I ask.

Lucy and Jack pick me up around ten. She's bubbly and beautiful in a pale green sundress. He, I've learned, is not at all like Barney Fife. Strong and wiry, soft-spoken and kind, Jack reminds me of a nineteenth-century, Old West cowboy. Salt-of-the-earth type. Fear the Almighty, work hard and love your woman.

In no time, we're beachside and pulling into Nance Park, where I see a sizable crowd has already gathered.

I stick on a smile and greet everyone. Tamara and Adriane arrive with their men. I'm like the seventh wheel. Third wheel is doable, the fifth is a little embarrassing, but the seventh? Downright humiliating.

Adriane introduces us to Eric Gurden, a floppy-haired

blonde who reminds me of Tom Berenger. Tamara cleaves to Sam as if she wants to be his permanent appendage and smiles so much *my* face hurts. They've been thick as thieves since running into each other that night at the coffeehouse.

At the last Single Saved Sisters meeting, I alone showed up, sipped half a white mocha and left.

The seven of us set up camp under one of the pavilions. Out on the beach, the volleyball is out and being tossed around. Now hear this—I stink at volleyball. Right down to my size-ten feet.

I watch the preliminary action, hoping no one remembers I'm five-ten. Every volleyball game is the same. Stick the tall girl in the front line and tell her to spike.

Tina Farrow harangued me during this inane game in eighth-grade gym class. Awkward and geeky with my new long limbs, I fumbled over my own feet during one game and landed in the net, arms and legs everywhere. Even our P.E. teacher faced the wall to hide her laugh.

After that, I refused to play such a cruel sport. In high school I was always sick that semester.

"Anyone for volleyball?" one of the guys hollers toward the pavilion.

"Macy's here. She can play," Lucy shouts down to them, pointing at me.

I gape at her. "Have you gone mad?"

"Look, a whole bunch of guys are here—Greg, Kip, Tomás what's-his-name."

I peer over the rail. No Velcro sneakers or bad comb-overs. Greg, Kip and Tomás are very cool—in fact, the largest gathering of cool I've ever seen at one of these things.

"Go on." She pushes me.

"No way." I grit my teeth. "You know I hate volleyball."

"Just stick your hands in the air and spike it."

"Come on, girl. I'll go with you." Tamara jerks me by the arm.

I don't know why, but I go. I'm an idiot.

"All right, Macy, Tamara," Tomás says, big white grin splitting his brown face. "I got dibs on Macy."

"I'm really awful," I confess, loudly, as a way of warning, watching Tamara cross under the net to the other side.

"Just stand in front and spike it." He takes my hand, walks me to the front center and gives me a thumbs-up.

This is not good....

We volley for serve, and fortunately the ball soars away from me every time. I stand there with my hands in the air looking ridiculous.

However, I am pleased to see that one or two on the opposing team are worse than I am.

Once the game starts and the first few passes fly right over my head, I relax a little. We're up three-zip.

Tamara claps her hands, admonishing her team. "Let's go! We can do this."

They serve. I tip my head back to see the ball coming right at me.

"It's yours, Macy," Tomás coaches. "Spike it!"

In that split second I get a *grrr* in my gut and decide, *Now is my time.* Eighth grade and Tina Farrow are twenty years behind me. Spike this one for yourself, Macy.

Eye on the ball, I draw back my arm. I leap. I'm spi-i-i-king.

The ball bounces off the net and into my face.

"Oomph!" The blow knocks me on my back, arms and legs flailing, the humiliation of junior high revived. I can't open my eyes. I can't look.

"Macy, are you all right?" Tomás is barely able to talk because he's stifling a big hee-haw laugh.

"I'm fine." I grab his offered hand.

Tamara hollers, "Way to sacrifice the body, Macy."

Tomás holds my chin and examines my face. "Let me see." He's highly amused by this damsel in distress.

"I'm fine," I repeat.

"I just want to be sure. No black eyes or anything."

"I warned you—I stink." There's an edge to my voice. Just because a girl is tall doesn't mean she's an athlete.

He grabs me by the shoulders and looks into my eyes. "Concentrate. You can do this." He gives me a light shake and goes back.

Concentrate. I make a face. What a novel notion. Einstein attributed his genius to concentration. Okay, this is not physics and I'm not Einstein, but I *can* do this. Concentrate.

In the next few passes, I set to Kip once, followed by a tip over the net. We score both times. Feeling proud and full of myself, I ready for the next volley.

I point at Tamara. "I'm gunning for you, Clayton."

"Bring it on, Moore."

I'm having fun now, sort of. The next volley sends the ball soaring my way. It's a little high and a little past me, but I can get it. I run back, concentrating, concentrating.

Maybe in the distance I hear, "I got it," but I'm concentrating. Eye on the ball. I'm going for it, erasing all my fears.

I draw my arm back, hand poised, aiming to pound that ball to south Florida, when all of a sudden my elbow slams into a brick wall.

In reality, it's Tomás's face. We tumble to the ground, me landing on top of him, blood gushing from his nose.

"Somebody get a towel," someone screams.

I scramble to my feet, humiliated. "Oh, Tomás, I'm so sorry," I sob.

"It was an accident. Don't worry." He presses the towel to his nose. "Didn't you hear me yell I got it?"

"No. Well, maybe."

"I think it's broken," someone declares after peeking underneath the towel.

"Broken!" I broke a man's nose? I fall to my knees, face in my hands. This is what I get for concentrating.

Tamara kneels next to me in the sand. "You okay?" she whispers.

"No. I broke a man's nose."

"Better go to the E.R. just in case," Kip suggests.

"I'll take him." I jump up and face the pavilion. "Jack, I need your keys."

Lucy is watching with her fingers over her eyes while Adriane cuddles with Eric in the corner, oblivious.

"It's all right, Macy," Tomás assures me. "I came with a date. She can drive me."

"Are you sure?" I help him to his feet.

"Yes, I'll need my car anyway."

Seeing the bloodstained towel, I start to cry. I can't help it. "Please forgive me. I'm so, so, so sorry."

He touches my arm. "Forget it. I told you to concentrate."

I grin through my embarrassment. "So, I guess this is your fault?"

On that lighthearted note, we help him to his car.

I return to the pavilion and sulk in the corner, aware that I single-handedly put a damper on the whole beach bash. And I didn't want to be here in the first place.

Lucy, Adriane and Tamara slide up next to me on the bench. "It was an accident."

"It's a barbaric sport."

"Girl, don't think about it."

I nudge Lucy. "I hope you're happy."

"Me?"

"Yes. This is all your fault for making me come, and then shoving me out there to play volleyball."

She brushes her hand over my hair. "I'm sorry. I didn't really think—" She stops talking to giggle. "When the ball bounced out of the net and into your face…"

Tamara looks the other way, biting her bottom lip, and Adriane wants to know what happened. She missed it all. Tamara recounts the whole thing.

I'm angry. Well, I want to be angry. However, the picture Tamara paints makes me laugh.

Despite the support of the single and saved, and all the great fun I'm having (not), I ask Jack and Lucy to run me home. Even cute Kip's big comforting hand on my shoulder doesn't comfort me. Breaking a man's nose is exhausting.

This, I promise Lucy, is my last singles event, *ever.*

"Definitely," she agrees. "Definitely."

* * *

Sitting at my computer desk, I check e-mail while picking at a two-day-old salad. Outside my window the sun paints the fading Memorial Day sky with a rich reddish hue. Nothing like spam e-mail and soggy lettuce to cheer a girl.

But I spot an e-mail from my old debate buddy, Kathy Bailey. Well, this is pleasant. I click to open her e-letter.

Dear Macy,
How are you? I saw your name on the class reunion flyer. I wasn't going to go this time, but when I saw you were emcee, I changed my mind. I can't wait to see you. I still think of how much we laughed in Mr. Ellison's class.

Married life is good. We love California, yet it doesn't feel like home. I'm pregnant with number four, but Mark and I agree this is the last. At my age, I have no patience for starting over with the diapers and midnight feedings.

Oh, gag. At her age. That's my age, and I haven't even started with a round of diapers and midnight feedings.

There's an attachment at the bottom of her e-mail. I click on it. A radiant Kathy smiles at me with Mark and the three kids gathered around. She looks fulfilled and happy.

First Joley, then Lucy, now Kathy. I exit e-mail, pick up my uneaten salad and head for the kitchen. Did I make a wrong turn somewhere in my twenties and end up in Old Maid-dom thinking it was Career Haven?

I know it's wrong to compare myself to others, but give me a minute. Kathy is content and happy as a wife and mom, raising kids that just may be president or the next Bill Gates.

I'm an unattached, unemployed nose breaker. That's it. I'm resigning as the emcee.

I dump the spotted lettuce and soft tomatoes into the garbage and jerk open the freezer door. What I need is a bowl of ice cream to soothe the black eye of my day. But the freezer is bare.

I'm pondering making a food run when my front door opens. Lucy and Jack, Adriane and Eric, Tamara and Sam tumble in, supermarket bags dangling from their hands.

"We decided you shouldn't be sitting home alone," Lucy informs me, dropping her plastic bag on my kitchen table. "We brought subs."

"What about the cookout?" I ask, my heart smiling, feeling the love. I am so blessed.

"You're more important."

I peek into one of the bags. Ice cream, Diet Coke and brownie mix. "Ah, you guys, my favorites."

Tamara holds up several DVDs. "Movie of your choice."

Adriane drops into the lounger, crossing her long legs. "I couldn't have fun thinking of you sitting here alone." Eric sits on the arm of the chair, his hand on her shoulder. He's quiet and observant, and I like him.

Jack explains, "The guys are going to the Sylvester Stallone festival at the Oaks and you girls will have ladies' night." Without much thought, he kisses me on the cheek.

"Thank you," I whisper. I like the glint in Jack's eye. Lucy's smart to fall in love with him.

Sam digs in one of the bags. "First let's eat. I'm starved."

"Yeah, let's get to it."

We sit at the dining-room table, eat and laugh, and tell

stories on ourselves. Since I gave everyone a visual today, I'm absolved from recounting.

Tomás calls to let me know he's all right. I apologize again for the umpteenth time and he assures me he's over it.

"Part of the game, Macy."

Still. I broke a man's nose.

We polish off the subs and the guys pile into Sam's SUV, leaving early so they have time to buy popcorn and candy.

Tamara holds up the DVDs while Lucy and I clean up. "We got *While You Were Sleeping, Sense and Sensibility* and *Mr. Deeds.*"

I make a funny face. *"Mr. Deeds?"*

"I like it," Lucy says.

"I wanted *Fiddler on the Roof,*" Adriane interjects, falling into the lounger, throwing a leg over the chair's arm.

"Sense and Sensibility," I vote, not sure I've seen it all the way through.

"Good choice. *Sense and Sensibility* it is." Tamara waves the DVD in the air.

While Lucy mixes up the brownies, I go upstairs and throw down a bunch of extra pillows for movie cuddling.

"I think I'm in love," Adriane declares from her chair, arms in the air, head back.

Tamara, Lucy and I look at each other. "Really?"

With an uncharacteristic smile, she gushes, "Really."

We cheer and dive on her. In a heap, we tumble to the floor wrapped in laughter.

"Off me." Adriane shoves at us, laughing, but she's finished fooling around. Getting up, she jerks her top in place and flops back into the lounger.

"I'm very happy for you. Eric is great," I say, arranging my pillows harem-style and covering them with a blanket.

"I know," she purrs.

Tamara pops in the DVD and takes a seat on the couch. While the player cues up the show, Tamara fires off a challenge. "Best movie of all time?"

"The Way We Were," I say.

Adriane objects. "Too sad. *It's A Wonderful Life.*"

Lucy votes. *"Gone With The Wind."*

We *oooh.* "Good one."

I hold up my hand. "I don't care what anyone says. I love *Remember the Titans.*"

"I've never seen that," Tamara confesses.

"What? You've got to see it," I insist, curling up on my pillowy bed.

"We'll watch it next movie night," Tamara suggests, and we all agree.

I get a little dewy-eyed. "Thanks again, you guys, for being here."

Lucy smiles. "Where else would we be?"

Chapter Twenty-Three

Tuesday afternoon I cruise home along the Indian River after a much-needed shopping spree (need new outfit for reunion, don't I?—plan ahead, plan ahead) with the Beemer's top down.

The reunion agenda calls for a fancy Saturday-night dinner, so I definitely need to look fresh, hip and in command. Can't have the emcee looking like a used shoe.

Overhead, the sun shines brightly in a very blue sky and the air is scented and salty. It's the kind of day that stirs my faith. Forget about Casper, friends with boyfriends and the gorgeous life of former classmates. I'm ready to get on with my own life—wonderful.

Still in the dark about Myers-Smith, I decide to call Peyton first thing in the morning if I don't hear anything by the end of the day.

Behind me, the plastic bag covering my new dress flaps in the wind. I use the rearview mirror to make sure it's safe. I should have stored it in the trunk. I smile. If Dylan liked me in the blue poplin, maybe he'll love me in this one.

When I pull into the garage, I catch sight of Drag loping across his little lawn, surfboard clutched under his arm.

"Hello," I call to him, unhooking the dress from the back-seat latch.

"You busy?" He tips his head to the side, eyes squinting in the sunlight, his sunglasses riding on his head.

I open the garage door. "I'm unemployed."

"Then can I talk to you?"

"Sure." This feels serious.

He leaves his board leaning on the outer garage wall and kicks off his worn flip-flops.

"Nice place," he says, making his way through the kitchen to the living room.

"Not much different than yours, I'd guess." I run upstairs to hang up the dress.

"Have you seen my place?" he calls after me.

"Actually, no," I holler down from my room.

"I have two lawn chairs, a plastic picnic table and a hammock."

I jog down the stairs. "Furniture is so overrated. Would you like something to drink? Water or Diet Coke?"

"No, thanks." He sits on the couch, scooping his long blond locks away from his face.

For the first time, I notice his aristocratic features. His nose, jaw and chin line up perfectly.

He notices me noticing. "What?"

I blush. "Nothing." I sit on the couch, facing him, curling my legs under me. "What's up?"

He leans forward and knocks his knuckles on the edge of the coffee table as if he's suddenly nervous. "I was wondering," he says, avoiding my eyes, "if you could tell me about Jesus."

"Jesus?" I repeat, as if I'm hearing the name for the first time—one of my more poignant "duh" moments.

"I've read the New Testament three times."

"Three times?" I'm impressed.

"Yeah, and I was—"

The phone's ring interrupts Drag's question.

"Excuse me," I say, reaching for the portable on the coffee table. "Hello?"

"Ms. Moore?"

"Yes." The voice is not familiar.

"Steve Albright from Myers-Smith in New York."

I leap off the couch. "How are you?"

"My apologies for taking so long to get back to you."

"That's all right." I motion just a minute to Drag. I walk to the stairs and sit on the bottom step.

"Our human resources manager is no longer with us."

"I'm sorry to hear that," I respond for lack of anything better.

"So was he."

I bite back a laugh. Poor Bob.

"Anyway," Steve continues, "I hear you interviewed in jeans and impressed the New York office."

I stand. All the blood drains from my brain. "What?" The word is weak and wispy.

"We'd like you to take a look at a job in our Chicago office. Director of customer service. It's a smaller operation than New York, but the Midwest market is booming right now. The department would be yours to run." He rattles off a potential salary, plus bonus, that knocks me back down on my derriere.

"I'm interested." My head is spinning.

"You okay?" Drag asks, low and sincere.

I nod and give him the just-a-minute sign again.

"Can you interview in Chicago the week of the twelfth? Sorry to wait so long, but Human Resources is being reorganized."

"The twelfth is fine." In fact, perfect. Right before the dreaded Beauty High reunion. That emcee job might not be so bad in this new light.

Welcome our emcee, Macy Moore, corporate director for Myers-Smith Webware.

Steve Albright and I talk dates and times. No need to jot it down or whip out my PDA—this information is forever engraved on my brain.

Steve confirms that his office will e-mail me an e-ticket from Melbourne to Chicago and the hotel information.

"I look forward to meeting you," he says.

"Same here. Thank you."

I press End. The phone dangles from my limp hand. I'm shaking.

"Good news or bad? I can't tell. Your face is white, but you're smiling." Drag watches me with a half grin.

I toss the phone onto the coffee table. "They want me to interview for the director position in the Chicago office. Chicago." I mute my squeal, but my insides are all swirly.

"Congratulations." Drag raps his knuckles on the table again.

I feel like calling someone. Lucy. Dad. Chris. Roni Karpinski. *How do you like me now, Attila?*

But Drag is here. Talking about the Bible and Jesus. Right. I come to my senses and plop next to my neighbor on the couch. "Enough about me. Now, what do you want to know?"

Drag's knuckle-knocking slows. "Is He for real?" No fooling around with this guy.

"Who? Jesus? Yes, He is."

"You're confident." Drag draws back, but his blue eyes are wide with wonder.

"Drag, you know everyone bets their life on something."

"True."

"For you, it's the next great wave. For my ex-boyfriend, it's the bull market." I catch my own wave and hang on for the ride to shore.

"My father lived for the bull market."

"And what did it get him?"

"A heart attack." Drag collapses against my couch and chews on the tip of his thumb.

"Jesus is the only way to true peace, the only sure thing," I say.

"To believe or not to believe. That is the question." Drag recites his own Shakespearean prose.

"Exactly." I tap my hand on his leg.

He gives me a small grin while still nibbling on his thumb. I have a profound thought and am about to share it when, of course, the phone rings.

"Hello?"

"Dinner?" Lucy asks with fabled familiarity.

"Absolutely."

"Be there in a few hours." I hear Lucy's remote key beep and her car door pop open. "I'll pick up something."

"Jack coming?" Why I bother asking I'll never know. *Jack* and *Lucy* are synonyms.

"If you don't mind."

I face Drag. "Do you want to stay for dinner?"

"Do I like to surf?" His Goofy laugh rolls out.

"Right." I nod. "Drag's joining us."

"Drag? What's he doing there?"

"I'll let him tell you."

"Macy…" she says in her what-have-you-done-now tone.

"Bye." I press End. It's then I realize this business with Drag completely eclipsed my Chicago, Myers-Smith excitement.

I'll meditate on that later. For now, it's back to Drag, Jesus and signing up for a spot in eternity.

"So, where were we?" I prod him.

"Believing or not believing." Drag sighs, then says, "I believe, Macy. I just wish I could see."

"Ah, that's what faith is all about. You must see with the eyes of your heart. You can't see the wind, you can't see love, but you know those things are real."

He regards me for a lingering second. "So what do I do?"

"Well, you read about Jesus, right? Tell Him you believe in what He said and did. Trust Him with your heart."

"Dude, just like that? Say it?" His tone rises at the end of the sentence as if he can't believe it to be that easy.

"Just like that. Speak from your heart, say whatever you

want." I stop short. I don't want my excitement to overwhelm him.

Drag slides to the edge of the couch, elbows on his knees, and locks his hands in front of him. He bows his head.

"Well, God, um, Jesus. Look, Dude, I believe You died for me, though I'm not sure why, but thanks. And forgive the bad stuff I've done. I want to be Your friend."

A *whoosh* feeling hits me and I start to snicker.

"What?" Drag peeks out from under his bowed brow, irritated. "You're laughing."

I button it up. "Just happy. Jesus is your friend and now you are His."

"Whoa, dude, heavy." Drag smiles and I know heaven has touched his heart.

If everything I endured the past few months was to help Drag find this place of peace, I'd take a deep breath and do it all over again.

Chapter Twenty-Four

The first weekend in June I drive to Beauty for…um, I don't know. Bored, I guess. Georgia on my mind, maybe. It's a beautiful weekend on the eastern seaboard and my Single Saved Sisters are otherwise engaged.

Lucy and Jack are spending the weekend at Disney with his parents and sisters. Tamara is in Live Oak visiting family with Sam, and Adriane is starting a new book. She's buried in the painful process of Chapter One and unable to communicate with any kind of human kindness.

So I throw a bag into the back of the car and head north on I-95.

I arrive in Beauty by late afternoon. Workmen are running a banner across Jasmine Street.

Welcome to Beauty Days.

Beauty Days start right after Memorial Day and go through Labor Day. June is Saturday In The Park month, where every Saturday the town gathers for the Beauty Games, craft showing and eating.

I cruise slowly down Jasmine, checking out all the shops and buildings, Saturday In The Park banners and balloons dancing in the breeze.

At the stoplight I have a perfect view of the park, where a small tent village dots the green lawn.

Well, if I was going to wander home for a weekend, this was a good one to pick. Saturday In The Park has always been one of my hometown favorite events.

As I turn onto Laurel, I catch a glimpse of the Braun Bikes tent. Right next to it, I see D. Sculptures. Dylan. The idea of seeing Dylan gives me warm fuzzies. Yeah, I know I'm moving to Chicago, but it is Beauty Days, and I can let my soul dream. A little.

A few minutes later I walk through the front door of 21 Laurel yelling, "Mom, I'm home."

I hear a clatter and a crash from the kitchen. She peers around the doorway, shocked.

"Macy, what on earth? Is everything all right?"

"Yes, of course. A girl can't come home for a visit?" I ask, arms wide. Yeah, I know, I can count on one hand the number of times I've done this in the past ten years, two of them being this spring, but since I'm no longer living life as if my hair's on fire, I find time for the simple things.

"Well, certainly you can visit. It's just not like you." She gives me a hug.

I breathe in her subtle scent and wonder if I've been

that distant. A surprise weekend home and Mom nearly ruins dinner.

While she bastes the roast and pops rolls onto a baking sheet, she catches me up on the town and family news (Aunt May got a new poodle.)

"Oh, Saturday In The Park starts tomorrow. You have to come out. Dad's donated all the sauce for the big grill-out."

I yank open the refrigerator for a bottle of water. "We'll see." The warm fuzzies I had earlier over Dylan have cooled a little. Why start what I can't finish?

An hour later Dad comes in and pretends my presence is expected, an everyday event. He tells us how many cases of barbecue sauce he delivered for the grill-out, how e-orders are up since *The Food Connection* linked their Web site to the Moore Gourmet Sauces site and how Rhine is calling him with ideas for showcasing the product.

"It's nice to have him so enthusiastic, Dad," I say.

"I'm not complaining," Dad counters, snatching a cooked carrot from the pan Mom's pulling from the oven.

We enjoy a nice, yummy dinner together, but by nine o'clock I'm asleep on the couch. Without a million to-dos or looming project deadlines, my mind is starting to unwind and sleep comes easily. A little after midnight I stumble upstairs and fall face-first into bed without changing into my jammies.

Well after noon on Saturday I wander into the kitchen and find a note from the folks saying they'd gone to the park. "Look for us at the Moore tent."

It's a cold cinnamon bun for breakfast, then hop into the shower, hoping to run into Dylan today.

It's a gorgeous day, and since the park is just down the street, I slip on my sneakers and head out on foot.

First stop, the Braun Bikes tent. Mr. Braun greets me as if I'm his prodigal daughter.

"Macy, welcome. Welcome home." He wraps his Papa Bear arms around me and motions to a half dozen motorcycles stationed around the tent. "What do you think?"

I walk among them. "They're amazing," I say, observing the fine detail and custom work applied to each one.

"Most of the handiwork is Dylan's," he says, obviously proud. "I do the grunt work. He makes them worth buying."

"I never knew he was so artsy," I say, running my hand along a hand-tooled leather seat.

"Closet talent, I guess. That boy can do just about anything."

A look passes between Mr. Braun and me, communicating something deeper than words can say, and it makes me squirm.

"He's over at the pie-eating contest," Mr. Braun says, tipping his head toward the tent door.

I grin. "Another hidden talent?"

He flashes the original Braun grin, rakish and white. "He's the defending champ."

"Well, then, maybe I'll go see."

"Better hurry. It's over by the barbecue grills."

I skip-hop-run over to the cooking area. Up on the stage I see the long table of pies. Bibbed men hover over them, hands behind their backs, waiting for the whistle to blow.

Ellen Van Buren, Beauty's mayor, is giving instructions, her loud, shrill voice causing the cheap sound system to feed back.

I spot Dylan on the end wearing a golden bib. I laugh. Pie-eating champ. Only Dylan. I shove my way through the crowd toward the front so I can say hi to him.

But yellow police tape ropes off the pie-eating area. "Can't go any farther," seventy-year-old Rover Whitaker says in my ear.

"Hey, Rover, how are you?" I ask, patting him on the arm.

"Good, though my rheumatism is acting up some."

Now, not that I don't care about Rover and his rheumatism, but I'm determined to get Dylan's attention before he pies his own face. From where I'm standing, about five feet back, I can tell his expression is intense—he's ready to win.

"You have one minute," Ellen hollers into the mike. "Get ready."

Dylan bends down, face toward the pie, hands locked behind his back.

"Dylan." I psst, leaning close. "Dylan."

He shifts his eyes to see who's calling him.

"On the count of three," Ellen barks, her whistle poised, ready to blow. "One!"

"Good luck," I say with a big smile and a thumbs-up.

"Two."

He smiles and winks.

"Three." The whistle pierces the air and Dylan's face is buried in a mile-high pile of whipped cream.

Everyone is cheering and laughing. I see something dangling from Dylan's mouth. He chomps it up and goes for another bite.

"Gummie worms." Rover chuckles.

Ew!

But before the whistle blows, Dylan jumps away from his pie plate. White cream covers his nose, cheeks, mouth and chin, but he's the winner. Once again.

"Dylan Braun, the defending champ, is our winner!" Ellen walks over to him, a blue ribbon in her hand.

Dylan shoots his arms into the air over his head as if he just won the Super Bowl.

The crowd starts chanting. "Dylan, Dylan, Dylan."

All at once his eyes are on me and he's pointing. Grinning. Well, I think he's grinning. Who can tell with all that white cream around his mouth?

I smile and wave back. He jumps off the stage and strides toward me as if he's Michael Vartan about to kiss Drew Barrymore in *Never Been Kissed*.

What is he… Realization dawns. I'm Macy Moore in *About To Be Kissed*. The whole town is watching. Oh, my word.

I walk backward, shaking my head. "Now, Dylan…" Dylan stoops under the yellow tape and closes the gap between us.

"Hey, you can't do that," I holler, pointing. "Police, police, he just crossed the line."

The crowd parts to let him pass, exposing me with nowhere to hide. Traitors.

They still chant his name. I turn to run. But he reaches out with one last stride and grabs my arm.

"Ack! Dylan."

He whirls me around and pulls me to him. For one brief moment his eyes search mine, asking permission. I'm pretty sure both eyes are saying yes.

"You could at least clean off your face," I murmur, feeling woozy. Umm, sandalwood and spices. My favorite scent.

"I could," he says, then lowers his lips to mine. His kiss is real, tender and very sweet and messy.

The crowd cheers. I burst into a giggle-snicker and wind up with a snort of whipped cream up my nostril.

"You have something on your face," he teases.

"Do I, now?" I can't stop smiling.

Someone—don't know who—hands him a wet towel. Gently he cleans my face. When he finally releases me, I almost fall down from the swooniness of it all.

He's so incredibly easy to be around, so incredibly easy to kiss. Yet he gets me so mixed up. Knocks my world off-kilter.

He cleans his face after mine and, taking my hand, walks me over to one of the park benches, tossing the towel onto the pie table.

We're about to sit when he presses his hand against my back and pushes me to him so he can kiss me again.

"I just wanted to make sure the sweetness was you, not the whipped cream."

My nerve endings are snapping and firing, but I laugh at his corny comment. Then, naturally, I panic.

"I—I'm fat," I blab.

"Wh-what?" His lips are millimeters from mine.

"I'm fat," I repeat a little more loudly.

He steps away and gives me the once-over. "No, you're just right. Better than right."

"Fourth grade. The haiku. 'I went out to play. I saw Macy Moore. She's fat.' Remember?"

Dylan sits and pulls me down to the bench next to him. "That was cruel of me and I'm sorry."

I try to respond with a clever quip, but the first syllable is a mere squeak. I clamp my mouth shut.

"Sometimes guys do dumb stuff." He places his arm around me.

"No problem," I manage to croak, relishing the sensation of his arm curling around me, cradling me against him.

The lake breeze brushes our faces and in the moment of silence, my mind records every vivid detail and sensation of his kiss.

The SSS will be thrilled.

He lifts his hand so the ends of my hair whisper through his fingers. "I've wanted to kiss you for a long time," he confesses.

I turn to him. "Why'd you wait?"

He shakes his head, spreads his arms along the back of the bench and with a sly grin, gives up his secret. "You were the untouchable Macy Moore."

"Untouchable?" I repeat. That's not the word I'd use.

He regards me. "You were larger than life, taking on the world, breaking all the rules."

"Me? No, you were the one larger than life. Football hero, Most Popular, dean's list. You had more girls huddling around you than players on the football field."

He regards me, his emotion reflected in his eyes. "I didn't see you crowding around."

Truly, he's melting my insides.

Wait, Macy. Stop swooning. I think. You're thirty three, not thirteen. I jump up, slipping my hands into the pockets of my shorts.

"I'm moving to Chicago," I say, matter-of-fact.

He leans forward, elbows on his knees. "I see."

I look toward the tent village. "I'm not with Casper anymore, Dylan. I'm interviewing with another Web software company. It's a tremendous opportunity for me."

"Is it what you want?"

"Of course." I think. Yes, of course. Isn't it the next yellow brick in the road?

He stands facing me. "Ever think of moving back to Beauty?"

"No, never." I tremble, hearing myself say no to him. I can't let a Dylan kiss derail me from landing my dream job. One confession of admiration can't melt my career goals like butter in the microwave. Or can it?

No, absolutely not. I have too much invested in my career and not enough in Dylan Braun. I have no basket in which to put my eggs.

"Macy…" He pulls me close and I press my cheek against his chest, listening to his heart beat.

"Dylan, hey, Dylan." Ellen Van Buren is huffing and puffing our way. "We need your photo for the paper."

He waves to her. "Okay, Ellen, be right there."

I lift my face toward his, waiting, longing, yet knowing.

"Good luck in Chicago." He brushes my hair away, then bends to kiss me ever so lightly on the lips.

Monday morning as I haul my stuff down the front stairs and out to my car, Dad meets me on the front porch.

"Let me help you." He grabs my suitcase and tosses it into my trunk. I drop my purse into the passenger seat.

The morning song of the birds is as fresh as the dew on

the trees and it's another great day. I pop the top on the BMW, figuring I'll start home with only the Georgia sky over my head. I look forward to the drive, a time to ponder and pray.

"Can I talk to you?" Dad asks when the convertible top is tucked away. "Let's take a drive over by the lake."

I stare at him for a nanosecond. He's up to something. "Whatever it is, the answer is no."

He chuckles. "I'll stop and get some coffees. See you at the lake."

"All right, but I'm dubious." I kiss Mom goodbye and head for the park and Crystal Lake.

"So, what's on your mind?" I ask Dad when he arrives. He hands me a coffee from a paper bag.

"I suppose you're looking forward to the Chicago interview."

We walk toward the benches under the mossy oak trees, weaving our way through closed tents and locked booths.

"I am." My insides leap at the thought. Chicago. My kind of town.

"I'd like you to consider something." Dad pauses to face me.

"All righty." I prep for some fatherly, businessman advice.

"Join me at Moore Gourmet Sauces."

"Huh?" I gape at him. What is he saying?

"Join me in the business." He cups his hands around his coffee.

"Move back to Beauty? Is this what you were talking to Rhine about?" What an unnerving notion. I let my mind picture Dylan for one teeny-tiny second, then shove him back into a dark corner.

"Yes. I mentioned your business skills to Rhine." He

flashes a fatherly grin. "Moving back to Beauty would be part of joining me in the business."

"After all the years, you think I'd consider moving back home?" I sound incredulous. I am incredulous. I love my father, but he can't be serious.

"It's a good business, Macy. A good life. I'd like to see the tradition continue."

"What about Cole?"

Dad shakes his head and pooches his lips. "He's working with Regis Gellar in the surveying business. He'll inherit that someday."

There is a sad echo in his words. I'm his only hope for keeping Moore Gourmet Sauces in the family. His only hope for maintaining the stellar reputation he's built with the business.

I ponder his recent deal with *The Food Connection* and feel queasy.

"This is really out of the blue, Dad." I fiddle with the lid on my cup before deciding to take a sip. Blech. It's black. No sugar, no cream. Doesn't Dad know I like my life with, er, my coffee flavored with sugars and creams? "Why now, Dad? Do you want to retire?"

"Mom and I have been praying about some things we want to do. I've always wanted you to have the business." *Whoa! News to me.* "With you between jobs and, well, not committed to your own family, it seemed like a good time to bring it up."

"I see." My own father, capitalizing on my failure. Pfft and huff. I stare out over the water and squeeze my coffee cup until I feel hot liquid on my thumb.

"And to make it a legit offer…" Dad pulls out his pen and little spiral notepad, and jots down a number. "This would be your annual salary."

Sly fox, my father. I peer at the paper he holds under my nose. I laugh. "That's more than I made at Casper."

Regarding me, he says, "Well, that does include your bonus, but it's a nice living. Of course, as *The Food Connection* sales kick in, the bonuses go up. A lot."

My heart thumps. "Right, of course."

"Do me a favor." He rips the paper from the little pad and stuffs it into my purse. "Please pray about it."

Oh. My. Word. I never, ever suspected Dad and Mom had built that little business into a cash cow.

And Dad wants to give it to me.

Chapter Twenty-Five

The drive home to Melbourne takes forever. I stop every two hours for a rest stop or to buy a Diet Coke. I'm tired and frustrated.

What is it about this time in my life that keeps giving rise to transition? Dad's little job offer looms like a giant California redwood over my thoughts and emotions. And is it the wind or do I keep feeling Dylan's kiss on my lips?

Focus, Macy, focus. You're a big girl. Not a giggly teen. Is Beauty, Georgia, part of God's plan to give me beauty for ashes? Does he actually mean Beauty—literally? In the back of my mind is there some dormant idea about Dylan? I hope not, because each encounter with him contained no promises, held no strings.

I pound the steering wheel. "God, I can't make this decision. I can't. You make it for me."

Cruising down I-95, the wind in my face, the sun behind me, I make a mental list of the pros and cons of moving back to Georgia.

Pros
A change of pace.
Simpler life.
Prayer in the morning at Beauty Community Church.
Being near family.
Nice salary.
Way less stress.
Dylan Braun. (But again, no promises.)

Cons
Moving back to Beauty. (I never, ever planned on returning.)
Missing out on a huge, huge career opportunity with Myers-Smith.
Missing out on Chicago.
If I move back isn't that like giving up on my life dreams?
The class reunion. (I can't tell my classmates I live at 21 Laurel Street, again. Not at thirty-three.)
"Well, if it isn't Macy Moore," someone will say. "What are you up to now?"
"I live in Beauty. Helping Dad run Moore Gourmet Sauces."

It's my worst nightmare realized. Maybe it's my pride, but I can't do it. I picture myself telling Dad, "No, I choose Chicago," and it hurts my heart.

Why did he do this to me? I bop the steering wheel with the heel of my hand.

I squirm and grip the wheel a little harder. A peek at the speedometer tells me I'm topping ninety, so I back off the pedal.

Okay, here's the deal. Decide after Chicago. Once I give Dad a glowing report on the Myers-Smith job, he'll pop his Proud Papa buttons and say, "That's fantastic, Macy. You must go to Chicago."

By seven-thirty I'm home, unpacked, showered and waiting for a pizza. A light knock sounds on my door and when I answer, Drag stands there.

"Hi." His hands are buried in his jeans pockets and his typically wild hair is combed and contained in a ponytail.

"Come in." I step aside.

"How was your weekend?" He pulls up a chair at the kitchen table.

"Quiet, relaxing. I drove up to see my parents in Georgia." I lean against the counter, unable to take my eyes off his face. He's practically radiant.

"That's nice," he says.

"How are you?" I half expect to hear he's been caught up and taken to heaven for a visit. He's provoking me and he hasn't said ten words.

"I called my dad this week." He fiddles with the napkin holder absentmindedly, his eyes fixed on some imaginary spot on the kitchen wall.

"Is that good?"

"It's the first time we've talked in almost two years."

"Really?"

"I'm moving back to New York to join him in the family business. He's always wanted me to."

His confession pierces my heart with the force of a thousand arrows. This cannot be mere coincidence. Not today.

As I listen to his story, I fuss in the kitchen, retrieving the cleaner from my cleaning bucket, powdering the already spotless sink and scrubbing with vigor. I ask, "How did you decide?"

He shrugs. "It's time to go home. After meeting my heavenly Father, my earthly dad didn't seem so intimidating."

I marvel at his insight. With a damp sponge in my hand dripping dirty green water, I join him at the kitchen table. "Is moving to New York what you want, though?"

"I haven't wanted much of anything, especially New York. But now I have this desire to make a difference in people's lives." He sticks his finger into a drop of greenish water. "But now that I have eternity in the bag, I figure I can venture out, take a chance."

"I'm proud of you, Drag," I say, returning to the sink to rinse away the green grit. I toss the sponge back under the sink considering the parallels of our lives. Me and Drag. I would never have imagined.

"My name's Pete Tidwell."

I smile. "Tidwell? Any relationship to Tidwell Communications?" What are the odds?

He grins. "That'd be my father."

"You're kidding." I dry my hands on a paper towel, my mouth open.

"Not kidding." Drag reclines with his arms over the back of the kitchen chair.

"You're a millionaire?"

"Well, my dad is."

For a split second I have this sense of destiny. My life intersecting with Drag's long enough for me to introduce him to Jesus. Wow.

Drag stands to leave. "I was wondering…"

"Yes." My eyes are wide. Is he going to ask me out? Doesn't every date invitation start with "I was wondering…?" I like Drag, maybe even love him in a sisterly way, but nothing more.

"Can I take your résumé to Dad? I can't promise anything, but…"

"Absolutely!" I throw my arms around him, smack his cheek with a kiss and run upstairs for one of my résumés.

I wake up the morning of my Chicago interview with a gargantuan zit on my right cheek.

I stumble into the bathroom, not quite awake, flip on the light and moan. "Ah, come on." This is not fair.

A stress blemish, I'm sure, though I can't discount the excessive junk food I've been consuming.

I sit on the toilet lid and slouch against the tank. Who stole my perfect life? I want it back. "Lord, I want my blemish-free, moneymaking, upwardly mobile, independent life back, please."

I figure if He returns it now, there will be no questions asked. We'll just shake hands, act as if nothing happened and move on.

I wait a few minutes. When the earth doesn't quake, I conclude I'm in the exact life God intended for me whether I like it or not. Who am I to argue with the Almighty Who loves me?

Think, Macy, think. My flight isn't until noon. It's a little after seven now. I have a few hours to combat the blemish before I have to be at the airport.

First I hop into the shower and steam my right cheek until it's sunburn-red. Next I zap the area with half a bottle of acne cream and pray for healing by the laying on of my hand. "Lord, make it go away. Please."

While the cream does its work, I dry my hair and slip into my flying clothes—a pair of jeans and a bell-sleeved top with a scoop neck.

I pack my wad-'n-wear Chico's suit for the interview and scoop the contents of my dressing counter into my toiletries bag. Keeping focused, I haul them down to the garage and toss them into the passenger seat of the car. I will not interview in my street clothes this time.

I flip through the morning talk shows and check e-mail while eating my breakfast of toast and Diet Coke. I have another message from Kathy. Shannon Parks is coming to the reunion, too.

Do you think we could have a debate-team minireunion? Maybe pick a topic to debate?

Yeah, sure. Let's debate my life. Resolved: Macy Moore is not a failure. Kathy can take the affirmative—she's good with the positive side. I'll take the negative.

Back upstairs, the only thing left to do is put on my makeup and go about my day as if this enormous imperfection did not light up the whole right side of my face.

At nine-thirty I run a mental checklist.

Interview clothes. Check.

Nightshirt. Check. Don't want to be sleeping naked in a downtown Chicago hotel.

Makeup and hair spray. Check.

Toothbrush, paste, perfume and deodorant. Check.

Clean socks and clothes to wear home. Check.

That about covers it. I settle at the kitchen table for a few minutes of prayer, though I'm too antsy to concentrate. At nine forty-five I grab my Birkin.

The phone rings as I open the garage door. "Hello." Please, don't be Mrs. Woodward. Not today.

"Macy, it's Adriane."

"What's up?" The SSS didn't meet on Tuesday because Adriane had some book business, Lucy was designing a special summer edition of the paper and Tamara got volunteered for a special work project.

They have yet to hear about Dad's job offer, Drag's true identity and the kiss. *The* Dylan kiss.

"I just called to say I hope you don't get the job." Ah, the real Adriane Fox stands up.

"Funny."

"I'm serious. What will we do without you?"

"You'll fly to Chicago and we'll have SSS reunions in a wonderful little bistro."

"Not the same," Adriane laments.

"I know. But this might just be impossible to turn down."

"I'm going to miss you."

My eyes water. "Me, too."

The flight to Chicago is uneventful. I pay special attention to the leg from Atlanta, since I might be flying this route often in the days to come. It's a short flight, as flights go, and on a bad day I could be in Beauty in less than five hours.

The moment I see Chicago from the air, I get that airy feeling of excitement in my middle and wonder if there is anything about this city I won't love.

It offers hundreds of amenities that Beauty or Melbourne could never, ever offer: theater, fine dining, art, the Cubs, museums, Oprah.

From the airport, I catch a cab to the Sheraton downtown. As the driver weaves through city traffic, I autodial Lucy from my cell.

"I'm in Chicago."

"How is it?" Genuine excitement reverberates in her words.

"Amazing. I've been here fifteen minutes and I love it already."

"Did you remember your clothes this time?"

"Yes. I didn't even check my bag. All carry-ons."

She laughs. "Good thinking."

I hear clicking in the background and know she's typing a story while talking to me. The cab pulls up to the hotel, so I bid Lucy goodbye and give Tamara a super-quick call.

"Can't talk. I'm here."

"Go get 'em."

The cabbie pulls up to the hotel and holds my bags while I find my cash stash. "Enjoy your stay," he says when I pay him for the ride, including tip.

"Oh, I will." But when he drives off, an odd alone-in-a-crowd sensation creeps over me.

Hello, cabbie, come back! You drove off with all my aplomb.

*I only brought one with me, and for some strange reason it's
in your cab.*

Suddenly a gigantic, Lurch-like uniformed bellman is
next to me. "Make I take your luggage, ma'am?"

I jump aside. "You scared me."

Emotionless, he says, "Step this way."

Well, then. He takes my luggage inside and waits while I
check in. I glance over my shoulder. He watches me. I snap
around to face the desk clerk.

"All right, Miss Moore. You're in room 222. If you need
anything, please let us know." She smiles and slides the
room key across the counter.

"Thank you." I move for the elevators, and Lurch follows
with my two little bags. He gets into the elevator car with me.

"Two," I say.

He pushes the button for the second floor and the doors
close. "Did you have a nice flight?"

I inhale and clear my throat. "Yes, thank you." I look up
at him. He must be seven feet tall.

Ding. The second floor.

Lurch leads the way to my room. When we arrive, I slip
my key into the slot and push the door open.

"All set." He backs away with a slight salute.

"Wait." I reach into my purse and pull out a few singles.

"Thank you, ma'am." He takes the folded bills.

"Thank you." I notice his dark blue eyes are framed with
thick lashes and topped with fuzzy gray brows. His name
tag reads Gabriel.

"Don't worry," he says as he tucks away his tip.

I view him from the middle of the hallway. "W-wh-what

did you say?" The door to my room closes, but I clutch the room key in my hand.

"God is with you." Gabriel tips his hat.

Tears puddle in my eyes and blur the straight angles of the hallway. Gabriel waves and disappears around the corner.

The Lord is with me. Take that, you zit of discouragement. He sent that tall, pale, gray-haired, albeit kinda scary, bellman to remind me He's watching out for me.

Chapter Twenty-Six

At eight-thirty the next morning I meet Steve Albright in the hotel lobby. I'm dressed up, hair properly coiffed and makeup applied with professional standards and taste.

I look for Gabriel, to tell him how much his words encouraged me, but two other bellmen work the lobby this morning.

"Macy Moore?" A sleek, tailored man with dark hair and narrow eyes approaches me with his hand extended.

"Steve?" I shake his hand. He's pleasant looking, but a cliché "suit." Right down to his manicured nails and Italian leather shoes.

"I have a car outside."

By car, he means limo. I climb into the backseat and sink into the very luxurious leather.

"Do you mind if we stop for a cup of coffee?" Steve asks,

reaching inside his coat pocket and pulling out a little packet of Tums.

"No, not at all." But I'm not drinking any. Coffee breath combined with the look-at-me zit would be my undoing.

Steve pops a couple of chalky tablets and conducts a cursory interview on our way to the Myers-Smith Webware office on Michigan Avenue, detailing the fabulous career I would have with Myers-Smith Webware.

"We're the industry leader," he says proudly. I know better, but I respect his loyalty. "It would be the perfect move for someone like you. Experienced and ready to blaze her own trail. The New York office will let the Chicago customer service director run things the way she sees fit."

"She?" Did I impress him with my attention to detail?

"I'll be honest. I set up this interview for my benefit." He keeps his eyes on me as he sips his coffee.

"Oh?"

"I wanted to meet the gutsy woman in jeans who bowled over the New York team. Plus, you need to see Chicago, meet the staff, understand what a great opportunity we're offering."

Hmm, smoothing it on a little thick, Steve. "Always good to meet the staff," I say.

From what I can tell, this job is mine to lose. All I have to do is be cool. I've heard of these things happening to other people, the ones with gold dust in their hair and golden starlight in their eyes of blue, but not me.

Steve continues, "Now that I've met you, I can see why they were so charmed."

I almost glance over my shoulder to see if he's talking to

someone else. I flash an awkward grin and focus on the Chicago landscape passing by the limo window.

In a few minutes the limo driver eases to a stop in front of a glassy high-rise. He opens our door and Steve leads me inside.

The office suites are amazing, overlooking the lake on one side and the city on the other. All the offices are modern and bright with lots of windows.

I try not to twitch like a kid at Christmas, but a small "wow" escapes my lips.

Steve grins, hands on his Italian-belted waist. "It's a nice setup."

"Very." I walk beside him, careful to keep that embarrassing blemish away from the unforgiving light of day.

"This would be your office." Steve walks me into a large corner office with a polished boardroom table at one end and a matching desk and credenza at the other.

One wall is windows, and another contains floor-to-ceiling bookshelves. It's decked out with all the amenities a director would need, including a flat screen computer monitor, leather chairs and a minifridge.

"You have your own private bath, too." Steve motions to a room behind the desk and credenza.

I look him square in the eye and stick out my hand. "Hello, I'm Macy Moore, formerly of Casper & Company. Are you sure Myers-Smith wants me for their director?"

"I'm sure." He smiles, shaking my hand. His hand is smooth and soft, but his grip is firm and sure. "We want a customer service director who can lead, who has experience and ideas. My guess is you'll be running the whole customer service show from New York in a few years."

"That would be my guess, too," I say like a true braggadocio.

"Glad we're on the same page." His eyes smile.

Why not run the whole show from New York? My biggest frustration with Veronica Karpinski demoting me was not being able to lead anymore. Being in the field is honorable work, but I want to lead, be in charge and empower others. I'm born to run the show.

Steve ushers me into the office of the Chicago vice president, whom I met and interviewed with in New York.

"Nice to see you again." I shake Paul Winter's hand.

"We'd love to have you join us here in Chicago." He's all smiles.

"Me, too," I blurt out, catching Paul cut a quick glance to Steve. Hmm, what's that about?

Next Steve directs me through a maze of cubicles and introduces me to various people. At a corner office he leaves me alone with the lead Web developer, Sonia Larkin.

"Sit," she says to me as if I'm a puppy.

I can't take my eyes off her. Around my age, she's locked in her teen Goth years. Her hair is dyed a flat black and her eyes are heavy with black eyeliner and mascara. Her lips are black, as well as her fingernails. To complete the death-warmed-over ensemble, she wears a black tank and black jeans.

I drop my pen to the floor so I can peek under her desk. As I suspected, she's wearing black army boots.

"So, what are your responsibilities?" I hold a serious expression, but fear I sound as if I'm trying out for the pep club. All I need is pigtails and a lollipop to ensure her complete and utter disdain.

"I'm in charge of all engineering projects. I'm head of development and product design for E-Z-Web." She resents telling me this, I can tell.

"E-Z-Web?" I jot it on a piece of paper Steve gave me earlier. Need to look knowledgeable. "What development tools do you use?"

She flops against the back of her chair, her expression asking *Are you kidding me?* Out loud she says, "Whatever's best for the product—Java, C Sharp or .NET."

"I see." Jot some more. "What tools are provided to the service techs to help in product support?"

She hooks her upper lip. "Whatever they need."

So goes our interview. I ask questions. She gives me stoic answers. I'm not an imbecile, but I'll never convince Sonia.

Steve bounces into Sonia's office twenty minutes later as if he didn't mean to leave me with her so long.

"She's lovely," I say to him as he steers me to the next cubie.

"You can handle her." He seems assured, but how does he know? I don't know if I want to handle her. Life is just too short for dealing with the Sonia Larkins of the world.

The rest of my meetings go well. I talk with a guy in marketing, a woman in sales and two people from the customer support team. They are a young, eager group.

"What are the goals for the Midwest office?" I ask Steve as we wind our way through the halls back to reception.

"Get our Web products in the hands of every person who uses the Internet. We want to take the fear out of using the Web and creating Web sites. We want our product in every small business in America. In the hands of the housewife who keeps the family newsletter, or the grandma who wants to put her grandbabies' pictures on the Web for her friends. If you can type, you can use E-Z-Web. No XML, no HTML, just our fine Web processing software."

Cold chills prickle over my scalp. Those words are replicas of Casper's W-Book marketing pamphlet. Almost exactly. Now I know why a jeans-clad girl gets a nod for a Myers-Smith director position.

They don't want me. They want Casper. Not my abilities, leadership or experience. Run the show? Ha! They want someone intimately acquainted with the competition.

Steve stops in front of the elevator. "Ready for lunch?"

"Sure." I force a smile. This is unbelievable. What do I do? I would love to stick it to Attila the Hun and Casper for treating me so callously, but deep down I don't want vendettas to govern my life.

But this is a career move, right? Myers-Smith knocked on my door first.

Steve tells me a little about Chicago on the ride down to the first floor, where the limo waits for us. Steve directs the driver to take us to a swank restaurant on La Salle Street as he retrieves the Tums tube from his vest pocket again.

A little heartburn, Steve? I ask a few questions about the Chicago office, hoping I don't sound as befuddled as I feel, wondering about their motive for hiring me. That glance between Paul and Steve was more than *Is she having a nice day?*

At the restaurant I excuse myself for the ladies' room and talk to God while freshening up.

"What do I do?" I powder my face and reapply my lipstick. "Do I join Casper's competition?"

My reflection in the mirror tells me I've returned to my savvy businesswoman appearance. The Chico's tunic and slacks are slimming and sleek. Even the right-cheek blemish has dissipated.

This is the Macy Moore I know and love. But I'm so conflicted. My thoughts are in disarray. Myers-Smith is offering me the job of a lifetime. They are picking up where Casper left off. I think I can do the job without disclosing Casper secrets, but you just know that's exactly what they want from me. I lean toward the mirror and shake my head. "They want you for all the wrong reasons."

I hurry back to the table where Steve waits. "I ordered you a glass of wine. Thought we could celebrate." A tall glass of milk sits in front of him, next to the wine.

"None for me, thanks." I spread my napkin across my lap. "I'm strictly a Diet Coke girl."

"My apologies." He motions for the waiter. "Cancel the lady's wine and bring her a Diet Coke." He glances at me. "Twist of lime?"

"Sure, why not?" I smile, but my insides tremble.

The waiter trots off and Steve zeros his energies in on me. "What do you think?" He reaches into his coat pocket and pulls out a packet of Tums.

I lift my hands, searching for words. "It's a fantastic job." I mean, right or wrong, they are offering the position to me.

He pops two tablets into his mouth and washes them down with a sip of his wine. "I'd love to phone New York with your acceptance."

Such a simple statement packs so much pressure. I stall. "Steve, what *is* the final offer?" He's painted a picture for me with broad strokes, mentioned a potential salary when we talked on the phone and baited me with a fabulous office, but…

He pulls a proposal package from his attaché case. "Here's the complete package. Salary, bonus, benefits, vacation and terms of employment."

My eyes stumble over the numbers and words on the page. My head spins. Almost double my Casper salary with a signing bonus. Add to that a 401K plan with 5 percent matching, stock options and a gracious three weeks of vacation for the first three years, then it bumps up to four weeks.

Unbelievable. I regard Steve, searching his face for the layer beneath. What's the true offer, the true catch?

"We feel we get what we pay for," he says as if reading my expression.

Ah, there's the catch.

Woo the client knocking their socks off, then work them to death.

Lunch is ordered and I review the package one more time and pretend I could actually move in next to Oprah.

"Do you have any questions?" Steve asks over our salads.

I shake my head. "I'd like some time to think about the offer." I sip my soda.

Steve holds out his hands and shrugs as if I'm an idiot. "You shouldn't pass on this opportunity. Casper would never give you the chance we are, Macy. Join us. Show them what they let go."

Okay, there it is, just as I suspected. Myers-Smith wants

Casper and I'm just the pawn they need. Yet, isn't this business? Isn't that how empires are made? How empires are crumbled?

Right in the middle of our main course and discussion of Myers-Smith, the maître d' approaches.

He stoops over and says my name with a French accent. "Miss Moore?"

"Yes?"

"You have a telephone call."

"I what?" He must have the wrong Macy Moore.

"You have a telephone call." He gestures with a white-gloved hand for me to follow.

"Excuse me," I say to Steve.

"Certainly." He rises from his seat.

Weirded out, head still spinning from the morning's revelations, I follow the maître d' to a plush parlor where I'm sure they serve cocktails to their more prestigious guests. The Frenchman motions to the only phone.

"Hello?"

"Macy, dude! It's Drag."

I smile and drop to the velvet seat next to the antique phone stand. "What are you doing?"

"I'm in New York, thought I'd give you a call."

"How did you find me?"

"I have my ways," he says with a solid, mature laugh.

"I see. The power of Tidwell is at your fingertips." His call comforts me like a home-cooked meal.

"It's both scary and amazing."

"How's New York, your dad?" I glance at my watch. I don't want to keep Steve waiting.

"Hard, but good. I pray a lot."

"Too bad you're moving to New York and me to Chicago."

"Just a flight away, Macy."

"Right, of course." I'm encouraged by Drag's confidence.

"Listen, I did have a reason to hunt you down. Your résumé impressed my father, which, believe me, is no small feat."

"Are you serious?" I'm on my feet.

"Would I hunt you down in Chicago if I wasn't?" Drag's surfer-dude accent has dissipated and he speaks like a seasoned tycoon.

"I have a great offer here. What would I do at Tidwell Communications?"

"Well, we'd have to discuss that, but Dad liked what he read. And that you are partly responsible for bringing his son back into his life."

"The Lord did that, Drag. I can't take any credit. Look at my life—part disaster, part ash heap." I fidget with the hem of my blouse.

He laughs. "Whatever. Anyway, I just wanted you to know Dad is interested just in case Myers-Smith tanked on you."

"Thanks, Drag. I appreciate it."

"See you at home in a few days."

"Yeah, see you at home." I drop the receiver on the hook, take a second to gather my thoughts, then make my way back to the table, Steve Albright and the offer at hand.

Chapter Twenty-Seven

As my plane taxis to the gate at the Melbourne airport and the captain gives the okay to turn on our electronic devices, my cell phone rings.

"Macy, you home yet?" Lucy is on the other end, animated and vibrant.

"Just landed." I've been gone two days, but it feels like forever.

"I can't wait to hear about Chicago."

"You won't believe their offer." I unclick my seat belt, stand and reach for my bag in the overhead bin. I pull it down and knock the guy behind me on the head. I wince and mouth, *Sorry.*

"Extra SSS meeting tonight at House of Joe's," Lucy informs me. "Can you be there?"

I fumble to look at my watch. Six-thirty. "Sure, but I've been there the last two times *alone*." I step onto the passenger ramp and head for the terminal. "And last week we didn't even meet."

"Adriane is engaged," Lucy blurts out. Bombs away without even opening the bomb-bay doors.

"What!"

The guy behind me, whom I accidentally knocked on the head with my bag, bumps into me—on purpose, I'm sure. My phone flies out of my hand and he *accidentally* kicks it across the aisle.

"Have a pleasant evening." He looks back at me with a snarky face.

Jerk.

"Macy, are you there?" Lucy's voice, small and far away, beckons me.

My cell is under a row of chairs. I scurry over to retrieve it. "I'm here."

"What happened?" She sounds concerned, which I appreciate.

"Never mind. What's this about an engagement?"

"House of Joe's. You can hear the details tonight at seven."

"Wild horses won't keep me away."

"I'm glad you're back," she says.

I hitch my bag onto my shoulder. "Me, too."

"Are you moving to Chicago?" She sounds sad.

"Details at seven."

"Hear ye, hear ye, I call this meeting of the Single Saved Sisters to order." Adriane raps her knuckles on the table as we gather around.

"Girl, get out." Tamara laughs and knocks Adriane with her shoulder. "Hear ye, hear ye…"

"Are you writing a book set in the eighteenth century?" I ask, settling down with my latte.

"No, just trying to be funny." Funny doesn't work with Adriane. Sarcasm and pessimism? Yes.

I look around the table with a feeling of melancholy. With Lucy and Tamara in serious relationships, Adriane engaged and me about to move to Chicago, it doesn't take a NASA scientist to figure out the era of the Single Saved Sisters is coming to a close.

"I'm sad," I say.

"Darling, don't fret." Adriane grabs my hand and gives it a concerned squeeze. "Your man will come."

"Not about that, Adriane. About the end of the SSS." I look at each of them. "The end of a great era."

"But a better era is before us," Lucy says. But by the look in her eye, I know she feels what I'm feeling.

We're quiet for a few minutes, then Tamara pierces our gloom with a vivacious "Let's see that ring of yours."

Adriane lifts her left hand, where an enormous diamond sparkles on her ring finger.

"You're joining the HEA club," I say, gripping her fingers for a better look.

"It's over a carat."

I gaze at her pretty, radiant face. "It's beautiful."

The conversation around the table is about diamond rings. Adriane promises up and down that she didn't want one, but how could she turn Eric down when he proposed with such a gorgeous princess-cut diamond set in platinum?

I'm jubilant and cheery at first, but when Lucy and Tamara gush about Jack's and Sam's latest romantic moves, I sulk in my chair.

A few short months ago Adriane practically despised all men. Now she's going to share a bed with one.

"Adriane, how'd Eric win you over?" I ask my dark-headed friend with the bright eyes.

"He just did." She sounds matter-of-fact, hand cupped around her coffee mug instead of propped for an imaginary cigarette. Her expression is dreamy.

"Did he do or say something?" I can't believe love happens in a vacuum.

"Yes, I suppose he did." Adriane sips her coffee. "He loves me. No matter how rude or trite I am, he loves me."

"Sam makes me feel so at ease, like my worst day is nothing to him," Tamara says, all smiles. "God knows what we need."

"He does," Lucy agrees. "Jack is my quiet strength. When he's around, I feel safe."

"That's how my dad is," I interject, not zeroing in on the fact they are talking about their future husbands and I'm talking about my dad.

But Tamara's comment gets me thinking. What do I need? Not what do I want, but what do I need? I don't think I've ever asked that before.

Now the couples chatter starts. How often can they get together? Jack is this, Sam is that. Eric just did such and such. Blah, blah, blah.

What I need is a double mocha with whipped cream. I leave the table to order. I'm the last-standing single of the

Single Saved Sisters, and I'm standing in the valley of decision.

Everything is changing. The Sisters are moving on with life while I run around in the backfield trying to recover a fumble. I have the Chicago offer, and Dad's. But is moving to Beauty and taking over Moore Gourmet Sauces the same as settling for a field goal when I could punch in for a touchdown on fourth and goal?

I drop my head to the café counter. "Macy, your double mocha." Zach nudges me.

"Thanks." I rejoin the ladies.

Lucy tosses me a bone and asks for a Macy Moore update. "What's the skinny on Chicago?"

I can't help but smile. "Well, the offer is amazing." I give them the high-level details, to which they ooh and aah.

After they settle down, I tell them about Dad's Moore Gourmet Sauces offer, to which they umm and ohh. Finally I tack on the news of Drag's identity, at which they utter nothing. Just stare.

"Unbelievable. What are you going to do?" Tamara asks.

"Beg God for wisdom," I say with a pound of conviction. "But there's more."

"Do tell." Lucy prods me under the table with her pointy shoe.

"When you all were gone that first weekend in June, I drove up to Georgia. It's Saturday In The Park month…" I pause while Lucy explains the Beauty Days tradition.

"I ran into Dylan after he won the pie-eating contest."

"And?" they chorus.

"His face was covered with whipped cream." I look

around the table. "He walked right over to me and kissed me. Cream and all."

Lucy slaps my arm. "You waited this long to tell?"

"What did you do?" Adriane gushes, leaning my way. Now that she has this romance thing bagged, she's into everyone else's stories.

"I said I'm moving to Chicago."

"Oh, now wait a minute." A debate over my life starts, which gives me a rip-roaring headache.

"You can't give up on Dylan. Not after all these years," Lucy says.

"I can't give up on Chicago. Not after all these years."

Then Tamara turns to me. "Tell me, was it a good kiss?" she asks, as if the question might help me determine an answer.

"The best."

"This is unbelievable," Adriane says. "I have to turn this into a book. But Macy, I wouldn't want to be in your shoes, even if they were thousand-dollar Pradas."

"It's not that bad," I protest. "Look, really all I have is two solid offers. Moore Gourmet Sauces and Myers-Smith."

"And Dylan?" Lucy kicks me under the table again.

I glare at her. "No, not Dylan." I kick her back. "I can't make my decision based on a simple kiss. He's, well, fabulous. But he's the past, not the future."

"Only God knows, Macy," Tamara says with authority.

I give them all pleading glances. "I could really use your prayers right now."

Adriane touches my arm. "We'll pray. Promise."

When the clock strikes ten, Lucy gathers her purse. "I hate to do it, but I've got to get going."

"Me, too." Tamara scoots her seat back.

"Shall we meet again?" Adriane grabs my hand and Tamara's. "Before Macy moves away?"

"Before you all walk the aisle?" I add.

We agree. "Yes."

Three years of great conversation and genuine laughter. My heart is sick. Tears burn in my eyes.

"To our time. Who we were, who we are and who we will become." Adriane raises her cup.

"To the Single Saved Sisters who follow after us," Tamara toasts.

"Hear, hear," we say in chorus and down the last of our coffees.

Feeling sentimental and weepy, I can't resist. "God bless us, every one."

It's June in Melbourne, Florida, and it's hot. But my condo is quiet and cool. I flip on a lamp and collapse onto the couch. I let my flip-flops drop to the floor and wriggle my toes in the fringe of the throw pillows.

In the silence, without the distraction of my friends, the dilemma of my life comes screaming into view.

Do I move to Chicago? Do I compete against Casper? Do I move to Beauty? Do I stay here in Melbourne and keep looking? Is Tidwell Communications a viable possibility?

Will I ever get married? Is there a man out there to love me? The memory of Dylan's kiss sends a shiver down to my toes. His kisses just might be worth the price of a Chicago job.

I bury my face in one of the throws and pummel the sofa cushion with my fist. Dylan cannot be a factor in my career decision, to which playground I take my marbles. I can't think of his lips on mine, that he said I'm beautiful or that he's 100 percent yummy and available.

"Lord," I say softly, "what do I do? What do I need?"

I think of Drag and his confidence. I get up and pace the length of my living room, praying, mulling it all over until the sun is tucked away beyond the western horizon.

Around eight, Lucy calls. "We're going to the movies with Tamara and Sam. Wanna go?"

"No, thanks, I'm praying over some stuff."

"Big decisions ahead, I know." Her voice is rich with sisterly concern. "Jack and I prayed for you today."

I tear up. "That means a lot to me." I can't imagine moving away from her. She's been my friend, my family and my confidante the past ten years. I wouldn't even be in Melbourne with a chance at a major corporate director job if it weren't for Lucy.

"Can we stop by later with a midnight pizza?"

"Thanks again, but no. I think I'll skip eating for a few days." I notice her fast-food ban has lifted since Jack entered her structured, sanitized world.

Lucy gasps. "What?"

"I need to hear from God, Lucy. My soul is making too much noise. I think I'll starve it into silence." I sink onto the bottom step of my oak staircase.

She muffles the receiver and says to Jack, "She's fasting."

"Lucy."

"Sorry," she says. "Call me tomorrow."

"Have fun. Hi to Jack and Sam. Kiss Tamara for me." I drop the phone to the floor. Chin in hand, I sit on the steps, pondering. I've had a good life in Melbourne, Florida. A great life. While I don't know if it's Chicago, Beauty or perhaps a chance at Tidwell's in New York, the Melbourne chapter of my life is coming to a close.

Tears slip down my cheeks and splatter onto my hand. They are tears of sadness, tears of goodbye, tears of hope.

"Okay, Macy, enough." I duck into the guest bathroom for a tissue. I blow my nose and wipe the mascara from under my eyes.

I'm relieved to hear the doorbell ring. Good, a distraction.

"Who is it?" I holler, tossing my tissue into the trash and padding across the living room to the front door.

"Adriane."

I check my appearance one last time in the mirror over the couch. No mascara remains under my bloodshot eyes.

I swing the front door wide and sing in my best opera voice, "What's up?"

"Oh, Macy, what have I done?" Adriane barges in, wringing her hands.

Chapter Twenty-Eight

Adriane paces around the coffee table, then stops with hands on her hips. "Got anything to eat?"

"What's gotten into you?" I want to laugh, but I can tell she's really bugged about something.

"Let's go out. My treat. Wendy's is around the corner."

She starts for the door, but I grab her arm and pull her back. "Sit down."

She plops onto the ottoman. I sit across from her on the edge of the coffee table. "What is going on?"

"This." Adrian sticks her hand in my face. I'm practically blinded by her herculean diamond.

I examine the ring. "Did you do something to it?"

"I accepted it. I can't get married, Macy. What was I thinking? I've known him for five months. Five months. I dated Travis for three years before I found out about him."

"Eric is not Travis."

"I know that." Adriane drops her head against the back of the couch. "But what secrets does he have?"

"You want a perfect man? One with no secrets? Please, Addy. You know Eric is not going to be perfect, but at least you two are starting out on the common ground of your faith in Jesus."

"Okay, that's a good point." She lifts her head and narrows her eyes at me. "What about Wendy's? You up for that?"

Normally this kind of offer would be too much for my weak, I-love-food flesh. I can't count the number of fasts I've started, resolved and resolute at 8:00 a.m., only to weaken and plan my lunch by ten.

But tonight feels different. I squelch the rebellious rumble from my middle with pressure from my hand. "I'm not eating. But I'll ride along with you if you want."

"Not eating?" Adriane furrows her brow.

"Not tonight." I go to the kitchen for a glass of water.

"Oh, I see, fasting," she says. "And listen to me, complaining to you when you have life-changing decisions to make, too."

"Thus the no-eating thing." I take a glass from the cupboard. "You want some Diet Coke, or water, or tea?"

"Diet Coke sounds good."

I pour her a glass of soda and fill mine with water. "What do you love about him most, Adriane?" I set her glass on an end table coaster.

A warm smile touches her lips. "It sounds silly, really."

"Tell me." I curl up on the couch next to her.

"He's kind, sincere, with the most soulful brown eyes

and the sweetest smile. And he loves me. I know he does. He loves me."

I nod with understanding. "Those are great reasons to get married."

Adriane sips her drink, still smiling. "Do you think I'm doing the right thing?"

"Yes, I do."

"Honest?"

She's usually so confident. It's odd to see her behave like a scared little girl. I slip my arm around her. "Honest."

Adriane takes a deep breath. "I feel better. I guess I panicked."

I rest my head on the back of the couch. "I understand."

She turns to me. "So what's going on with you?"

"Myers-Smith called me again." My words are slightly slurred. Nine hours of fasting and I'm a little light-headed already.

Adriane makes a frowny face. "What do they want?"

"They offered a five-grand signing bonus."

She leans forward to set her drink down. "What did you say?"

"I told them I'd let them know."

"Tell me why you're hesitating." The Adriane I know comes to life and drills to the core of the issue.

"I'm almost a hundred percent sure they only want me because they are launching a Web product that rivals Casper's."

"And you want them to hire you because you're a corporate genius?"

She has such a knack for putting me in my place. I guess

I did it for her—she can do it for me. "No." My stomach rumbles, so I cradle a throw pillow in my lap to muffle the sound.

"If you want to live in Chicago and work for a major corporation, then you accept their offer." Adriane rises with her empty glass in hand. "I'm getting another soda. You want one?"

I look at my bland glass of water. "Yes."

When she returns, I ask, "Why can't they hire me because I'm good at what I do? Because I'm a leader, a decision maker?"

"Macy, you're missing the forest for the trees."

I swat at her with my pillow. "That's profound, Professor."

"It's like dating, right?" she says, clearly an expert after five months.

"How so?" I pop the top of my Diet Coke and pour it over the melting ice in my water glass.

"Women want men to love them for their mind and heart, what's on the inside."

"Absolutely."

"But sometimes it's the sweet-smelling perfume, the pretty face, or the lovely dress that draws a man close enough to *see* all the beauty on the inside."

I'm astounded at her analogy. How true, how true. "I interviewed in jeans and a T-shirt, and they're pursuing me like paparazzi."

"The forest, Macy. Look at the forest. They want you because you can give them an edge on the competition. That's the perfume and pretty-face part. You go in and show them the real Macy Moore."

I like her thinking. "I want to say yes, but I don't know…"

"What are the pros?"

"Great money. Incredible bennies."

She nods.

"A chance to build and lead the customer service department of a major corporation."

"Excellent." Adriane hops up, striding for the kitchen. "Got any peanut butter and jelly?"

"Yes, but no bread, only saltines."

"Perfect. Any more pros?"

"Travel. Opportunity for advancement. Living in Chicago. Great culture and shopping."

She laughs. "Great shopping. A must for every female corporate executive."

"Exactly." I take a sip of my soda before all the ice melts.

"So, what are the cons?" Adriane comes in with a plate of crackers, the peanut butter and jelly jars and a knife. To my starving eyes, it's a king's feast. My stomach screams, "Feed me."

"The cons are working a gazillion hours a week. Stress. Starting over with a new company, new friends and new church. Did I mention stress?"

I slide to the edge of the couch. "I'll be married to the job. My friends, my love life, my relationship with God, everything will take a backseat. At least for the first few years."

"That should tell you something." Adriane puts peanut butter on a cracker.

"What do you mean?"

"Plenty of good Christian men and women run successful, high-powered businesses and maintain a deep, personal relationship with God. But listening to you, there doesn't seem to be grace for it. Not in a Chicago kind of way."

I twist my lips, thinking. "I never thought of it like that, but…" Adriane brought the forest into view. I can see it now instead of the trees. So does that mean I don't move to Chicago?

Pillow to my face, I mutter, "Nothing feels right."

"What about your dad's offer?" Adriane asks.

I move the pillow away. "It's a consideration. And very generous. Nice money. Be my own boss."

I tell her all about Drag, aka Peter Tidwell, taking my résumé to his father.

"So, that's a possibility. I always thought Drag was a druggie on the lam."

I shake my head. "We all did, but he's on his way to being a communications exec."

"You can never tell a book by the cover," she says with a glint in her eye.

"Said like a true author."

Adriane waves the knife at me. "Exactly. That's what I mean about Eric. What if there's some hidden layer?"

So we've come full circle. I knock her leg with my foot. "Stop. He's marvelous. Fabulous. If you have any concerns, you're going to have to go to the Lord with them. And talk to Eric."

She makes a face. "I hate when you're right."

I laugh. "Okay, now tell me what to do with my life." I'm half kidding, half serious.

She answers without hesitation, with authority. Downright freaks me out. "Return to Beauty."

* * *

Return to Beauty? How did Adriane conclude that from our pros and cons conversation? And so quickly. Her words haunt me the rest of the night and all day Saturday.

I continue my fast, prayerfully going about my weekend chores. I mull over the Lord's verse to me the past few months, "...beauty for ashes." Couple that with Adriane's profound statement, *Return to Beauty,* and I'm befuddled.

I can't put my finger on it, but these two ideas are the same, but different. That's right, the same but different. Clear as mud.

On one hand, I understand Jesus is the beauty in the ashes of my life. But do I literally return to Beauty, Georgia? Do I get a *city* for my recent ashes?

That is the million-dollar question.

Mrs. Woodward calls in the afternoon to tell me she bought a new refrigerator and it just arrived.

"Come over, dear, and see it."

I rush across the street to celebrate with her.

"Isn't it lovely?" Her hand rests on her pearl necklace, her eyes bright.

"If you're into refrigerators, yes." I wink down at her.

"Do you mind?" Mrs. Woodward motions to the piles of frozen food, meats and vegetables on her counter.

"No, not at all." I arrange her refrigerator while she tells me stories of her youth. Another time, another era, Mrs. Woodward would have been a spunky member of the Single Saved Sisters.

With the kitchen all cleaned up, she makes tea and we sit on her davenport, talking about my Chicago interview.

"Well," she says with a light pat on my knee, "I shall miss you if you go."

"I'll miss you, too."

I hate goodbyes.

Lucy telephones around five Saturday evening. "How's it going?"

"Good." I fill a tumbler with water.

"Eating yet?"

I hesitate a moment to consult my spiritual barometer. "I'm ready for dinner." The fast is over.

"Chinese? Pizza? Salad?" She knows me so well.

But I don't want Chinese. "How about Wendy's?" See, the last food I hear mentioned during the fast is always the first one I want when the fast is over. Speaking of that…did Adriane eat all the crackers?

"We'll meet you at the one by your house. Six o'clock?"

We hang up. I take stock of my refrigerator and decide I need to make a supermarket run. Diet Cokes are running low and ice cream sounds like a yummy late-night snack.

I check to see if I need anything else, like toilet paper. I've been caught on that one before. I'm about to dash out the door when the phone rings again. I reach without checking caller ID.

"I'm making a run for ice cream."

"I like double chocolate chip mint."

I steady myself against the kitchen counter. "Dylan, hi."

Chapter Twenty-Nine

"Hello." His tone is intimate.

My limbs go weak and I hold on to the counter. My pulse is doing the salsa and my tongue sticks to the roof of my mouth. Feeling woozy, I reach for the saltines. "How are you?"

"I'm good. And you?" he asks.

Crackers are a bad idea. "Fine," I mutter, spewing cracker dust, fumbling for a glass of water.

"How was Chicago?"

"Umm." I take a gulp of water. "Great."

"You think you'll take the job?"

The rhythm of my heart slows a little. "Thinking I might."

"You have a second to talk about the reunion?" Ah, the true point of Dylan's call. I'm disappointed. I don't know what I wanted the call to be about, but I can guarantee I didn't want it to be about the reunion.

"Okay."

"If you take the Chicago job, will you still be able to emcee?"

Well, Macy, there you go—your chance to resign just waltzed in. But deep down, I don't want to say no. "I'm sure I can make the weekend."

"Good."

I shove my hair away from my face. Maybe it's the fast, maybe it's Dylan, or maybe it's the anticipation of Wendy's, but I'm trembling and ready to bare my soul.

"Dylan, I'm a failure. You should know. I'm not the big success you and Joley think I am."

"What are you talking about?"

I let the tears come. "I got fired from Casper, my boyfriend dumped me for another girl, and my bank account is empty. It's June already and my credit card is still maxed with Christmas cheer. And the only reason Myers-Smith wants me is because I worked for Casper, their competition."

I sniffle and wipe away tears with the bottom of my shirt.

"So what?" He exudes confidence the way most people exude fear or insecurity.

"So what?" I parrot. "What does all that spell, Dylan? Failure."

"No, it doesn't. Not for the Macy Moore I know. Isn't she the one who turns lemons into lemonade?"

"That is so corny I'm tempted to hang up on you."

He laughs. A sound I like a lot. "Don't hang up," he says. "Look at all the new opportunities you have now. Pioneering a new career just like you did ten years ago. The thrill of finding a new love, and joys of learning to live on a budget."

Now he's got me laughing. "I guess you're right. But finding a new love?" I move to a kitchen chair. "Last time I went fishing, there weren't many biting."

"Maybe you're fishing in the wrong pond." There's no missing the smile in his voice.

"What pond do you recommend?"

"I hear they're biting just fine in Beauty."

His comment rockets my heart right out the top of my head. "You don't say?" My knees go soft.

"Scout's honor."

"Next time I'm in Beauty, I'll have to check it out."

"You should."

Well, I'm stumped. Since I don't know where else to go with the pond thing, I steer back to the reunion. "So, in light of all I just confessed, you still want me to be the emcee?"

"Absolutely."

His confidence gives me courage. If my classmates whisper behind their hands about the Most Likely To Succeed failing, then so be it. Whatever doesn't kill me only makes me stronger.

Whoever came up with that slogan obviously wasn't dying at the time.

"Good. And, hey, just to clarify, you know what I meant when I said they're biting in Beauty, right?"

"Just to clarify, why don't you tell me what you meant?" I go over to the refrigerator with my water glass. This ought to be good.

"Me, perhaps."

I drop my glass. It crashes to the floor, but doesn't break. Water runs under my bare feet. If I'd had socks on, he'd have blown them off. "You?"

"Yeah, me. But we can talk about that some other time.

Just wanted you to know there's at least one fish in Beauty waiting to be hooked."

I'm almost undone by his brazen honesty. "Good to know. What kind of worms does the fish like?"

He laughs. "Ones that come from Melbourne."

"I'll keep that in mind."

"Are you considering your dad's partnership offer?"

I swallow hard. "You know about that?"

"Your dad and I golf once a week together."

Dad *golfs?* How did I not know that? "You and Dad?"

"He's a good friend."

"What do you think I should do?" I hadn't planned on asking him, but now that I have, I really want his input.

"Ah, Macy, don't ask me. I'm prejudiced."

Can a girl fall in love over the phone? I think I am. "Tell me anyway. I want to know."

"Return to Beauty, Macy."

"What did you say?"

"I said return to Beauty."

His answer raises the hair on my arms, and goose bumps run down my spine. "A friend of mine said the exact same thing to me last night."

"Then what are you waiting for?"

A lightning bolt, a clap of thunder? How about a shooting star or maybe a rare comet bearing my name?

Adriane tells me to return to Beauty at the beginning of my fast, and now Dylan says it at the end? More than mere coincidence?

But where's the booming confirmation to move to Chicago? Hmm? Come on, God.

Returning to Beauty, a place I couldn't wait to leave, would be like doing a mile on the treadmill when I know I can do two, maybe three. Jogging a mile is good, some days downright amazing. But pushing my body to jog two is an accomplishment. Jogging three is outstanding. Chicago is like the three-mile jog.

"Macy?" Dylan calls me, his voice full of soothing intonations.

"I'm here. Just thinking."

"Are you thinking you can't move back to a place you couldn't wait to leave?"

Creepy. How does he do that? "Well, sorta. I don't want to take the easy way. Chicago is unbelievable, Dylan. My dream job. If I move back to Beauty, am I quitting?"

"Quitting what?"

"My life. My dreams." I stoop to pick up the water glass.

"What dreams do you think you're giving up, Macy?" He leads me, draws me out.

"Life beyond Beauty. Being a successful businesswoman." I grab a wad of paper towels and mop up the floor.

"Maybe it's time to see life from Beauty."

"Maybe." I toss the wet paper towel in the trash.

"Look, focus on what God is saying now. Life happens in stages. Sometimes you're running at Mach ten, other times you're sitting on the front porch watching the sun set." He sounds so experienced and wise. "And Mace, from what I can tell, running Moore Gourmet Sauces would make you a very successful businesswoman."

"Good point." The more he talks, the better I feel. "Thanks for your sound advice."

"Anytime."

Dylan's advice echoes over the valleys of my mind as I grab my wallet and car keys.

My heart and head are all over the place by the time I get to the grocery store. I couldn't be more wired than if I stuck my finger in a light socket and drank a gallon of coffee. I'm in the checkout line with three gallons of ice cream (indecision reigns), two cases of Diet Coke, a bag of celery and a bag of apples (cancels the guilt from the ice cream) when Lucy rings my cell.

"Where are you?"

"Supermarket. I'll be there in a minute."

"What's taking you so long?" In the background Jack asks her what she wants to eat.

I give her the quick explanation of my call with Dylan, to which she responds, "Ooh, la, la."

"Stop," I retort. "I have to run home first. I bought ice cream."

"Good grief, girl. We'll talk when you get here."

Over dinner, Lucy and Jack come to the same conclusion as Adriane and Dylan. Return to Beauty.

I sigh and snap the lid off my chicken salad. "Chicago is too incredible to turn down." I'm being stubborn, I know.

What I need is challenging what I want.

"If you ask me, Beauty is too incredible to turn down. You have way more opportunities there, Mace. The six-figure salary can't buy love, or peace, or contentment."

I concede with a soft "Maybe."

Lucy grins. "Sometimes it's okay to let your heart decide. It's not about appearances, or climbing the corporate ladder or living up to your reputation. Say yes to your heart. Return to your first love."

I get what she's saying. It's what she told me months ago when Chris and I broke up. Returning to my hometown will enable me to return to a deeper relationship with Jesus. The rest is gravy.

By eleven, I'm exhausted, stuffed and ready for bed. I pick up my journal from the day I tried to get a tan and burned myself to a crisp. I open to the list, *the* list.

Things I want in a husband
Committed to Jesus
Handsome (at least to me.)
Sense of humor
Sense of seriousness
Kind
~~*Rich*~~
~~*Poor*~~
Somewhere in between rich and poor
Love fast food
Love my family
Nice teeth (I have a thing about teeth. Ever since junior high hygiene class.)
Loyal (Chris was not)
Smart; common sense
My best friend

I dig for a pen in my nightstand drawer. Reading the list one more time, out loud, I add another item. In big bold letters: "Dylan Braun."

Shocked by my self-confession, I rip out the page, and there is my other list.

Things I want in a job
Attila-free zone
Mike-free zone
Respect
Respect (worth repeating)
Opportunity for growth
Challenging and creative environment
More money
Good money (as long as the work is satisfying)
Cozy office
Decision maker
God first, work second

Oh, wow. I'd forgotten about this list. I read it again. It sounds way more like Beauty than Chicago.

Okay, God, what are You saying to me? Do I return to Beauty? Please...clap of thunder, bolt of lightning here.

I kid you not. In the distance I hear the rumble of thunder. I scramble out of bed and peek out my window, clutching a pillow. It's dark, I can't see much, but the stars do not twinkle along the horizon.

Somber, I crawl back into bed, the choice of Chicago or Beauty ricocheting around in my head. I've pondered this decision so much I ache. Yet somehow I know that it is mine to make. Chicago if I want. Beauty if I want. God in His loving kindness will back me up either way.

Chapter Thirty

Sunday morning I back out of the garage on my way to church and see Drag perched on my front stoop. At least, I think it's Drag. I do a double take.

His long blond locks are buzzed and styled with just the right amount of gel. The white oxford he's wearing is crisp and tucked into a pair of dark dress slacks. And he's got the world's biggest Bible tucked under his arm.

Grinning, I slide down my window with a touch of a button. "What are you doing?"

"Going to church with you." He passes by the back of my car to the passenger door, his dress shoes thudding against the cement.

I've never, ever seen him like this. "When did you get home?" I shift into First and drive west over the causeway.

"Last night."

I reach out and pat his hand. "You look fantastic. It's good to see you."

"Good to be seen."

I enjoy introducing him around church, because he's proof that God is a God of miracles. It's funny how quickly we forget that fact.

During worship, Drag belts out each song at the top of his lungs. At first I'm a little embarrassed. His timing is off and his raspy voice is not in the right key. But his noise is joyful and before long, I'm caught up in his enthusiasm.

After the service, a group of us troop over to Bennigan's for lunch. Several of the younger single ladies invite themselves along, giggling over the "new guy."

While we're ordering waters and iced teas, Drag's gaze catches mine and I suck in a deep breath. His eyes are so blue. I think it's my imagination, but he looks remarkably like Brad Pitt.

He whispers in my ear, "That's why I grew out my hair."

I wrinkle my face and squint at him. "What are you talking about?"

"I look like Brad Pitt when my hair's cut."

"Really?" I hide behind my menu, embarrassed to be caught staring. I mutter, "I guess, maybe, yeah, a little."

Poor Drag. He's doomed. If I noticed the BP look, so did the single chicks. They'll be circling like hungry sharks.

In the middle of lunch my cell chirps. Dad is on the other end. "Hey, Pop, what's up?"

"Can you come up to Beauty?"

"Um, why? When?"

"Today?"

"Now?" My stomach lurches. "Is everything all right?"

"I'll see you when you get here."

At a quarter to midnight I cruise past Beauty's city limits and down Jasmine. The shops are quiet and dark, asleep until Monday awakens them for a new business day.

There's Jasmine's Gallery, Mabel's Country Christmas & Crafts, the post office and courthouse and all the other quaint shops that make Beauty Beauty. Freda's Diner is at the end of the row right as I turn down Laurel for Mom and Dad's. Her outside deck, tucked away under the pine and oaks, is a dreamland with a thousand tiny white lights.

I slow down as I round the corner. I remember when Freda hung those lights ten or eleven Christmases ago. Every April she says she needs to take them down, but every August she says, "What's the use—Christmas is just around the corner."

She inspired me one year to think about stringing lights around the perimeter of my back porch. I bought a slew of tiny white lights at an after-Christmas sale. Six years later they're still in the box, in the dark, under my bed.

That screams volumes about my life. I'm so preoccupied with my pursuits, with corporate ladders and whatnot, I never took time to string pretty white lights around a fifteen-by-twenty-foot porch.

I press gently on the gas and shift gears. In the whole vast scheme of things, what does it matter? Does it have an impact upon my destiny? Probably not. But it has an impact on my soul. I must take time for the beautiful things like white lights dangling from my porch ceiling, investing in elderly neighbors and millionaires masquerading as surfer dudes.

Beauty, I conclude, is about discovering contentment and realizing with every part of my being Jesus is my soul's satisfaction. I can find beauty in Chicago. I can *make* beauty happen. Plan, schedule, live by the PDA.

I turn onto Laurel Street. Five houses down on the right, my parents' home is lit up like the aurora borealis. I roll into the driveway and prepare to enter the zone.

"Macy." Dad steps off the veranda. "Welcome." He reaches for my single bag.

"You guys are up late," I say. This is spooky. The last time my parents were up this late on a work night, Cole came screaming into the world.

"Waiting for you. Come on in—your mom is making cookies."

"At midnight?" I trail Dad from the front foyer through the family room into the kitchen with a big question mark on my brain.

"Hi, Macy, darling." Mom motions to me with a spatula in her mitt-covered hand. "Earl, take her suitcase on up to her room."

"Good idea, Kitty." Earl trots away like a good little bellman.

"Would you like some cookies? They're fresh from the oven."

I perch on a stool at the breakfast bar. "S-s-sure."

She slips a couple of chocolate chip, peanut butter chip cookies onto a plate.

"How 'bout some milk?" she asks. "Oh no, you're a Diet Coke girl."

"How's it going in here?" Dad enters with a clap of his hands.

"Earl, can you run out to the garage? Get some Diet Cokes for Macy."

"Sure thing. Back in a jiff." He disappears through the side garage door and returns a few seconds later. "You want a glass with ice, Mace?"

"Hold it!" I hold up my hands. "Who are you people and what have you done with my parents?"

"Oh, Macy." Mom chortles and shushes me with a wave of her spatula-wielding hand.

"No, seriously. What are you two doing up so late? Dad, don't you have to work tomorrow? Mom baking cookies at midnight? Growing up, you wouldn't let me microwave popcorn after eight."

"Things change." She slides another sheet of cookies into the oven.

"I'll say." I bite hard into a warm cookie. "But mutate into weird? I don't know."

"Here ya go, kiddo." Dad hands me a glass of ice and pops open a can of soda. He perches on the stool next to me and asks Mom for his own plate of cookies, which she supplies.

I take a long sip of my drink and consider my next move. If these people are in fact my parents, and not aliens, how am I to respond to this? Usually they are responding to me, my idiosyncrasies, my oddball notions.

"How was your drive?" Dad shoves a whole cookie into his mouth, then goes to the fridge.

"Fine." I watch him take a swig directly from the milk jug. That confirms it. An alien has replaced my dad.

"Oh, Earl, here. Use this glass." Mom shoves a tumbler into his hand and plants a kiss on his lips.

I almost slip off the stool. A public display of affection? "What is going on here?" I pound the countertop.

"Eat your cookies." Dad alights on the stool next to me.

"Is one of you sick, dying, ravaged with cancer?"

"What?" Mom stands up from where she's bending over the oven, shuffling cookie sheets around.

"Cancer?" Dad echoes.

"Yes, cancer." Have they gone deaf, too? "Either of you dying in six months?"

"No, no, darling. No one is sick or dying. At least, not that we know of." Mom comes over and pats me on the arm as if that news would be the last straw.

"Then why did you call me up here? Why are you making cookies at midnight and running around like teenagers?"

Dad's hearty chuckle rumbles from his chest and Mom tee-hees behind her mitted hand.

"Should we talk now or wait until the morning?" Dad addresses Mom.

"We can wait until morning."

"Absolutely not," I protest. "Are you trying to kill me? You made me drive all the way up here, so you're gonna tell me, now."

"Let's just put it on the table, Kitty." Dad motions for her to pacify me with more cookies.

"Whatever you want, Earl." Mom drops a chewy, gooey cookie onto my plate.

"Out with it, Earl," I say, tipping my head and eyeing him from under my brows.

He claps his hands together. "We want you to come up and take over the business."

I choke and swallow. "That's what this is all about?"

"Yes."

"I told you I'd pray about it." Their gazes are locked on me and I'm feeling a little squeezed.

"And?" Mom asks, her voice like a first soprano.

"I don't know." Am I yelling? 'Cause it sounds to me as if I'm yelling.

"How did the Chicago interview go?" Dad inquires.

"Great, actually. They offered me a ton of money and a grab bag of corporate perks."

"I see." A shadow of disappointment falls over his face.

"What's the rush about the business, anyway, Dad? You're not going to retire, are you?"

"Your mother and I found out today we have an opportunity to go to England."

Mom's eyes light up like a firefly, her round cheeks rosy from the heat of the oven.

"So? Go to England. Sharon can manage the business for a few weeks." I pick up the last cookie on my plate, my absolute *last* cookie. The five I just ate will be moving into my hip area any moment now and it'll take a month of Sundays to jog them off.

"Not a few weeks," Dad says. "Six months. At least."

"Six months?" I echo, flabbergasted. "You just signed a deal with *The Food Connection* and you want to leave the business?"

"*The Food Connection* agreement has been in the works for a long time. I just saw it through."

I'm baffled. "What will you do for six months?"

"Be missionaries," Mom blurts out with a small squeal.

"Since when did you want to be missionaries?"

"We've been praying about what we should do in our senior years, after we retire. We don't see ourselves playing shuffleboard in Florida or puttering around the house."

I laugh. "Me neither."

"Your mom's been e-mailing her old friend Rita about a prayer ministry in England."

I hold up my hands. "Dad, there are prayer ministries in this country. Stay here and pray if that's what you want to do."

"We thought of that." Mom stands by Dad, her arm around his shoulders. "The ministry in England also shelters refugees from the Middle East. We want to be a part of that work. Rita called after church to tell us about a staff opening…."

Dad takes up the story in his pragmatic, businessman's voice. "Frankly, this is the only door that has opened to us. My spirit tells me it's the right choice."

I sigh, actually a little envious of their confidence. "I'm proud of you. It takes guts to make such a major life change."

"But?" Dad reads my hesitation well.

I slide off the stool. "I just can't see myself moving back to Beauty."

Lucy's, Adriane's and Dylan's advice, *Return to Beauty* is a distant reverberation in my head, like the thunder from the other night. I plug my internal ears.

"Not what you pictured yourself doing at thirty-three?" Dad glances at Mom. "Macy, if you don't want to come back, we understand. You do what the Lord calls you to do—that's certainly what we're doing. But we wanted to offer you the business first."

"First? Who's second?"

"Selling it."

"What? Sell Moore Gourmet Sauces?" I'm yelling now and I don't care. He's crazy. He can't seriously consider selling his life's work.

Dad nods. "Sell it."

Chapter Thirty-One

I lie in bed, awake, staring at the ceiling. Moonlight peeks through my window and highlights certain aspects of my room. My Georgia pennant, a gold medal from the year the debate team won regionals, frayed pep-squad pom-poms from my junior year.

I smile, remembering. I let Lucy talk me into the pep squad because I thought I'd see Dylan more—him being the star quarterback and all. The pep squad was the closest I'd ever get to being a cheerleader, so I gave it a go.

Way too much stomping and clapping and shouting, "Go, go, go, Eagles!" for my taste.

I stuck it out that year, but ran the other way when the pep squad's draft team bounced my way the fall of my senior year. Life is just too short. It's against natural law for a debate team member to moonlight on the pep squad. Besides, shouting "Dylan, Dylan, he's our man…" did nothing to boost my esteem in his eyes. Or so I thought.

Of course, umpteen years later I find out he did notice me, but did nothing about it. It's odd to know how Dylan felt now that we are so far away from high school and college. I wonder how my life would be different if he had expressed his feelings for me back then.

I sit up in bed, plump my pillow behind my back and recline against the headboard. In a way, I'm glad he didn't. I wouldn't be me, the person I am today. Weaknesses and failures aside, I like my life so far.

My thoughts segue to Dad and Mom's news. Moving to England, wanting me to take over the sauce business. The notion gnaws at the deepest part of me.

Unable to stand the mental swirling, I get out of bed and click on the light. A soft white glow warms the room and the monsters of choice retreat under the bed.

I pace. "Lord, Lord, Lord. What do I do here?"

Waiting, I try to listen to my spirit. My head is no good to me now. The past few hours of mental debating warn me not to believe any thoughts I "hear."

"God, You speak in a still, small voice. Forget the thunderclaps and bolts of lightning. You have my attention. What do You want me to do? What do I *need* to do?"

I sit on the floor, my back against the bed and I reach for my Bible. I don't advocate spiritual roulette, but I take a chance and toss out a fleece. "Lord, let me open to Your answer for me. Your Word is my light."

I close my eyes, let my Bible fall open and jam my finger

on a page. I hope it's not a verse about the curse of Edom and the fall of Moab, or the recompense for the wicked.

I glance down and read. "Your nose is like the tower of Lebanon which looks toward Damascus."

I laugh. Who says God doesn't have a sense of humor? I think for a sec, then flip over to the only verse resident in my mind at the moment. Isaiah 61. I skim down to verse three. "To console those who mourn in Zion, to give them beauty for ashes."

What time is it? Is it too late to call Lucy? Surely she's awake at… I squint at the clock. Yeah, surely she's awake at 4:00 a.m. Not.

Unable to distract myself with a call to Lucy, I talk to Jesus about the meaning of beauty for ashes.

Several hours later I wake up to a tap, tap, tap on my bedroom door. I'm curled on the floor, hugging my open Bible.

"Macy?" Dad sticks his head in the door.

"Yep, come on in." I sit up, blinking the sleep from my eyes. I touch my hand to my hair. A rat's nest, I can tell.

"Did you sleep on the floor?" He steps inside and props his hand on the edge of my little-girl desk.

"Long story." I hate it when my hair looks like a rat's nest.

"I'm going over to the church. Want to come?"

"Um, okay."

"Meet you downstairs in five minutes."

The image in the dresser mirror is not pretty. Hair ratted and frayed, ends flying away, mascara residue under my eyes as if I hadn't bothered to wash my face before going to bed, which I did. Lovely. Just lovely.

My outer self appears to be in disarray, but in a strange turn of events, my inner self is at peace, sensing resolve. I haven't decided what to do yet, but my answer is on its way. I'm sure.

Driving to church with Dad, I decide. Chicago. In the clear light of day it makes sense. Right? The Windy City. My kind of town, Chicago is. I'll make it work. I'll make time for friends, family and the beauty of the Lord.

How can I turn down Myers-Smith? Macy Moore, Director, Myers-Smith Webware. Yes, *that* is the Macy Moore I want emceeing Beauty High's class of 1991's fifteen-year reunion.

Holding my head high, I follow Dad into the sanctuary. Halfway down the aisle, I hear someone whisper my name. It's Dylan. Oh, gag, I didn't plan on seeing him here. I don't need him mucking up my senses.

"Sit." He jerks me down into the pew.

I have no idea where Dad snuck off to, but I'm betting he's beseeching heaven on my behalf.

"You're a million miles away," he says, his eyes searching mine. He smells wonderful, like—I don't know—the morning breeze. Fresh and clean.

"Chicago." I dip my head, intent on praying and not furthering this conversation.

"Still Chicago?"

I peer up at him. "Yes."

"Did your dad talk to you?"

I nod, but keep my head down.

"And?"

"Shh, I'm trying to pray." I peek over and my gaze meets his. Bad move. Oh, bad move on my part. Orbs of greenish blue are gazing at me with an expression I can't explain. My heart is moved and for ten or fifteen seconds I am clutched in his visual embrace.

I break the magic by bowing to pray again, but it's too late. All I see is Dylan's face. All I sense is the warmth of his presence.

He sits peacefully next to me. This feels like the stance of a seasoned married couple, mature in love, grounded in mutual admiration.

He leans my way. "Piper and Angus Purdy are selling off the second story of their old mansion. It's gotta be 2500 square feet."

I *love* the old Purdy mansion on Whisper Willow Lane. It's an old place with high ceilings and hardwood floors. Chicago is slipping away by the second. *Excuse me, Lord. Be right with You.*

"Why are they selling?" I whisper out of the corner of my mouth.

"Angus says it's too big, too much to keep up."

"How much do they want?" I can't believe I'm asking, but I am.

"You know Angus, Macy. He'd give it away if Piper would let him."

Ack! I *must* get out of here. I press my hand on his arm. "See you." I jump up and out of the pew.

Crystal Lake is a few blocks away, so I jog over, my mind reeling with the idea of Angus and Piper selling. They've talked about it for years, but never, ever actually put it on the market.

Until now.

I collapse on the bench under the oak, winded. I really do need to start exercising more.

"You hurried out of there fast."

I look up to see Dad standing over me.

"Pressure," I say, staring at the smooth surface of the lake.

Dad chuckles. "Decisions can be hard."

"And this is a hard decision."

Dad sits, resting his elbows on his knees. "Macy, if you truly feel the job in Chicago is for you, then take it."

I pluck at the moss swinging from the trees. "It's just that I've worked ten years for an opportunity like Myers-Smith."

"I understand." Dad is calm and collected, and it's really irritating me. I'd prefer a lecture or sighs of disgust. Then I'd be justified in my decision.

We sit in silence for a minute, then Dad stands. "We better get you home so you can head out before I-95 traffic gets too bad."

When we pull up at home, Mom meets us at the front door with an anxious smile.

"Well?" She's clutching a dish towel and her eyes are alive with expectation.

"Chicago it is," Dad tells her as if that is the answer they wanted.

"Good for you, Macy." Mom kisses me on the cheek, but I can't help but notice her death grip on the dish towel.

"Thank you, Mom."

We stand in the foyer in awkward silence until I glance at my watch and say, "Look at the time. I need to get going."

I run upstairs for my things. Below, Mom and Dad wait

for me. I'm dazed by their demeanor. I'm saying no to Moore Gourmet Sauces. They will have to sell.

I sit on the side of the bed. Am I making them sell? Isn't this their choice? I can't build my life around them. Right?

Guilt. I feel guilt.

I definitely gotta get out of here. I grab my suitcase and sweep the bathroom for my toothbrush and contact lens solution.

"I'll see you." I pass Dad and Mom standing in the foyer exactly as I left them. Mom's hand still has a vise grip on the dish towel. I'm not sure, but I think I see a few tiny threads break off and fall to the floor.

"Drive safe, darling." Mom kisses me on the cheek.

"Of course," I answer, giving her a hug that lets her know this decision is nothing personal. When we break away, I point to the towel. "Be kind."

"Oh," she says with a simple laugh and releases the terry cloth. I regard her for a second, noticing how young she looks for fifty-nine.

"Bye, Macy." Dad's goodbye is loaded with emotion, and when he wraps his arms around me, tears flood my eyes.

"I'll miss you guys when you go." I step toward the door with a covert swipe at my tears. "But Chicago is a quick flight." Forget I'll be too busy to vacation for the first year or two, or five, or ten.

"Absolutely." Dad takes my luggage and motions that he'll walk me out.

I pause by the driver's door, head hanging. "I'm sorry I disappointed you, Dad." My vision blurs with unshed tears.

"You haven't disappointed me, Macy. Your mom and I took a chance in asking you. We knew that."

I force myself to look at his face. "Don't sell the business."

"I don't want to worry about the business while I'm away. We feel our life is in a new season and sauce-making is a part of the past. Time to press on."

I acknowledge with a nod. "Now it's your turn to run away from Beauty."

He laughs. "Beauty is beautiful. You should try it."

I open the car door. "On that note, I'll say goodbye." I kiss him on the cheek.

As I drive away, Dad stands in the yard, hands buried in his pockets, watching and—if I know him—praying.

I press a little harder on the gas.

Chapter Thirty-Two

❧

"Steve Albright," says the voice on the other end of my cell phone.

"Steve, it's Macy Moore."

"I thought I might hear from you today." His tone carries a lilt and a confidence. A word comes to mind. Arrogant. I shove it aside. Why shouldn't a man in his position be a little arrogant? He's earned it.

"Are you still looking for a customer service director for the Chicago office?" I take the humble approach.

"Only if that director is you." He's pleased with himself.

"Then you have yourself a director." As the words flow, panic hits me.

"Outstanding. We need you in Chicago on Monday. Midwest sales meeting and market planning."

"Next week? I was hoping for some time to get my condo on the market and…" And say goodbye. Tie up loose ends. Get my mind wrapped around the fact that I'm moving. Perhaps make sure I'm sure? I've been expecting change, but now that it's here, it feels overwhelming.

"Monday, Macy. I'll e-mail the official offer letter today."

"I don't have a place to live." I toss my first wrench to see if I can stop up the works.

"You'll stay in the company apartment. We'll sign a real estate agent to sell your Florida home. We have a contract with Century 21." Ah, clever. He not only deflected my wrench tossing, but turned up the pressure a little.

One verbal "I will" and they own me. Just like that. And women complain about marriage and men "chaining them down"? The institution of marriage has nothing on the institution of corporate America.

"Time to hit the ground running, Macy. If you can't handle it…"

I answer with what he wants. "Monday it is."

"Good. You'll have up to a year to live in the company apartment." I hear desk drawers opening and closing. "Greta, where are my Tums? I need my Tums."

Egad. My stomach curdles. "A year?"

"You'll be pretty busy…." Steve is full of overwhelming information.

Who placed this call? Steve or me? Ah, yes, I did. Gripping the wheel until my knuckles turn white, I wonder if I just left the frying pan for the fire.

But this is what you want, Macy. Go for it, face-first. Any other way and you're a coward.

"Arrange your flight for Sunday and we'll reimburse you."
Steve is nailing down the details. He's hooked his big fish
and is twisting the barb deep. "I'll have a limo take you to
the apartment. It's on North Lake Shore Drive, Macy. Stunning view of the city."

"Fabulous." I exhale and make myself relax a little, ad-
justing to the new pressure and pleasures in my life.

We exchange a few more details before hanging up. I
toss my cell phone into the passenger seat. "I'm moving
to Chicago."

A little before six I arrive home, exhausted from two days
of driving. Before going inside, I stand on the edge of the
garage and survey my Gables community. There's a light coming from Mrs. Woodward's window, while Dan's place is dark
and barren looking. I've barely seen him or Perfect Woman
since the night they drove me home from the Sun Shoppe.

I look to the spot on the pavement where Drag and I
watched the stars, and where I met Lucy's Jack Westin for
the first time. Those are forever memories.

From inside I hear my house phone ring, so I end the reminiscing and run to answer.

It's Lucy. "What are you trying to do, kill me?"

I laugh. I'm so going to miss her. "I'm sorry I didn't call."

"So, what's going on? Why the rush to go home?"

I sit on the step into the garage. "Dad and Mom are moving to England."

"Oh, wow. Jack and I are going to a couples' home group,
but we'll be over soon afterward."

"Thanks, Lucy."

* * *

I unpack and change into a pair of old shorts and a T-shirt that has seen better days. I toss my clothes from yesterday into the laundry, contemplate doing a load, but change my mind.

In the bathroom I wash my face and pull my hair back into a ponytail. When I lift my arms, I see the forgotten hole under the left sleeve.

(Mental note 8,590: throw this shirt away. Too ratty for a Chicago executive.)

In the kitchen I spread peanut butter and jelly on two slices of light bread and settle on the couch with the TV remote. Through the porch doors I catch a glimpse of the Florida horizon, ablaze with orange, red, gold and blue. I'm acutely aware that views like this are numbered and fading.

I'm moving. Leaving. Ending a very long and wonderful chapter of my life.

Something bothers me, but what? I mute the TV. Is it moving? Leaving Lucy? Rejecting Dad's offer? Letting the family business go on the auction block?

I recline on the couch and stare at the ceiling until the motion of the fan makes me nauseated.

I know what bothers me. Antacid-chewing Steve Albright. I said I do and he said, "Here's the ball and chain." It's fancy and gold plated, but it is a ball and chain nevertheless. I've sold myself into corporate slavery.

I'm not afraid of hard work. I'm afraid of work making me hard. Steve's declaration that I needed to be so dedicated it would take a year to find a place to live gives me great pause. If I don't have time to find natural living quarters, how will I have time to find a spiritual home?

How can I make time for beauty if every ounce of "beauty" is bought and paid for by Myers-Smith? I'm cognizant of the corporate mind-set. They own you. They aren't buying forty or fifty or even sixty hours a week. They're buying your heart and soul.

I feel shaky and unsure. I let my relationship with God stay status quo for the past few years, but deep in my gut I don't want to do that again. I want to discover the deeper layers of His word, understand the tender mercies of His heart.

A knock on the front door hauls me away from my mental discourse. Under the porch light is a distinguished man in an Armani suit (or I'm not Macy Moore).

"Can I help you?"

He offers me his hand. "Fallon Tidwell."

Oh, wow. "How do you do?" I warble. I'm about to shake Fallon Tidwell's hand when a breeze passes under my arm.

Whoops, my T-shirt. I tuck my left hand under my armpit, pressing the ripped edges of my shirt together. "Sir, come in."

"Thank you."

I close the door on the mosquitoes. "Was I expecting you?"

He chuckles. "No, forgive me. Pete told me where you live."

Ah, yes, Pete. The real Drag. "Please sit down." I'm desperate to run and change, but I can't leave Fallon Tidwell sitting alone in my living room, not for one minute.

"My son's in the hospital." His voice weakens a little.

I sink slowly to the couch. "What happened?"

"He went surfing after the storm yesterday and a shark got his left calf."

Bile forms in my throat. I feel green. "Is he all right?"

Mr. Tidwell settles into the lounger as if he's commanding a boardroom meeting, elbows resting on the chair's arms. "Hurting, but recovering."

"Shark attacks can happen in turbulent waters." I sit on the edge of the couch, stiff as a board, afraid if I move without careful calculation, my ratty T-shirt will expose more of me to the communications tycoon than necessary.

"So I'm told. The doctors have patched him up, but the calf is damaged. It will take a while to heal."

I press my palms against the sides of my face. "How painful, utterly painful. May I see him?"

"I'm on my way over now. Would you care to ride with me?" Mr. Tidwell stands.

"Yes, please." Now I hurry to change.

Mr. Tidwell's rental car is fragrant with the new car smell, and a hint of cigar smoke. I sink into the cool leather seats, acutely aware that I'm riding with one of the richest men in the country. But I try to keep my attention on whispering prayers for Drag.

"My son speaks highly of you."

"Thank you, Mr. Tidwell. Drag, um, Pete is a good friend."

"Call me Fallon."

"All right."

"Thank you for helping my son find his way home."

In the dimly lit room I can see Drag's pale face. His half-eaten leg is bandaged and elevated slightly. Tubes and wires connect him to blue-lighted monitors.

As I step toward him, he appears so calm and peaceful. If I didn't know better, I'd think he'd just woken up from a really great nap.

"Hey, Macy." His voice is low and raspy, tired and bruised.

With tenderness, I clasp his hand in mine. "Hey, you're not supposed to feed the sharks."

He musters a grin. "I should have known better."

"I'm glad you're all right." I squeeze his hand a little tighter.

He motions for me to draw near. Whispering, he says, "I saw Him."

I pinch up my face. Are the meds talking? "Saw who?"

"Him. Jesus."

I jump back and regard Drag—I know it's not the meds talking. "You saw Jesus?" I've never heard of such a thing.

"Right after the attack, when I was tumbling in the water."

"What did He do? Did He stick out His hand and say, 'Take My hand, My beloved son'?" I used my best King James voice. "Or bonk the shark on the nose?"

Drag gives me half a chuckle. "No. He touched my heart with His hand."

"Touched your heart?"

"Yeah." Drag lifts his hand ever so slightly and settles it on his chest. "Right here."

"Was He in the water with you? On top of the water looking down? How did He do that?" I flit and flutter, unsure what to think.

Drag shakes his head once. "I don't know. Suddenly I see Him and He touches me."

"Wow." I sink onto the chair by the bed. Tears creep down my cheeks. "You really saw Him?"

"I'm undone, Macy. Undone. Tumbling in the waves, trying to find my way to the shore, I thought I was going to die. Then there He was." He pats his heart once.

"What did He look like?" I picture the painting of Jesus that hangs in the foyer of Beauty Community Church.

"Radiant," Drag says. "The most beautiful person I've ever seen. Full of goodness and light." He pats his heart again. "I'm undone."

I rest my chin on the edge of the bed, his hand still clasped in mine. I'm one degree of separation away from actually seeing Jesus with my eyes. Who cares about Six Degrees of Kevin Bacon? I'm touching a man who physically saw Jesus. And I'm jealous.

Drag's known Jesus a few weeks and already he has this incredible encounter. I surrendered my life twenty-five years ago and I've seen Him only with the eyes of my heart. What's it take for a girl to see her Lord face-to-face? A shark bite?

"Then what happened?" I plead. With a quick motion I glance over my shoulder toward Fallon, but he's gone.

"My buddies pulled me ashore, my leg half gone, gushing blood like a fountain."

"Will you surf again?"

"Better believe it. I'll have a big dent in my leg, but the doc says I should be able to stand on the board—eventually."

"But you saw Jesus. I can't believe it."

"I saw Him first with my heart. You showed me the way."

His voice is weak and his words stick to the sides of his drying mouth. I offer to help him with a sip of water.

"Thanks," he says after a long drink. "Dad's been great.

When I leave the hospital, I'm flying to New York with him."

"Good for you."

"He and Mom want me home for recovery. And then I'll start working at Tidwell Communications."

"You're doing the right thing." More tears leak out and run down my cheeks.

"What about you?" Drag gives my hand a little squeeze and tug. "Chicago? Don't forget my dad is impressed with you."

"I accepted the Chicago offer." Then I confess as if caught red-handed. "My dad wants me to move home and take over the family business."

"Moore Gourmet Sauces?" He remembered.

"Yes." I lift the water cup to give Drag another sip.

"Why don't you take up that offer?"

I set the cup down and fall against the back of the chair. "Because it's going backwards. I never, ever planned on moving back to Beauty. Maybe I'm being stubborn about Chicago, I don't know."

"Macy, look at me." I sit forward. "Look how fragile life can be. One minute I'm catching the biggest wave of the season. Next minute I've got shark teeth ripping my leg apart."

The imagery makes me quiver, but he's right. Life is full of the unexpected. I don't know what tomorrow brings.

"Choose what's important to you, Macy. Not for the moment, but for eternity."

I lean close. "How do I know?"

He taps his heart, then says, "What's in here?"

I return to the chair, catching my reflection in the window. For years I've prided myself on my appearance (right down to designer socks), my talents, my career status, even the type of car I drive and how much I pay for a haircut. I supported all my worldly achievements with a very shallow pool of inner beauty and in some cases, shallow character.

"My gut tells me taking over the sauce business will reap a different kind of reward than I've been seeking. Perhaps the Lord will touch my heart in such a way that I can say like you, 'I'm undone.'"

I desire to be undone.

"There's your answer." Drag's reply is barely audible, but I hear loud and clear.

Fallon returns with two large coffees in hand. "Visiting hours are over." He motions to the door.

I lean over and kiss Drag on the cheek. "Thank you, friend."

"See you soon." His energy is zapped. Here I am wasting it on my problems.

Fallon hands me a coffee as we walk down the corridor together. "Pete tells me you're looking for a job." His gray eyes spark when he speaks and I can tell he is a man who sees as well as looks.

"Well, sir, I have a job."

"Pete mentioned a possibility in Chicago."

Without a thought or hesitation, I blurt out, "Not Chicago. Beauty. I'm going home to Beauty, Georgia."

We stop at the elevator and I press the down arrow, feeling perfect. Absolutely perfect.

"All the best to you, Macy."

I don't care if he is Fallon Tidwell, communications tycoon. I celebrate my decision and throw my arms around him. "All the best to you, too."

"Yes," he croaks, backing away, straightening his collar.

I'm going home. Riding the elevator down, my heart soars. I'm returning to Beauty.

I call Dad as soon as I get home. "Where will I live?"

I glance at the clock on the stove. Lucy and Jack should be by soon.

He clears his throat. "Our house will be empty, of course. But you know Piper and Angus are selling off part of their Purdy homestead."

"Dylan told me." I plop into one of the kitchen-table chairs and draw my knees up to my chin.

"Who do you think put him up to it?" A sneaky snicker threads the tone of his voice.

"I am not surprised."

"A man's gotta do what a man's gotta do to wage war against a fancy New York software company offering the world to his daughter on a Chicago-style platter."

"Any cheap, low-down trick will do, eh, Dad?" I see Lucy and Jack pass by the window with paper bags of Chinese food.

"I'll take the cheap shot if that's all I got."

"You know how much I've always loved Piper and Angus's place." I get out silverware, napkins and plates.

"So what are you telling me?" Dad asks.

I hear the front door open and Lucy's familiar hello. I take a deep breath. "I'm returning to Beauty, Dad. I'll take over the business."

There's a long pause from Dad's end. Lucy is in the living room, flipping on lights.

Finally Dad chokes out, "Are you sure?" The emotion

in his voice runs down the wire and splashes over me. My eyes well up.

"Yes, very."

Chapter Thirty-Three

⚭

August 4

On the veranda swing, I wait for Dylan. He's picking me up on one of his custom bikes—which he's trying to sell to me, by the way. He's crazy. Gorgeous and crazy. My new best friend.

We're meeting Lucy and Jack at the corner of Jasmine and Lily Avenue and heading over to the lake for a picnic. Jack just bought a Braun bike.

Oh, before I forget. The class reunion was a blast. I'm proud to say I attended as a hometown girl and the new proprietor of Moore Gourmet Sauces. I emceed with great poise and hilarity, even if I say so myself.

I couldn't believe how many of my old friends patted me

on the back and congratulated me about moving back to Beauty. There was no humiliation. No teasing. No eating crow.

"We always thought you'd be the Moore of Moore Sauces one day."

Did everyone know but me?

Kathy Bailey and I spent an hour talking, catching up, being jealous over each other's lives and promising to keep in touch. Resolve: good friends are worth the trouble.

Dad bought Cole a Braun bike the same time Jack bought his. Part of Cole's inheritance, Dad claims, but I'm finding out that my former-hippie-turned-Jesus-freak-turned-Southern-bourgeois-capitalist-turned-missionary father is incredibly generous.

For me, he put a down payment on the Purdy mansion. Absolutely blew me away. He's all but giving me the business, then goes and buys my dream home.

"Signing bonus," he said when he handed me the keys.

I cried. Yep, cried in front of the boss. But at Moore Gourmet Sauces crying executives are not frowned upon. I stood there in my new pleated skirt and curled my toes against the soles of my flip-flops and cried a nice, businesswoman cry.

Be true to you, I always say.

Lucy hooked me up with one of the newspaper's advertising real estate agents, who advised me to rent my condo. It made moving so much easier, and the rent covers my mortgage and then some.

Piper and Angus sold my half of their home for a song. Dad tried to give them several thousand more, but Angus refused.

"The money makes Piper crazy," he told Dad, chewing his chaw, then spitting in the dirt.

I'll spend the next four months remodeling, and that expense is entirely on me. Until then, I'm unpacked and living in my old room.

Dad and Mom leave for England in a few weeks and are as giddy as a couple of teenagers. They inspire and challenge me with their yielded, unselfish hearts.

But Dad's concentration level is worse than a child's. I have to snap my fingers under his nose to get his attention. "Tell me how to do this!"

I'm slightly panicked. The day they leave, I debut on *The Food Connection*. Butterflies launch themselves across my middle at the very thought.

Six months ago, if someone had told me I'd return to Beauty as the new owner of Moore Gourmet Sauces, I would have laughed and called the paddy wagon. Absurd. Unthinkable.

Steve Albright lit into me when I called to say I would not be taking the Chicago position. Ooh-wee, he was mad. Worst case of the mean-'n-nasties I've ever heard. In my honor, I'm sure he consumed a whole packet of Tums.

I apologized profusely, offering to pay for any expenses I had unduly caused Myers-Smith. *That* he took as an incredible insult and all but hung up on me.

After that episode, I fell on my knees and thanked God for rescuing me from what would have been a bad, bad move.

I left Melbourne with all my loose ends tied and tidy. I stopped by Casper & Company on my way out of town, the back of my Beemer loaded with suitcases and boxes.

Roni jumped to her feet like a frightened cat when I appeared in her office. "Macy." Her smiling lips quivered.

I walked across her office as if I owned the place and gave her a big hug. "I'm moving back to Georgia."

She gawked and gaped, but I thanked her for all she'd done for me. And I meant every word. She and Mike were the first to throw the burning match on the wood, hay and stubble of my life and I'll always be grateful.

Keeping my word, I gifted Jillian with the Gucci boots. She cried and threw her arms around me, promising to take good care of them.

"I know you will, Jillian."

"Did you hear about Attila and Mike?" she whispered, checking over her shoulder.

"Jillian, stop using that name. I should never have invented it."

"Please, Macy. Everyone uses it. Anyway, she and Mike—"

I held up my hand. "Don't want to know." I hit the front door with Jillian trailing behind me, desperate to gossip. But I refused to hear. What good would it do me?

Drag is settled in New York, and healing. He's e-mailed a few times and called once. When he joined Tidwell Communications, CNN ran a quick news brief and a head shot. Drag in a suit looking like Brad Pitt. I'll never forget it.

Mrs. Woodward, at seventy-seven and free from gallbladder attacks, bought a Mustang convertible and joined the Red Hat Society. Every Tuesday, Thursday and Saturday, she and three other beauties in purple dresses and red hats pop the top and vroom away.

Finally, but not least, Adriane, Tamara, Lucy and I said goodbye in style the night before I left. The movers had taken the last of my furniture, so the four of us sat cross-legged in the middle of my empty living room, laughing and reminiscing, eating Carraba's takeout, listening to the echoes of our hearts against barren walls.

"To the Single Saved Sisters," I said, raising my glass when we quieted down. "Jewels in my heart."

"To the Single Saved Sisters."

Then we got all mushy and cried for a while until Adriane reminded us we'd be together in October for her wedding. We brightened for a moment, then cried again.

I waved tootles to Dan Montgomery and Perfect Woman as they pulled away one morning. I'm not sure they even knew I was moving.

In the distance I hear the rumble of Dylan's bike. He continues to make his intentions known while giving me space to figure out this new chapter of my life.

I watch as he coasts up the driveway and parks. My heart does the hundred-yard dash as he takes the veranda steps in one large leap and strides my way.

He pulls me to him and kisses me. Not a howdy-do or by-your-leave kiss, but a nice manly man's kiss.

I swoon. Sure as shooting, I swoon. "Hello to you, too," I whisper when his lips leave mine.

He wraps me up in his arms and I bury my head in his chest and breathe in sandalwood and sage. He strokes my hair. "Hey to you, blue eyes."

I am so in love.

"Ready?" he asks when he releases me.

"Yep." I shut the front door and take his hand.

Riding across Beauty with Dylan, my arms around his

waist, my cheek pressed against his back, my hair dancing in the wind, I can't remember why I wanted to run away from this place. Life is funny, isn't it? Like Dorothy in Oz, I've searched for my rainbow out *there* somewhere when really all I wanted was right here in my own backyard.

I lift my head and laugh. The Lord has given me Beauty for my ashes.

* * * * *

Questions for Discussion

1. Macy shows up at work on a Monday morning to find out she's been demoted—over e-mail no less. Is her response Christ-like? How would you respond in a similar situation?

2. Our society focuses a lot on food as an emotional medication. Macy falls into this trap when she learns about her job situation. What would have been a better comfort?

3. Macy dated a man who was not a Christian. She let her desperation to be married dictate her heart. Have you ever found yourself in a situation where you were compromising your faith with a nonbelieving boyfriend? What advice would you give to a person in that situation?

4. Macy and Lucy have a long-term, special relationship. How can you be a better friend? Friendships must be about giving as much as receiving.

5. Macy's career became her idol. She forgot to consult God about her plans. Are there plans in your life that need to be submitted to the counsel of God? Why or why not?

6. We have three commodities in this life that we can exchange for eternal currency: time, money and words. How does Macy realize she's not used some of her "currency" wisely? In what situations does she realize she needs to make a change?

7. Even when we are adult children, the Lord may use our parents to speak His will into our lives. Does this happen to Macy? What is her response? Has this happened to you? How should you respond?

8. When Dylan Braun shows up in Macy's life, it messes with her heart's desire to be a Chicago executive. How is Dylan a Christ-like picture of love, patience and acceptance?

9. Once Macy surrenders her will to the Lord, what happens to the desires of her heart? Has this happened in your life? If not, are there issues you need to surrender?

10. Discuss the end of the book where Macy leaves Melbourne for Beauty. Think of situations in your life where you've closed one door and walked through another. What lessons have you learned? What lessons did Macy learn?

A NOTE FROM THE AUTHOR

Georgia on Her Mind *was written by one, but birthed by many. My journey is fragrant with the love and support of many people. Below is my humble attempt to share my gratitude.*

To my friend, Jesus, the creative genius behind anything I write or say. Mistakes are mine. The beauty is all Yours. I am absolutely nothing without Your love and affection. You're my beloved and my friend.

My husband and best friend, Tony, who brainstorms with me, encourages me and does final editing. You cover me, encourage me and give me wings to fly. Your devotion to Jesus, to prayer, to staying the course when it's hard overwhelms my heart. Jesus is my King, but you are my Prince.

Colleen Coble, your constant encouragement and belief in me is a beautiful thread woven through the tapestry of my life, forever. We could live on the opposite ends of the earth, and I'll always treasure the labor you extended on my behalf. You have a unique and beautiful gift from the Lord to encourage and mentor writers, and you use it wisely. I know the Lord is saying over you, "Well done."

Kristin Billerbeck, you've also encouraged me beyond belief. I love your heart and spirit, and zeal for the Lord. Especially for young women to rise to a higher standard. We are so on the same page. Thank you for "discovering my chick voice" along with Colleen and for being a signpost on my journey. I'm honored.

Karen Solem, my agent. Thank you for mentoring me and finding the "diamond" in the rough. You are a wonderful gift from the Lord.

Joan Marlow Golan, who listened to my story ideas during a conference dinner and said, "I think you've got a chick voice." Thank you for going to bat for this story and for believing in me. I really appreciate you.

Krista Stroever, my editor, inspiration and the one who made Macy's story shine. I appreciate all the labor you've given to this project. Yeah, I know it's your job, but you never made it seem that way to me. Thank you, Krista, for being available to brainstorm and answer questions. You've made me a better writer.

Christine Lynxwiler, friend and author extraordinaire, who took time from your busy schedule to read and critique...one more time. Thank you for your friendship and constant encouragement.

Tracey Bateman, with your timely phone calls, constant friendship and encouragement. I love your heart. Thank you for making me a Pinkie. And Susan May Warren and Susan Downs for being available on IM or e-mail when I needed a friend. You are jewels in my heart.

Ted Travers, you let yourself be used by God in the most extraordinary way. You came back to church that morning after prayer and spoke the Word of the Lord to me, and dropped a plumb line in my writing life. Thank you for being my friend, my brother in the Lord and an example of wholeheartedness.

My family, I love you all so much. We endured hard days last summer when Dad died and I remember thinking there's no family like mine. I'm sure, as you all read these pages, you will find glimpses of yourselves because you are so much a part of who I am. Thanks for a lifetime of warm, fond memories. Mom, you're so much stronger than you know. I love you.

Dave McMillen, who gave me the W-Book idea. And to Chuck, Jim, Hyer, Darryl, Ralph, Steve W., Richard, Dan, Roy, Joallyson, CJ, Tim D., Pam, Gail, Terri, Juli and Teresa, who filled my software days with genuine friendships and at times with downright, laugh-out-loud fun. "Well heellllooo."

Lynn Coleman, thank you for all your encouragement.

Deb Raney, for listening so patiently as I went on and on about writing chick lit during the Orlando CBA. Your beautiful smile is an encouragement in itself.

Meredith Efken and Mary Griffith for reading the story in a "before" stage. And to my laugh-buddies from the 2003 Houston Conference, Patti Hall, Sandra Moore and Allison Wilson, who inspired the Single Saved Sisters idea. Thank you.

Sheree Stebbins, Carrie Campbell and Elizabeth White, for letting me know if Macy made sense. Thank you. I love you, my friends and daughters!

And to all the Fire Dwellers! Thank you for the Friday nights of worship and intercession, for not letting go and for pulling me out of author mode into my true identity as Lover of the Bridegroom. We're camped on the mountain until He comes. Javi, Don, Matt and Tony—I'm honored to be named among you. We say yes to the dirge and the dance.

Chelle, Tricia and the Tapper girls for praying for me. I love you.

The Faithchick.com bloggers, especially Mary, who came up with a great idea. Blog on, my sisters.

ACFW! Wow, what an amazing organization. I wouldn't be here without you.

My NCFLife family who gives me a home and a place in the body of Christ.

And for anyone I may have forgotten, my humble apologies, but very sincere thanks!

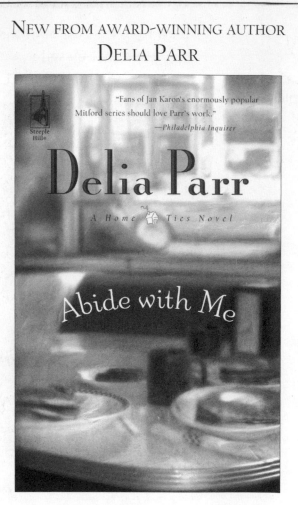

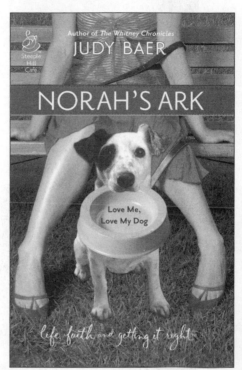